Something to Call Your Own

by

Marc Krulewitch

Smashwords Edition

1

The headline from 1930 read, "CAPONE READY TO KICK ELLERSTEIN OUT OF POLITICS," and "20th Ward Boss Due to Fade from View." Fade from view. How wonderful the phrase sounded to Jules who wanted nothing more than to simply fade from view.

The article arrived as Jules was recovering from a breakdown of sorts, provoked by his first job out of graduate school. At the time, he never considered Al Capone sharing a headline with his great-grandfather a blessing. But he had not been lingering much over blessings, choosing instead to devote his attention to the workings of the brain, particularly how thoughts sprouted from the movement of chemicals traveling between neurons. What could such a complicated science have to do with blessings?

***

His crisis began at the commercial lending firm of Nathrop & Moore, where he had arrived from a small Midwestern business school and distinguished himself quickly, earning a promotion after only six months in the field. The advancement was unexpected and, perhaps, a blessing. Had he not been within ear-shot of Mr. Warner, another auditor would have discovered Tri-Cal borrowing money based on phony assets and someone else would be calling themselves an "account executive."

His promotion caused more than a little fur to fly since he was not only the newest auditor but the youngest of a group including several crusty veterans. The fact Jules was tall and thin and wore English suits while his short, plump, graying co-workers wore synthetic fabrics in dark maroons, had already created a resentful atmosphere. Behind his back they whispered his last name had more to do with his advancement than anything else since diversity had been in vogue and Nathrop & Moore's roster read like the passenger list from the Mayflower. Inevitably, these rumblings found their way to Jules, who became more determined to write off the cheap insinuations to petty jealousy. Despite leaving the

2

auditor's pool sans friends, his enthusiasm and excitement eclipsed the bitter taste.

Jules knew nothing of blessings the first morning of his new job. He knew only of being escorted by his manager, Mr. McNally, a tight-lipped middle-aged man with a shock of white hair, and being told "welcome aboard" by several other men whose names he quickly forgot. He was shown to an office composed of wood-trimmed partitions with large windows, where McNally announced he would meet someone named James Williamson, who was also new to the firm but most capable of advising him on the ins and outs of asset-based lending.

McNally smiled broadly, suggested to Jules that he try to relax. Williamson would be around any moment to begin orientation. When McNally was out the door before hearing Jules' "thank you," he laughed to himself, leaned back in his new chair, a brown leather high-back conference chair, and let his knees knock against the oak veneer desktop, a substance far superior to the imitation walnut Formica of the auditor's pool.

He thought of his father schlepping bulky garment bags around the Midwest. It was an honorable occupation, but to Jules, the traveling salesman's life was depressing and dowdy. Instead, he pictured himself walking from his apartment to the subway dressed smartly in one of his three Gieves & Hawkes suits or even the Hickey-Freeman he had recently purchased. He loved the look of English suits and sometimes imagined himself modeling them with their single-vented backs, peak lapels, and flapped pockets with piping. English suits were the ticket to success, he knew, but still he dreamed of the day he could afford a Fiorvanti. Gratitude washed over him for a generic form of Providence that had blessed him with a career. His stomach rumbled, reminded him he had been too nervous to eat breakfast. He looked at his watch, wondered what time he would be able to break for lunch, longed for the day when he could take his lunch whenever he pleased. Training could take months, he knew, but what were a few months in the life of a career?

It was when he let his head fall back against the neck cushion that he saw the figure of a gaunt young man staring at him while standing near the water cooler outside his office. The man's suit was dapper yet comical, hanging loosely on his skinny frame like a child dressed in his father's clothes. What's this? Jules thought. Somebody's son, or—worse yet—an intern? Did he know how ridiculous he looked? The stranger's crossed arms conveyed a sense of confidence suggesting he had been the subject of the stranger's gaze for some time.

Jules nodded at the stranger whose expression then turned serious as he walked into Jules's office, hand extended. His unblemished face, framed by blonde hair tapered perfectly behind small ears, had an almost pre-pubescent purity. But it was the man's blue eyes that struck Jules as most peculiar, how they held a fixed look of woeful resignation, as if destined to carry a heavy burden. Jules was shocked to see the suit hanging on this skinny frame looked Italian, Zegna perhaps.

"Nice going at Tri-Cal," the man said in a tired voice. "You're Ellerstein, aren't you?" He pronounced each syllable slowly, as if English had not been his first language.

"Yes," Jules said, surprised but flattered, then annoyed the stranger did not respond with an introduction of his own but walked slowly past Jules' desk then stood behind him. Jules swiveled his chair around. "And you are?"

The stranger looked Jules over, first at his wingtips and then up to the knot of his tie.

"Call me Izzy."

"Izzy?"

"Yes. Short for Isadore."

Jules was stung by a sense of the familiar. The strange intonation of Izzy's voice evoked black-and-white images of bearded men he'd seen in documentaries.

"My grandfather's name was Isadore," Jules said, pleased with himself for remembering.

This interested Izzy. "Where from, if I may ask?"

The question took Jules by surprise, not only for its incongruity, but again for the stranger's inflection, a way of speaking that seemed unnaturally old. "Poland...I think."

"Ah," Izzy said, nodding his head. "Your mother's father?"

Jules agreed it was his mother's father, wondered why Izzy had assumed as much.

"And where is she now, your mother?"

"Deceased."

Izzy had an odd way of standing which gave the appearance of leaning backward. The oddness was enhanced by the way he kept his hands buried deep in his pockets. The pockets seemed to engulf half his arm. "And how long dead?"

How is this your business? "Twenty-three years, this October."

Izzy produced a note pad from his breast pocket, scribbled something, then waved his hand dismissively.

"So, what do you do here?" Jules asked.

"Loans, what else?"

"You're an account executive?"

Izzy closed his eyes and shrugged. "So hard to believe?"

"It's just that you look so—young."

"Yes, I know. I finished school at eighteen. A burden, really, to be so young in the world. But as burdens go, I didn't do so bad."

Jules agreed, struggled not to laugh. "You finished college at eighteen?"

"MBA. They called me a prodigy. Fun at first but made me old before my time."

Jules nodded, pretended he understood the pain in Izzy's voice. If this little man was telling the truth, he could be making six figures already.

"And how long have you been at N&M?"

"Depends," Izzy said, then fell silent. This annoyed Jules.

"Depends on what?" Jules said with enough edge in his voice to cause Izzy to hold up his hands in a mockingly defensive posture.

"Easy, Ellerstein, you got plenty of time to dislike me."

That he could so easily hurt the little man's feelings annoyed Jules even more. "Sorry. I'm just a little nervous."

"What can I say? They called me a prodigy." Izzy paused, then said, "How do you think N&M got so prestigious anyway? They recruit, of course. Me they started in elementary school."

He was recruited, no less. "And how did they come to know about you?"

"Chess."

"Chess?"

Izzy shrugged again. "When an eight-year-old check mates college professors, people notice. Back to your question, I'm here only three days. Before that, three years in Cleveland."

Jules knew of the Cleveland branch, a thriving office distinguished for having the most improved new-business-to-default ratio. "Why did you leave?"

"I, too, was promoted, and by the way," Izzy lowered his voice to a whisper, "pay no attention to the rumor-mongers. You deserve to be here. Your work at Tri-Cal was first class."

Jules thanked Izzy and wondered if he had misjudged him, if in this odd boyish man he had an ally.

"But keep in mind you're the only one here."

Jules ignored the remark. "So we'll be working together?"

"Of course, why do you think I'm here?"

"I was told Mr. Williamson would start my training. I guess he's—

"You don't have to tell me about Williamson. Williamson will be here at 10:00."

"He told you this?"

"Of course."

Of course. "So what do you think of Williamson so far?"

Izzy kept his vision focused out the door. "How should I know?" he said, yawned.

"But what's your sense of him? Will he be difficult to work with?"

Izzy turned back to Jules, blinked twice. "Take my advice Ellerstein, and relax. I'm here to help you, but with a heart attack we both lose."

Lose what? Jules tried to focus back to Izzy but heard only that irreconcilable inflection—with a heart attack we both lose. "Well," Jules said, "maybe I'll run downstairs and grab a sweet roll before my meeting." As he moved toward the door Izzy touched his elbow.

"Listen, I just got here, and without a nickel. I got money, of course, but no time to open an account. Loan me a few, just to buy a lunch."

Jules reached back for his wallet, then his hand wavered—an innate reaction to strangers asking for money. He gave him ten dollars anyway. Izzy looked at the money and then back to Jules. "Tell me what kind of lunch you can get for ten?"

The remark rendered Jules momentarily speechless.

"You think I'm not good for at least twenty? Listen Ellerstein, if you can't trust me who do you think you can trust?"

The comment confused Jules, but he did not ask for an explanation. Instead, he grabbed the ten dollars from Izzy's hand and replaced it with a twenty dollar bill.

"Have a great lunch," Jules said then moved quickly away, turning back once to see Izzy standing in the same position, staring at the money.

***

Upon returning from the cafeteria Jules stopped in the men's room to check his appearance. He pushed his hair around, laughed at his nervousness, reminded himself that Williamson was just another account executive for chrissake. When he returned to his office he found Izzy leaning casually against the front of his desk.

"Still here? Are we both meeting with Williamson?"

"Relax Ellerstein, I am Williamson."

Jules studied the little man's face for the slightest sign of humor, but saw only the sad blue eyes and sober grin. He felt justified by his anger but managed to keep his voice in check.

"Why did you tell me your name was Izzy?"

"I said call me Izzy. There's a difference."

Jules tried to think of a reason not to be angry. "Isn't your name James? Why the hell would you want to be called Izzy?"

Izzy nodded, returned to his odd stance. "It's a devotional name. A testimonial, if you like."

When he didn't elaborate Jules was not surprised. "A testimonial to what?"

"Isadore Himmel was his name. I'm right now having mine legally changed."

"You're taking the full name of another person?"

"It's a testimonial to the dead, not the living."

"Why this man?"

Izzy's face lit up momentarily, and for an instant, Jules thought he saw the little man as he truly was—youthful, enthusiastic, unburdened.

"Himmel was made into ashes by Nazis," Izzy said. "I arrived at his name from an obscure book of lists that somehow found its way to the library. The lists were of Hitler's victims from various German towns. I sat in a far corner of the reference floor, my eyes moving past name after name. You could've pushed over a bookcase and I would not have flinched so transfixed I was. I happen to know some German and when my eyes saw the name

Himmel, I stopped. You see, Himmel means 'heaven,' and I found the irony of this image touching. Himmel having gone up the chimney in the middle of a forest."

Jules thought of his descendants, all of whom had immigrated decades before Hitler's arrival; although he remembered a story from his father's cousin who thought there was an uncle who stayed and perished.

"You're Jewish?" Jules asked.

Izzy hesitated, then snapped, "Next you'll be wanting to see my papers?"

Jules shrank back, unsure why he felt shame. Izzy conceded.

"Forgive me Ellerstein, you have the right to ask such a question, and for you I will tell quickly my story." Izzy moved to a small leather couch, sat with one leg draped over the other. "I knew nothing of Jews," he began, "until I one day went to a Catholic wedding where I was to be an usher. It was there while standing with the priest and several members of the wedding party that I heard the priest ask the groom if he had gotten a 'Jewish deal' on something he had purchased." Izzy stopped, unhooked his legs and slouched on the couch with his head back. "As I said before, I knew nothing of Jews, but I was familiar with stereotypes and I knew a disparaging remark when I heard one. And it struck me that if a priest could so deftly embrace such an ancient, unflattering image of a people, then anything was possible."

Jules wanted only to admire the good intention of Izzy's story, but saw affectation as well. Nevertheless, a mass of outrage welled up into his chest over the priest's remark. It was true Jules had not been subjected to much anti-Semitism, but over time he had become familiar with the verbal subtleties of language, the disparaging overtones, the pejorative inflections. He had been acquainted with the phrase, "Jewish deal," but only in the archaic sense as a passé term from a bygone era. His father despised the term and also took deep offense to anyone who employed the word, "Jew," as a verb.

"I even lit a candle on his Yahrzeit—using an assumed date of course," Izzy added.

Yahrzeit. Jules had heard the word before, tried to recall where.

"When you light the candle," Izzy said mildly irritated. "On the death anniversary. Surely you know that much."

Wanting to avoid what he did or did not know, Jules tried to keep the focus on Izzy. "Do you define yourself as Jewish?"

"Don't talk to me of definitions. I studied the culture. The more I studied the more I became."

A secretary tapped her foot on the wood partition panel, breezed into the office holding a stack of paper. She smiled quickly at Jules, dropped the stack on his desk, then reminded "James" of a two o'clock conference call before strolling out.

"You haven't told the others of your name change?"

"In time they'll know."

"But you told me right away."

"You I am right now working with. And, of course, you would understand."

"You want me to call you Izzy in front of the others?"

"Of course."

"And what if they ask me about it. Or you."

"We tell the truth."

"Aren't you concerned what they will think?" The word "they" sounded strange to his ears.

"And what will they do? Sack me for not liking my name? They have laws nowadays for this. I'm bearing witness to the dead, Ellerstein. To the dead who have no one alive to remember them."

Jules nodded, although adopting a dead person's full name still did not sit well.

"What about that priest? Did you ever say anything to him?"

Izzy said nothing, stared out the door. Jules waited. "Better we move on," Izzy finally said, "to your new job."

2

At the time of his promotion, Jules was living with his girlfriend, Marla, an arrangement tolerated by the couple's parents who viewed cohabitation as the next step in a romance nurtured in the playpens of suburban Chicago. No one had really expected their mutual fondness to survive the commotion of elementary school or the trials of adolescence, but when it did, when Marla and Jules began dating in high school and it was supposed they were investigating the sensual aspects of life's mysteries, the schmaltzier side of the adults re-emerged with the hope of an old-fashioned neighborhood alliance.

At first, Jules thought he would enjoy characterizing this strange little man to Marla. Walking to the subway, he practiced imitating Izzy's speech pattern, embellished on Izzy's mannerisms expecting Marla to convulse with laughter. But that evening, when she anxiously asked to hear about his new job, he could only recount the mundane aspects of his first day— the countless introductions, explanations of procedures, talk of preparation for his training. Purposely, he omitted using Izzy's name, referring to him only as his "supervisor," until Marla interrupted and asked if his supervisor had a name. Lacking the energy to again conjure up an accurate image of such a bizarre man, Jules said "James," and asked Marla about her day at the art gallery.

"The new exhibits just arrived," she said, and Jules pretended to be interested in an obscure French proto-fauvist painter whose vivid use of color and free treatment of form resulted in a "wonderfully vibrant and decorative effect." Jules had simpler tastes, preferring Hopper's use of dark complementary colors.

"…He ushered in a whole new movement…" Jules tried his best to follow, but a heavy fatigue had settled in, unmoored his mind to drift back to interactions with Izzy. And due largely to his weariness, Jules's guard lowered enough for the image of Izzy's tie hanging below his belt and the cuffs of his slacks enveloping the heels of his shoes, to provoke an unexpected chuckle.

"What's so funny?" Marla said.

"I'm sorry, continue," Jules said.

"You've never respected my work," Marla said.

Respect had always been important to Marla. When she had chosen art history as her major, her parents tried to hide their concern that she was pursuing a degree not very "marketable." Marla sensed how they felt but refused to consider spending four years studying a subject solely for its ability to earn money. "How much is respect worth?" she often said to her father when the subject came up. "Can't you respect someone who doesn't make a lot of money? Hitler made a lot of money. Does that mean you respect Hitler?"

Jules had always admired Marla's outspokenness, especially her Hitler analogies. In high school, after the Soviets invaded Afghanistan, there was talk in the Carter administration of reinstating a military draft to include women. Marla was the lone female voice among her peers who welcomed the idea, enthusiastically pointing out if women wanted equal rights they needed to prove themselves on the field of battle. "That's how respect is earned," she had said. Even as a child, Marla had an uncanny precociousness with regard to social issues, going as far as setting one of her mother's brassieres on fire in front of her fourth grade class.

When her schooling finished, when the financial reality of what was required to live independently in a major metropolis while maintaining a cultivated lifestyle was suddenly obvious, when the absoluteness of the world abruptly exposed itself as being, at best, indifferent with regard to Marla Greenbaum's respectability, she hit a wall. Jules watched helplessly. He tried talking to her, but as her depression deepened so did Jules's own insecurity.

"Don't worry so much," Jules had told her. "When I get a job we'll get our own place."

Gradually, Marla softened and became more accepting of the way things were. She resigned herself to living with her parents while working at the gallery—this despite her father's offer to subsidize a city lifestyle, a proposal that infuriated Marla. "I will not be a princess!" she insisted. Over time she would learn respect was shown implicitly to those who approached their jobs professionally, with a degree of enthusiasm. Fortunately, her brain adapted, allowed her to recognize when circumstances warranted a change in attitude, that conceding old contentions in the short term kept alive hopes of fighting another day.

"I'm not laughing at you. It's that supervisor I told you about. You wouldn't believe this guy."

"Try me."

"I was told that his name was, 'James…'"

With renewed energy, Jules began describing this absurd apparition who wanted to be called Izzy. He did his best to imitate Izzy's peculiar posture, his anxious countenance, his immigrant accent. But at the moments Jules had expected audible expressions of amusement, Marla offered only concern.

"It's hard to explain but picture a twelve-year-old wearing a fifteen-hundred-dollar Italian suit! He's just bizarre. Nobody of his background or age should act like that. It's some weird trip he's on. Like what the hell is he trying to prove?"

"And how will you deal with him?"

"I never said I couldn't deal with him."

"You're angry."

"I'm not."

Marla looked thoughtfully at Jules. "Can you work for this Izzy guy and do as you're told without melting down on me?"

"Melt down on you?"

"Melt down on us. We're at a critical point now, Jules. We're not kids anymore."

Notwithstanding their parent's wishes, Jules had never thought Marla would view their relationship as being contingent upon anything. And despite the sudden wave of nausea moving through him, he said, "I'll do fine," then reassured Marla, told her that in the grand scheme of his career path, a character like Izzy would be of no consequence.

To Jules's surprise, Izzy demonstrated the skills of a patient and compassionate instructor. He answered Jules's questions—sometimes more than once—without the slightest loss of temper or least bit of condescension. He castigated himself for harshly judging Izzy—although he was still unable to grasp why Izzy's manner of speech should be that of an immigrant.

Jules was also wrong in assuming Izzy's name change would be met with suspicion and puzzled looks. On three occasions he watched Izzy give lengthy explanations of his adopted moniker; explanations that became involved discussions of National Socialism and Teutonic folk lore. And although Jules was present throughout these discussions, not once was he asked for his perspective.

Purposely, Jules kept their conversations strictly professional. In particular, he left the subject of Himmel alone, and did his best to appear no longer interested. Izzy, too, seemed to take this approach. Only on occasion did he state innocuously, "I see Hanukkah arrives late this year," or "I watched Schindler's List last night," and never did he pursue Jules's polite indifference.

But it wasn't until he saw Izzy through the glass walls of the conference room that he realized the scope of respect the little man commanded. Standing in his singular posture with one hand in his pocket and the other pointing, writing, summing numbers, Jules's mentor was clearly in charge, an equal to his white-haired audience. Still, he couldn't comprehend how this strange voice in a baggy suit could be taken seriously.

Eventually, Jules was "cut loose" with three accounts. His co-workers took him out to lunch, and later McNally stopped by to offer words of encouragement. With his hand on Izzy's shoulder, McNally emphasized "James" would still be available should Jules run into trouble.

In very little time Jules realized his clients were low maintenance accounts requiring only "check-up" work equivalent to re-adding the entries of a trial balance and, if necessary, confirming with an auditor the claimed receivables. His first real test came when one of his accounts requested an emergency loan to cover payroll. The money was delivered, but when the same request was made two weeks later, he decided to send in the auditors who discovered the client's largest customer had shut its doors. This discovery led to a declaration of insolvency and the transferring of the account to the bankruptcy division. While Jules was pleased with himself for potentially cutting the firm's losses, he was anxious for more challenges since his client base had been reduced by a third.

"Bad timing it seems," Izzy said, reclining in his high-back chair looking like somebody's visiting son. "But your decision was the correct one. And these things also get noticed by the higher ups." Izzy assured him he would speak with McNally, and matter-of-factly claimed, "You'll have more work than you'll know what to do with."

Jules thanked Izzy, but as he turned toward the door Izzy said, "Just a minute, Ellerstein. I understand the significance of next month. No doubt, you will soon become preoccupied. Let me know when the day is forthcoming. I will not expect to see you in the office."

Izzy waited for a response but when a light bulb didn't go off in Jules's head, he shouted, "Ach! C'mon, Ellerstein. Surely you must know what I am talking about!"

Stunned by the vitriol in Izzy's voice, Jules peered out the door to see if anyone was looking. "Jesus, Izzy, what are you talking about?"

"I don't mean to yell Ellerstein. But if one were to ask me who contributes more to society, the peddler turning his fingers into bones to make a small living, all-the-while conducting a respectful pious life, grateful for the little he has; or the successful banker whose thoughts rarely dwell on his actions outside of the pursuit of money, I say the peddler is the first to reach heaven."

Jules nodded, fearing any other response would make things worse. He wanted to know what Izzy's comment had to do with the significance of an October day, but for the moment he was compelled to search for the meaning himself.

"There's more to life than money," Izzy said. "This you might know in your head, but you'll be judged on your actions and not what goes on in your head."

Izzy's voice penetrated Jules like a deep burn, and for the first time in his life he felt old. Not the knowledgeable and sagacious kind of old, but the old of weakness and vulnerability. And in that moment, all he had accomplished now seemed tenuous and fleeting. It was just possible his career—his life, no less—could hinge on whether he discovered the significance of one particular day in one particular month.

"Think about it, why don't you," Izzy said quietly and turned his attention elsewhere.

Over dinner, Jules foolishly told Marla what had happened. "He yelled at you?" she said without looking up from her plate.

"He snapped at me."

"And you responded how?"

That her gaze was still directed toward her spaghetti spoke volumes to Jules, and it became suddenly obvious he had brought up the subject with the hope of eliciting compassion.

"Do you mind looking at me when we talk?"

Marla apologized and set down her fork.

"I asked him to explain this particular accounting method again. And then we tried the procedure again and it worked out. That's it. Not a big deal."

Marla stared at Jules for a moment and then took a breath. "It sounds like a big deal. I mean, you make a mistake and he yells?"

"Maybe I exaggerated the yelling part."

"Well, he did something to upset you."

"I probably overreacted."

"And you're just realizing this?"

"After talking about it, yes."

Jules put a forkful of pasta into his mouth and chewed, hoping his appetite would return to facilitate swallowing.

"For God's sake, Jules. How are you going to deal with a job where you get yelled at for adding up the wrong numbers or something?"

He choked on a laugh, which only made things worse. "You think this is funny?" Marla leaned back and folded her arms tightly against her chest. She couldn't continue. Her emotions now stuck in her throat, she sat quietly and blinked back tears.

"Marla, I'm doing fine."

"It doesn't seem like you're doing fine."

"How could you possibly know? You'd think by now you would trust me a little bit."

Marla let her head go slack allowing her chin to rest against her chest. Jules watched, afraid to speak.

"What's wrong with us?" Marla said.

"What do you mean?"

"Everyone we know has direction, they're doing something, and I'm just sitting here waiting and you're in this job that you're figuring out and I feel like we're just wandering…"

Jules listened as Marla purged herself of pent up anxiety and revealed insecurities long buried within her idealism, a parade of horribles kept safely hidden in the sanctuary of her father's suburban house. As she spoke, Jules could not help but become cognizant of a change taking place in his body, as if some ghostly part of him was molting. An overwhelming sense of responsibility took hold and a heavy burden manifesting in a rash of sweat crawled up his spine and spread across his shoulders.

"What's wrong? You've turned white."

What was wrong? It was a trick question. On the surface, nothing was wrong. That is, Jules saw no reason for anything to be wrong. In his view, they had made it. He had a career. They had an apartment with closets full of beautiful garments, and walls covered with contemporary art. In the not-too-distant future, he saw a BMW parked in the garage off the alley. Marla, too, had employment, albeit not by itself a "living," but a respectable vocation for an educated woman. Together they could easily get by. All this he knew intellectually. His body, however, spoke through heart palpitations, a disappearing appetite, and a tightness in his chest.

"Jules? Are you OK?"

Jules was fine. This, too, he knew intellectually. His head was the jurisdiction he trusted most.

"There's nothing wrong," Jules said and began skillfully outlining his case, first reiterating the positive events of the past year, then, reaching deep into their history, resurrecting the childhood mythology their parents had created. He reminded her how inseparable they had been as children and how as infants just learning to creep, they would lift their heads and smile at each other.

Whether the softness of Marla's brown eyes and her subdued smile was evidence she, too, treasured their past and regarded it as an indication of the future, Jules couldn't be sure. But for the moment, he chose to ignore the potential ambiguity and wait for her response which came quietly as, "I'm sorry." Although happy to hear the words, Jules was unprepared for the equivocal tone in which they were offered.

"I'm sorry, too."

***

After a fitful night's sleep he arrived at work to find Izzy standing in front of his office. "Now that you've had time to think," he said, "what have you remembered?"

Jules ignored him and collapsed into his chair. "I haven't remembered."

"It's for your own good that you should feel so lousy. One day you will thank me."

Thank him for what? Jules looked at the little man in his baggy suit, an image hard to fear first thing in the morning. "Jesus, Izzy, what do you want? Am I not performing my job? If not then tell me, otherwise leave me alone. It's hard enough learning a new job, I don't need games."

"Are you performing your job? That, only you can answer. Maybe better to ask: What is your job?"

Silence fell between them until Izzy said, "You are a man before you are a job. Maybe better to ask: What is your occupation?"

"All this because I can't tell you why some day in October is so goddamn important? Why don't you just tell me already and get it over with!"

"Calm yourself," Izzy said and casually peered out the partition door. He moved a few steps toward Jules and reached into his back pocket. After removing a twenty dollar bill from his wallet, he placed it neatly on Jules's desk and said, "Here's your loan. My apologies for taking so long to repay." Then he walked out, leaving Jules to stare at the money he had all but forgotten.

3

The week passed without further incident. Occasionally, Jules said hello to Izzy and Izzy would nod in his peculiar business-like fashion and the two of them would act as if nothing had happened. The mysterious October day, too, passed as any other.

When the following week ended and Jules still saw no evidence of more accounts, he thought he would approach Izzy for a friendly chat, but discovered he was out of town. Instead, Jules decided to approach McNally, figuring he had nothing to lose by displaying a desire to work. McNally appeared pleased with his initiative and instructed his secretary to schedule a meeting that afternoon. Jules's spirits soared, and at the appointed time, he knocked on McNally's door with restored confidence.

"How are you getting along, Jules?

"Fine," Jules said, and proceeded to explain his desire to take on more responsibility. When he finished, McNally's head continued nodding until he cleared his throat and said, "James tells me you're doing a crack job. He says you're ready for more accounts."

Jules agreed and sat patiently while McNally talked at length of the prodigy, James Williamson, and how lucky the firm was to have him. Jules detected a slight impatience in McNally's voice, just the barest hint of condescension. But only when he started to lecture him on the importance of cooperation did he begin to wonder if Izzy had complained about him. "You can learn much from a man like Williamson," McNally said, "He's a team player..."

Had Izzy told McNally he was uncooperative, not a team player? McNally stood and extended his hand. Jules shook it and walked out. That evening, he awoke in a fever, and in the sweaty darkness he thought he heard Izzy say, "Calm yourself Ellerstein."

The next morning Jules entered his office to find a large manila envelope lying on his desk. Taped to the envelope was a note from McNally. "To present at Friday's meeting." From the envelope Jules pulled out a thick computer readout containing the account receivables list of a large manufacturer of abrasives. Another note inside explained his task was to study the list and determine if the cash-flow projection presented by the manufacturer was accurate. It was a formidable assignment—he had only three days to prepare—but one offering the promise of redemption, and, perhaps, a chance to move beyond the influence of Izzy.

He set to the task by submersing himself into the receivables record, breaking down the companies by how much they owed, circling in red those longest in arrears. By mid-morning he had barely dented the list, but told himself to relax, that he'd work eighteen-hour days if needed.

At 1:00 he broke for lunch and bought a box of colored pencils before returning to his desk to color code the companies in similar industries—should one go under, what was the probability related companies would follow? It was the kind of reasoning he would—under normal circumstances—run by Izzy, although that was now out of the question. "Trust yourself," Jules thought, "go for the details." It was just a test after all, a way for McNally to see if he had what it took.

He spent most of the evening in the business library researching various companies and making profuse notes about how to structure a draft of his presentation. He arrived home well after 11:00, exhausted, but for the moment, content. Marla was already asleep.

***

That was Tuesday. On Wednesday, he awoke at 4:00 a.m. with a sour stomach. Unable to fall back asleep, he arrived at work extra early, surprised to see several others already drinking coffee behind their desks. After consuming the day with more organizing and researching, he decided he could finish the bulk of his work on Thursday. Since the meeting was scheduled for two o'clock Friday, he would then have Friday morning to tie up loose ends. Again, he arrived home long after dark, only to trudge back to the office after another restless night.

His routine firmly in place, Thursday proved to be his most efficient day. Friday now became extra time he would use to finish his presentation and make the appropriate copies. Flushed with confidence, he quickly put together the report for the following morning and called Marla to suggest she meet him at an expensive Italian restaurant. Unfortunately, Marla had eaten a late lunch with her mother and the two had arranged to go shopping. Jules wished Marla well in her shopping endeavors and told her he would dine alone. The prospect of being seen among the privileged clientele frequenting this particular restaurant was enough incentive to overcome any self-consciousness.

"It sounds like you had a good day," Marla said.

"I did," Jules said and promised to tell her about it.

The restaurant had been an old fashioned Italian storefront grocery with all the original architecture and charm of the early part of the century. The ornate brass and black marble bar, along with the reputation for their homemade sauces, had created a certain aura Jules found irresistible. When he arrived, there were

21

still plenty of tables available, although the bar was already two deep with happy-hour revelers. The hostess seated him at the front, next to the enormous picture window, and after ordering a plate of ravioli, he sat comfortably and stared into the busy street. He pictured himself pulling up to the restaurant in his BMW and handing the keys to the valet who would promise to take good care of it. While he reflected on the intensity of the previous days, he was filled with a joyful sense of accomplishment and thought back to his first day on the job. He remembered wishing he could transport himself forward in time, to the point where he would be working on his own after having proved himself capable. So keen were Jules's thoughts, his realization of having reached his goal captivated him within the dissociative nature of "time." Jules, himself, became a part of his own investigation, dissolving into the background cacophony as he pushed his examination deeper into the unanswerable.

The ravioli's arrival broke the spell. He ate passionately, spearing several squares at a time while his mind downloaded any thoughts his gray matter had to offer. From the abstract notion of time he moved to the concrete emotion of joy, the kind of happiness associated with absolute security in one's station in life, a frame of reasoning that enabled Jules to enjoy his ravioli in complete surety he deserved it.

With the onset of twilight, the window began mirroring the busy restaurant behind him. Jules enjoyed seeing himself in the same reflection with a room full of professionally dressed people and thought of his father, who at Jules's age had already spent several years eating his dinners at roadside diners. He felt tremendous admiration for his father's thirty-plus years of traveling and selling. Jules marveled that his father never swayed from his chosen livelihood and did what needed to be done to make a living. And he felt tremendously relieved for not having a career dragging garment bags around the Midwest.

He looked back to his plate and speared another piece of ravioli but hesitated before lifting his fork. It seemed the joyful anticipation now combined with the heavy meal to beset him with a fatigue that squelched his appetite. The waitress dropped the check and dished the rest of his meal into a doggy bag. Jules stood and faced the crowded restaurant. Every table was occupied. The bar buzzed with sharply dressed women surrounded by men in gray, black, and navy jackets.

He viewed the scene as an outsider, as someone who much preferred a quiet lounge to sip brandy. He thought back to his high school days, his choice of dating the same girl throughout and the ridiculously poor odds this same girl would stick with him all these years. Now that he was older, he knew how uncommon it was for childhood sweethearts to stay together. While watching the exertions at the bar, the looks of rejection and isolation, Jules felt all the more fortunate.

As he reached for the doggy bag an opening through the crowd caught his eye. Initially, it was the whiteness that captured his attention, as if a bobbing ball of light hovered over the black counter. But in the same instant he recognized McNally's white hair, he also saw Izzy's profile. Jules watched hoping to glean some information from the two heads. His initial paranoia was quickly overcome by the knowledge that he had genuine research in the form of a completed project full of real numbers. And they all knew numbers didn't lie. He took a deep breath and walked out.

***

As he stepped through the front door of his apartment, he thought of the doggy bag sitting on the table at the restaurant. The apartment was empty. Marla's shopping plans had momentarily slipped his memory. He slumped into his reclining chair and surfed the television channels. Jules was not an avid TV watcher, preferring instead to fill his evenings with books about European history, particularly the Second World War. Jack was surprised when his son chose to major in business and admitted privately to his brother, Solomon, that he was disappointed Jules did not aspire to study the humanities. "Why not make a living at something you find interesting?"

When Jules did watch television he usually sought out documentary programming, which on this night he found, the

23

Battle of the Bulge proving to be the perfect diversion. It was his Uncle Solly's war, but not quite his father's war, but everybody's war in some way or another. The battle footage and interviews of surviving soldiers riveted Jules, but soon he was fighting a battle of his own as his eye lids grew heavy. He drifted off to black and white images of advancing troops, liberated towns, and finally, to the death camps where Izzy stood waiting. Jules watched this bizarre hallucination of a man as he looked over the starving, shivering multitudes, his gray suit immaculate, his face the mournful judge of mankind.

When he opened his eyes it was eleven o' clock. He shut off the television, stumbled to his bedroom and crawled into bed. When he was about to drift off, it occurred to him in a dreamy, irrational way, Marla was not beside him. But his concern could not bring him back—she was with her mother, after all—and once again he drifted into sleep, this time a prolonged, agitated slumber that took him all the way to the sound of his alarm clock. After silencing the noise he reached to Marla, touched her shoulder, then slid out of bed.

***

He walked briskly through the office, smiled at various administrative staffers, and felt confident enough to veer toward Izzy's office for small talk. But apart from the briefcase sitting on his chair, there was no sign of him. And it was while considering the pros and cons of discussing his presentation with Izzy, he entered his own office to discover the report missing from his desk. Months later, when he thought back to this moment, the room appeared imbued with shades of pastel hues, a hallucination he attributed to shock.

It took a while, but eventually Jules was able harness a rational thought and it came in the form of the janitor cleaning his office. But when he checked the logical places—the floor, his chair, the credenza, file drawers—the report was nowhere to be found.

While standing in the elevator, he had trouble focusing on the matter at hand and for some reason began assigning personalities to the numbers on the floor-selector panel. The nine was happy, the seven laughed, the six was frightened. The letter, "B" lit up as Jules pondered the disposition of a four. Bud, the chief custodian, was sitting in the boiler room office reading the newspaper.

"I'm missing my report," Jules said. "I think a janitor threw it away by mistake."

Bud rested the paper on his lap and stared thoughtfully. "Couldn't have happened," he said.

"How do you know?"

"Odd floors are on Tuesdays and Thursdays. Tonight the twelfth gets cleaned."

Hearing his only logical explanation so easily dismissed brought to Jules a second round of visual chromaticity, this time filled with white flashing spots.

"Couldn't they have done the twelfth by mistake?"

"Never happen," Bud said and pointed to the cleaning schedule.

"But how do you know? You're not here at nights, how do you know what the night shift does?"

Bud frowned, picked up the phone, and dialed a number. "Helena, it's Bud—I know he's sleeping but we got a problem." Bud leaned back in his chair and waited. "Dushko, what floors did you clean last night? But not the twelfth. I know, I know. OK, Dushko, go back to sleep."

Bud hung up and looked at Jules. "Dushko's the night supervisor. He's Russian. Does a good job. He says nobody touched the twelfth floor last night...."

Without another word to Bud, Jules looked at his watch and dashed back to the elevator. For the moment, he let go of the janitor theory and tried to think of other possibilities, but nothing made sense. Who else would enter his office over night?

Then it occurred to him the theft hadn't happened over night but before the business day had ended. It had only been four o'clock when Jules had left the office. And suddenly, despite having nothing to substantiate his hunch, he couldn't help but feel suspicious of Izzy. He recalculated his time spent at the restaurant and approximated when he finished the meal and stood to see the back of McNally's head. There had been plenty of time for Izzy to have stopped in the office before coming to the restaurant. But if Izzy, why? Out of resentment, perhaps, for his ignorance of what was to take place on a given October day? The memory of Izzy and McNally's bobbing heads brought back his nauseating paranoia and Jules was once again a vulnerable child watching as the two discussed his future. It seemed implausible, ridiculous, but as hard as he tried, he could come up with no other reason.

He checked first with the administrative staff. One declared to have done no work for Izzy in a month, another said she was ninety-nine percent sure she saw him early that morning, perhaps holding some papers. They suggested Jules approach McNally, but this was a terrifying proposition since McNally would certainly inquire about the state of the presentation. Instead, he asked McNally's secretary who confirmed Izzy had been in the office and remembered him leaving for the health club.

Despite his corporate membership, Jules had never been to the club, and feeling the pressure of time more acutely, he lost his temper at the smiling young woman behind the desk when she asked him to fill out various forms and questionnaires before entering. A manager intervened and when Jules insisted he only wanted to view the facilities, he was allowed to enter. But where to look? What sort of activity would interest Izzy? Racquetball came to mind although Jules had trouble picturing Izzy moving quick enough for this game. Nevertheless, he checked each of the glass enclosed courts, but to no avail. His luck was no better at the tennis courts or swimming pool, and after scanning the weight room he walked back to the lobby where he bumped into another account executive, Gilbertson, who smiled and expressed surprise at seeing Jules at the club. He ignored Gilbertson's remark and said, "I need to find Izzy. Have you seen him?"

"I saw him in the sauna, but that was an hour ago. S'matter Jules. You don't look so good."

That Gilbertson could make such an irrelevant comment angered Jules. "I've got to go," he said and ran off.

When he arrived at the twelfth floor it was almost eleven o'clock and Izzy's office was still empty. Panic and confusion now fused, becoming one with Jules. The thought of going to the meeting empty handed seemed beyond reason. How to explain such a thing? The report was missing, he would say, and then what? And, worse yet, how long would it take to regain their confidence? Perhaps never.

When the administrative staff had nothing new to report, Jules started running door-to-door, knocking on office partitions, until another account executive, Pelc, out of legitimate concern for a younger colleague, demanded to know what was wrong. Jules told him about the missing report and asked if he had seen Izzy.

"I saw him leave for the airport," Pelc said.

At first, Pelc's words hovered in the air for Jules to watch, lingering on an anemic backdrop of pink. Then they started moving, dancing, twirling, to the roaring of the conch shells Jules imagined were being held to his ears. He tried to shrug them off, push the hands away from his head, but his attention turned back to the changing colors as they faded into a pure, white light.

"What time is it?" Jules heard himself say.

"The color is coming back to his face," someone said.

"Do you want an ambulance, Jules?" another voice said.

An ambulance? "I'm not crazy," Jules said, struggling to get back to his feet. "I'm as normal as any one of you."

"Nobody thinks you're crazy, Jules," Pelc said. "You just fainted, though."

Jules focused on Pelc's face and then realized he was being supported at the arms by two other co-workers.

"I did not faint. You can let go of me."

"Yes you did," Pelc said and four others voiced their agreement in unison.

Jules looked at their faces, saw legitimate concern in their eyes, which, for the moment, he found comforting, although they knew nothing of the gravity of his situation. They had no idea their colleague was on the verge of losing his career. Everything at stake abruptly resurfaced and whatever camaraderie, charity, or friendship his colleagues had to offer was lost in a fresh wave of dread. The conch shells were back on his ears, the roar now the accompaniment to Jules's drama, his brain a projector showing an actor running down a hallway leading to an airplane staircase on which Izzy ascended.

Thus far, Jules's life had been logical, maybe too logical. It was true he had lost his mother at an early age, but death seemed logical in that people died at all ages, all the time. After she died, the attention from relatives and friends seemed just as logical, even to a five-year-old who just had the rug pulled out from under his life. Upper-middle-class suburbia of the late 1970s did not expect much of white males except to reap the benefits sown by their urban-raised parents. Go to school and become successful was all Jules was guilty of, which made the missing report seem all the more illogical.

Perhaps life was more susceptible to blessings than logic, although neither blessings nor logic commanded Jules's attention as he struggled to find the slightest optimistic route in the noise and colors that now made up his world. Years later, looking back on this moment from a medicated point of view, Jules will acknowledge that as he stood among his co-workers, in the depth of his crisis, this moment represented a last stand of sorts. That is, his brain, for the last time before his collapse, would correctly and accurately sling the proper neurotransmitters from one neuron to the next thus producing a triumphant insight: he was no worse off. Not really. He was still young, educated. Still a good investment. He would calmly explain everything to Marla's father who would understand. All was not lost. There were other companies, other ways to stay on the right path. Of course, Pelc could be wrong about Izzy going to the airport. It even occurred to Jules he might be wrong. Perhaps Izzy had nothing to do with the report disappearing. But what did it matter now?

"OK, I'm fine, really," he said, straightening up, shrugging off the grip of his bewildered co-workers. "Thanks for your help. I appreciate your concern. But I'm fine, really. Let me get some air. I'm fine."

And he was off, wanting nothing more than to walk the streets a free man, prepared to accept his fate.

4

Although clouds covered the sky, they were thin and high and the day appeared bright. Jules chuckled with gallows humor at McNally's reaction should he not show up for the meeting. Then he fantasized emerging unscathed after discovering dozens of reports were found to be missing from dozens of desks and he was simply one of many innocent victims. His daydream held until he thought of the work itself, the long hours of industrious labor and painstaking detail; effort wasted for a reason he may never know.

He entered a coffee shop and sat at the farthest table in the back. For several minutes he stared through the room, watched patrons come and go, observed others sitting at tables, reading, writing, or like him, just watching. He asked himself what these people did with their lives, why they should be casually drinking tea or coffee in the middle of the day. He wondered what they saw when he became the object of their gaze. Jules knew wearing a suit and tie cast him as the figure of the conventional young urban dweller of the late nineteen-eighties. He liked the image although he couldn't help but feel like a fraud.

His victorious perception was fast succumbing to the reality of professional failure. He fought to regain a semblance of the glorious mood that twenty minutes earlier had lifted him from his co-worker's arms. He could not yet know he was failing his first cerebrally crucial test as an adult. His neurotransmitters were hesitating, his neurons were unreceptive. His brain settled upon images of the tragic hero basking in the romantic notion of sitting idly in a coffee shop while heading for disaster, a state of mind lasting until Jules asked himself, Am I here?

Jules needed movement. Outside he blended into the lunch-time crush, unsure of where to go, but feeling better just being among a mobile crowd. He wasn't so different from everyone else. He could deal with life's consequences as others did. He would survive and eventually prosper as so many before him had done. He thought of his grandfathers, how they started as peddlers, lived relatively long lives and died with plenty of money in the bank. He had done everything correctly, he had played according to the rules. There was no reason he should not eventually become successful.

At one o'clock he found himself close to a museum he had yet to visit, and after crossing the street his eye caught a familiar posture leaning against an enormous concrete lion—a coincidence hardly believable and one he refused to accept until he recognized the suitcase and the raincoat bunching around the figure's ankles.

So engrossed with allaying fears of what awaited later that afternoon, Jules had all but forgotten the person most likely responsible for his distress. He approached his mentor slowly, peripherally, not wanting to pounce, but to advance calmly.

"Greetings Izzy! I spend half the day looking for you and when I give up, here you are."

Izzy looked at Jules and then away.

"May I ask where you are going, Izzy?"

"New York."

"Important business, no doubt."

"My nephew's first communion."

"Really?" Jules laughed.

"This you find amusing?"

"Kind of a strange place for a Holocaust survivor to be."

Izzy ignored the comment. "By the way Ellerstein, did you happen to remember what you missed in October?"

"Ahh, things that are missing. An interesting subject. You see, I am to give a presentation in less than an hour. Perhaps you heard?"

"Why should I?"

Jules threw up his hands. "Beats me. It's just that the presentation disappeared off my desk this morning."

Izzy craned his neck to look down the busy avenue.

"The events of your morning are none of my business. Excuse me." Izzy broke forward a few steps and waved toward a taxi, but too late. "It's a pity Ellerstein," he said after rejoining Jules. "I'm sure McNally will understand."

"Oh cut the crap! Just tell me why. For God's sake is that asking too much!"

Izzy grabbed the handle of his suitcase and began a fast walk toward a line of taxis now pulling over on the next block. Jules kept pace with him. "I told you," Izzy said, "what you decide to think—"

"You win Izzy," Jules said, amazed at how fast the little man could move with a suitcase. "Just tell me why. What did I do?"

Two of the taxis began pulling away from the curb and Izzy began sprinting the last stretch. Jules fell back panting and watched him catch the last taxi and open the door.

"Just tell me!"

This time Izzy turned around, and before getting into the taxi called back. "The candle, Ellerstein. The job was consuming you; took you away from even lighting a candle. Some day you'll thank me."

Jules made a final dash but could only watch the taxi pull away as the window came down and Izzy's face stared back. "Respect needs to be earned," Izzy shouted. "The anniversary of your mother's death. You missed her Yahrzeit."

***

Had Jules showed up for the meeting he could have explained what had happened, he could probably have kept his job. And even if McNally had not believed him, he would have seen the shame on Jules's face and knew something out of the ordinary happened— that Jules's MBA, his arrival at N&M, his promotion, all had not happened by accident.

31

But long after Izzy's taxi disappeared into traffic, Jules remained on the sidewalk transfixed by the way the daylight drained into the cars and shops until the buildings themselves grew brighter with each passing moment. It was here Jules first became acutely aware of moments, how moments were all he was made of, how each moment built upon the previous moment until everything had been transformed.

Moments are the worms of time, he thought standing next to the street. And why not? Worms, those miraculous creatures, so reviled in their lowness in life's hierarchy, living amongst the dirt and slime, but performing the most essential of functions, creating the very dirt that grows the food we all depend upon. And so it was with moments—fleeting, innocuous, invisible, but the structure of time itself.

Everything had changed. Jules knew this as he watched the final remnants of light empty from the sky. But despite the day's confusion, everything seemed very clear. His job was gone, of this he was sure. Marla, too, would be gone. Having juxtaposed herself with Jules long enough, the collective fantasy of a childhood union will finally play itself out with a not-so-sudden grasping of the scope of Jules's failure. His inability to cope with the missing report will become the touchstone to which Marla will silently compare Jules's life during the weeks to come.

"You just stood there?" she will say over and over. "You just stood there on a street corner while the meeting came and went?"

And Jules will have no choice but to agree with Marla, that he did exactly what she described. On one occasion, he will try to explain what happened inside his head, how for some reason he simply could not move when the taxi pulled away, and perhaps he had suffered some kind of breakdown. But his reasoning will sound pathetic to Marla and she will nod her head slowly for several minutes before walking away.

5

"I'll teach you the line," Jack Ellerstein said, referring to his ready-to-wear business. "It doesn't have to be forever. But it'll get you out of this box, help you snap out of it. People like you Julie, you know that. You're a natural you know. You could be a great coat salesman if you wanted. I've always said that."

Jules was sitting at the end of his bed. He had heard, "I'll teach you the line," often in his adult life, although the phrase changed slightly when Jules announced he wanted to get an MBA and his father replied, "I'll teach you the line, and for a lot cheaper than business school." Jules wanted to be a businessman, not a salesman of women's clothing.

His father's voice resonated deeply with Chicago, the Chicago of men who reached maturity in the late forties, men who may or may not have served in the Second World War, men whose fate had been determined by accident of birth with those born before 1927 defined in some way by their participation in the war.

Those who didn't wear the uniform finished high school, entered college, walked among the droves of returning boys who had found their way from the battlefields to the campuses, some still limping, some still wearing the boots in which they plodded around Europe and Asia, many only a few months older than Jack Ellerstein whose draft date had been set for a few weeks after Germany's surrender. And along with millions of other men blessed enough to have been born after 1927, Jack Ellerstein witnessed history from the sidelines of 1940's America, enjoying everything available to a white Chicago teenager. The war hit closest to home when his older brother, Solomon, was drafted shortly after D-Day and served as a medic from the Battle of the Bulge to VE day.

"He must've seen some horrible things, Solly did," Jack had told Jules who wanted to know about his uncle's war. "Ask him. He'll probably talk about when he bumped into that German Lieutenant while looking for wounded during the Bulge. It's the only story he tells."

Jules asked and Solly did as his father predicted.

"The son-of-a-bitch spoke perfect English," Solly said. "He asked me what I was doing and I told him I was looking for wounded and he told me to go back to my lines. And then he

walked away! Unbelievable. He could've shot me. The krauts
didn't give a damn if you had a red cross on your helmet."

Jules waited to hear more but when Solly remained silent,
when he averted his gaze, Jules knew better.

"Solly will tell you what Solly wants you to know," his father
said later. "I wasn't there, Julie. It's not for me to tell."

It's not for me to tell. Jack's generation knew so much, had
seen so much, how could Jules resist when the voice declared him
a natural salesman, insisted he would teach him the line? Sitting at
the end of his bed, the idea seemed logical if only to give him
something to do. Maybe it was the time to immerse himself into
his father's world. Many before him had finished law school,
earned their CPAs and MBAs, only to work in the family business.

But why? That is, apart from the voice extolling his attributes,
the voice's insistence his son had a propensity for sales, that he
was a natural. From his father's own words Jules knew the garment
industry stunk. "They're all whores," Jack had said often. "Coat
manufacturers? They would sell their own mothers to make a
buck!"

Even before he was old enough to understand what a
manufacturer's representative was, the dominant image of his
father at work had been a furrowed brow shaking his head in
disgust. Tagging along while Jack inspected endless rows of coat
racks, young Jules saw his father with an unlit cigar gripped
between his teeth, holding a coat sleeve with both hands, rubbing
the material between his fingers, repeating the words "shit" or
"pure shit" under his breath. And even if the line wasn't "shit" the
traveling apparel salesman constantly dealt with cancelled orders,
disappearing stores, and buyers routinely ignoring appointments.
The buyer. The word itself had mythological qualities to the
apparel salesman, the buyer being the person who held all the
cards, the person whom the salesman was completely dependent
upon for their livelihood.

But even when things went well, even when Jack Ellerstein
arrived home after a week or two on the road with his briefcase full
of orders, it could be months before he received his commission

checks. And sometimes the checks never came, sometimes the manufacturer suddenly had no idea who you were. On top of it all was the traveling itself, the Midwestern bleakness, boredom, loneliness of motel living, contending with blizzards, ice storms, driving rains, and tornadoes.

"It used to be every town had at least one good store," Jack would say, and by the time Jules was a teenager he knew his father was talking about a world before shopping malls and corporate chain stores that bought their merchandise only in New York. In New York the buyers had one-stop shopping, what did they need the traveling salesman for?

"I'm not kidding, either," Jack would then emphasize. "Even the smallest, pissant little town had at least one good store or specialty shop, and everyone knew the owner and what to expect. After a while, they got used to seeing me come through every year and they treated me like an old friend. This salesman from Chicago they would have over for dinner."

And then he would talk about the New York of this period, the New York of the fifties and sixties, home to the biggest manufacturing whores but also the place where Jack Ellerstein had the most fun. And when his father talked about those days, the nightclubs, music, parties, a traveling manufacturer's representative sounded like the greatest job in the world.

That world was gone. Now you had mostly big department stores and maybe a decent store in Peoria or Rockford or Joliet, small cities with enough population to stay alive, enough people to consider buying from the place with the kitschy-looking storefront that folks over forty would point out nostalgically to their children who will never set foot in the store with the old saleswomen in their wool skirts. The traveling apparel salesman could still hope to make a few bucks from such cities, but anything smaller, Vandal, Benton, Centralia, Shelbyville, forget it.

This was the world Jack Ellerstein wanted his son to join, and as Jules sat on the end of his bed listening to the voice, his brain tuned in long enough to know his father wanted only to help, to give him something to do, to get him over this business at the

commercial lending firm and not because there was a great future
in wholesale apparel or because Jules was a natural, but because it
was familiar. It had been a part of his family, his culture. It was
full of people who knew him, people who had watched him grow
up, people he referred to as "Uncle." Whether Jules's brain was
wired for this world Jack Ellerstein could not have known, would
not have even thought to ask himself. It wasn't a question of brains
to Jack Ellerstein; what could brains possibly have to do with
selling?

6

Jules was late for an appointment. So late that when he
stepped outside into the bright sunshine, he declared the
appointment officially missed and spent the rest of the afternoon
emptying his bucket of compost in different parts of the city. He
chose small places, like a plot of grass surrounded by a black iron
fence or the overgrown weeds of an alley, or a thick juniper bush
that could swallow a withered vegetable and keep it forever hidden
in the shaded mud below. It wasn't the first time he'd missed an
appointment. And on those days, Jules sometimes hid apple cores
and spinach stems and collected dog excrement to mix into the dirt.
It felt good returning organic matter to the soil. The earth
fascinated him, how she simply took care of its refuse, blending it
in for nourishment, wasting nothing.

His father would want to know what happened, why he missed
the appointment. It was an important client, after all. Marshall
Field no less. The appointment had been his father's way of
showing confidence in Jules. It was also an opportunity to make up
for the last missed appointment. He knew he would have to explain
to his father why he couldn't make it. But since it was a beautiful
day and his thirtieth birthday, he walked to the park and lay
comfortably in the shade of a giant elm—a majestic old survivor,
defiantly flaunting its limbs—and pondered his new girlfriend's
advice to get off the medication. "Let me be your drug of choice,"
Bronwyn had told him.

Choice. Since the moment Jules stood on the curb staring
down the avenue, the concept of "choice" had become more an
abstract notion than a word with unambiguous meaning. The

36

change began with his father's urging to join him in the apparel business. The ardor in Jack's voice had been something Jules was not used to, something that triggered an intensely sentimental reaction. It was time, he decided, to embrace his father's judgment. He thought he owed it to Jack to give it a try since his father had the experience, after all; his father should know what he was talking about. What choice did he have but to trust his father?

So he did as Jack suggested and before he knew it he was on his way to Milwaukee where Jack had several old accounts, men who had owned specialty shops that for many decades catered to the smartly dressed women of Milwaukee, but whose stores now occupied moribund strip malls in "transitioning" neighborhoods. Those same dapper women were now aged ladies, but still venerable and loyal and making their way across town to shop from men they had known for three decades as Sheldon or Irv or Sam. "It's a good trip to get your feet wet," Jack told him. "These guys are all sweethearts."

Sheldon was a sweetheart in his brown pinstripes, his ear-to-ear grin, and the way he cupped Jules's ear and rubbed his head. But his kindness intensified the shabby surroundings and filled Jules with a suffocating sadness. He managed to maintain a polite façade, laughed at Sheldon's stories of his father and the "guys" living it up in New York, but when Sheldon's gray-haired assistant returned, baby-stepping in her droopy stockings, Jules could bear it no longer.

"I have to go to the bathroom," he said and excused himself to a closet of a room where he sat on the toilet and stared at the marbled glass of the small window. Oh God, was all he could think as panic welled up into his throat. He stood, paced, took deep breaths, tried to will his heartbeat to slow down, tried to assemble a course of action.

A knock on the door. "You OK in there?"

With Sheldon's voice Jules saw the now familiar spots against a whitening background. He pulled on the window and got it opened about a third of the way. He pulled harder, slugged the frame with the heel of his hand and then rammed it with his shoulder until the frame bent and the glass exploded. The screen fell away easily with a shove of his elbow and exposed a portal to freedom through which Jules squeezed himself head first, delivered from the world of ready-to-wear.

The king-sized bed at the Holiday Inn was firm, comfortable, a luxurious raft upon which Jules floated while repeating, Am I here? It was relaxing, especially when compared to the rudeness that awaited him, the pounding on the door, the strange faces hovering about, the lifting, the pulling, the pinching of his skin.

Laying comfortably under the Elm, Jules wished he could call Bronwyn and tell her he was off the medication and then tell her about the day. But it seemed much easier to sleep than talk, and he drifted off remembering his hospital bed and how he watched his father's bewildered face as an Indian man who called himself a neurobiologist spoke of isomers and their spatial arrangement of atoms and how they held the promise for many medications. The doctor compared Jules's thoughts to electrical impulses choosing negative pathways instead of positive ones. "Isomers can help your son," the doctor said. "They can help Jules choose the right pathway."

***

A soft breeze blew through the leaves of a lovely summer day. Everything made sense in this day, including the sudden feeling of not being alone, a feeling of "otherness" Jules incorporated into his dreamy world, as if joining fellow hitchhikers on a celestial journey. They whispered at first, or tried to whisper, as if out of respect for the sleeping—which flattered Jules—but eventually their voices grew louder, until they talked comfortably as if in their own backyard.

"I know what he's sayin' Bea," a male voice said. "But that don't change nothin'. The masters say ego ain't gonna budge on you 'cause all the momentum of human conditionin'."

"Like I says, you ain't been listenin' white man," a female voice said. "Don't tell me about no human conditionin' neither. Masters also say we's here now. An the only way we's gonna git free is to shit-can that ego."

38

Jules enjoyed how innocent and genuine they sounded.

"I ain't dissin' you on ego, Bea. But we barely survivin' with it. How we gonna get by when we waste it? You know, then we'll be walkin' around all happy-like. A man's gotta eat don't he?"

"If you been listenin' instead of drinkin', you'd know it don't make no difference once you done with ego. You won't need no damn job 'cause you git everything you ever want. Like Christmas every damn day..."

Jules half-opened his eyes and saw a grocery cart glimmering in the grass not ten feet away, filled with cans, a filthy sleeping bag draped over the end. He turned his head slightly and saw his fellow travelers: a thin black woman, early forties, wearing a yellow construction helmet, and her partner, a short paunchy white man in a pink tank-top, probably the same age. What was left of his blonde hair he combed straight back. He was lying on his side with his elbow lodged in the ground, his head resting in his hand. She sat cross-legged in front of his face, a grimy white gym bag beside her.

"Hey there little bro!" the female voice shouted. "How you doin'?" Jules focused on the woman and smiled. "Couldja spare us a little change, my brother?"

Jules sat up and looked at the man who nodded his head and rubbed together the tips of his fingers.

"Money, my amigo," he said. "Can ya help us out a little bit?"

The couple stared at Jules as if their lives hinged on his next move. Jules took out his wallet and extricated a folded bill that he placed between two fingers before extending his arm. The man pushed himself into a sitting position and began crawling toward the money. When he was within a few feet he stopped and cautiously plucked it from Jules's hand. Upon recognizing the denomination he cursed loudly.

"What's goin' on, Leroy?"

"Twenty dollar bill is what's goin' on, Bea"

The woman screamed and fell over laughing while her yellow helmet tumbled away. "I knowed it," she shouted. "I be manifestin' all day fo that money and there it comes, like manna from heaven."

Jules watched the woman and started giggling himself, to the point he needed to rub the tears from his eyes.

"I'm Leroy," the man said and wiped his hand on his shirt before offering it to Jules. "And this here is Bea."

Jules took Leroy's oily hand. Bea waved and retrieved her helmet.

"You got a name little bro?" she said.

Jules looked into her brown eyes and couldn't remember when he last spoke.

"Don't talk much, do you my brother?" Bea said.

"Nothin' wrong with that neither," Leroy said. "No sir, a man say more by what he doin' than by what he sayin'."

Jules opened his mouth slightly which sent a ripple of anticipation through his new companions, and upon hearing his own name, "Jules," emerge from his mouth, he smiled in amazement it could be so simple. Bea and Leroy couldn't help but smile too, creating a scene in which the casual passerby would be blameless for believing there existed a long and deep-running friendship.

"Is that a Euro-pean name?" said Leroy. "You a Euro-pean feller?"

Jules wanted to answer, but instead the question provoked vague recollections of voices and faces; a man speaking a strange language from a book, a woman waving her arms over candles. "Yes," he finally said.

"Don't matter none if you is or isn't," Bea said. "We just 'preciate yo help. Leroy and I gettin' tired a'eatin' church food."

"An we been fixin' to save up for a good meal, but they only givin' twenty-five cents for a pound of cans," said Leroy, grabbing the front of the grocery cart and shaking it.

"S'cuse Leroy with all his talk. We just happy to know you Jules. An it don't matter if you don't speak 'cause maybe it ain't you language. Maybe you one of them refugees we hear about. And if you is, well God bless you for it. Either way it don't matter. But for now, Leroy and I got a powerful hunger. Ain't that right Leroy."

"Yes, ma'am."

"An it only be fittin' that you join us in a meal. A Thanksgiving in July."

Jules liked the idea of Thanksgiving while it was still warm, the leaves dry on the trees instead of wet and decayed on the ground. "Yes," Jules heard himself say, and as a gesture of trust, Leroy told Jules to keep an eye on his grocery cart and jokingly warned him not to run off with the cans. Jules lay down again and enjoyed the feeling of the cold grass on the back of his neck. He imagined his neurons triggering one-by-one, giving the signal to his brain to feel cool.

***

When he opened his eyes again it was early evening. He looked east and saw the lake had taken a darker, more ominous appearance. In an hour it would be ink-black except for the occasional light moving slowly across like a phantom.

He stood and yawned, raised his arms over his head, and surveyed his environment: The statue of Göethe was silhouetted against the sky, featureless and grotesque. The traffic was somehow quieter, as if the coming darkness served as a volume control for the city. His eyes locked on to the grocery cart and he tried to remember its significance. Leroy's face popped into his head and then Bea's and the chain of events starting with the missed appointment and the summer day under the giant elm. He scanned the park thinking they might be lurking around, but the darkness had now turned all objects into fleeting shadows dashing about. The cart troubled Jules. He felt obligated to take it with him and pushed it across the grass and on to the sidewalk along Diversey. From there he pushed it past the discount health and beauty aid store, across the Walgreen's parking lot, and through the outside door of the Art Deco style low-rise building where he lived. The ancient elevator—with its heavy hinged door and collapsing iron gate—was too small to accommodate both passenger and cart, so Jules left it in the lobby where it seemed curiously at home with the scratchy checkerboard tile and red velvet love seat.

At the fourth floor he stepped off the elevator and opened the door to his studio apartment. The light from the hallway in the next building shone brightly through his only window, casting shadows over the brown tweed carpet. He pushed the flashing number "3" of his answering machine and waited for the clicks and beeps to reveal the first voice, Uncle Solly. "Jules, Ira just called me from the Apparel Center wondering where you are. Wondering if he was ever going to see the line. And all I could do was wonder too, Julie. Is it happening again, Jules? Your're father, he's a wreck, but I told him it's probably nothing. That it wasn't starting again..."

Jules couldn't help but smile while Solly spoke. His thoughts turned to days spent hanging out at the showroom with his father and Solly, Solly's old friends stopping by to kibbitz; retired apparel men, worn-out fossils sporting Fedoras and black or brown pin-striped suits.

Solly trailed off to another beep from which a voice emerged evoking a vague sense of familiarity despite sounding absurdly incongruous. "Six months gone already," the voice said, "and what do you have to show for it? Perhaps you are in a better place— although this I very much doubt. Perhaps you are earning your living by pushing a wagon and shouting that someone's knife you will sharpen for a pittance..."

Jules knew the voice as one knew an annoying song constantly on the radio. "...Listen Ellerstein, the earth will spin with no regard as to your opinion of it. At the equator you will spin fastest, at the North Pole not at all. As The Name told Adam, 'I set before you two possibilities...the blessing and the curse. Choose life.' So you should too, Ellerstein. That is, choose life."

I could kill him, Jules thought but had trouble conjuring up images of himself committing a violent act against such a pitiful figure. Izzy's voice was cut off by a prolonged "beep," and then Bronwyn's voice emerged. "Jules, please pick up," she said followed by her breathing. "I can wait Jules, 'til you're ready."

Bronwyn was thirty-eight a personal transformation therapist, divorced, a devotee of an eclectic spiritual practice taught by a woman who "channeled" a disembodied spirit called "Jahmal." They had met in a coffee shop when she approached Jules and asked if he wouldn't mind sharing his table. He saw a lovely face with large brown eyes bordered by long chestnut hair.

"Please sit," Jules said and Bronwyn sat, peered at Jules occasionally while she sipped a latté and worked on knitting Sanskrit words across a sweater. Occasionally, their eyes would meet and they would both smile, until finally Jules asked what she was knitting and Bronwyn uttered the curious-sounding phrase. Jules asked what language she had spoken, what the phrase meant, and for what reason she would choose to know how to utter such sounds. Bronwyn answered in short phrases—"it's my teacher's mantra"— until Jules asked enough questions to warrant a lengthy discourse on the teachings of Jahmal, and her quest for "enlightenment". The conversation progressed throughout the afternoon with Bronwyn's explanation of enlightenment proving too irresistible for Jules's troubled mind to disregard—the "freedom" of which Bronwyn spoke sounded like a state of mind that would solve his problems.

The silence was again broken with "Your uncle called me Jules," which was significant since both Solly and his father couldn't help but consider Bronwyn a part of Jules's problem. And the idea of his "problem" pulling Solly and Bronwyn together to confer as allies, brought another smile to Jules's face.

"It's actually beautiful what you're doing," Bronwyn said later that evening after Jules called her. "You're soul has been repressed, and now it's expressing."

"I missed another appointment."

Bronwyn giggled and sighed happily. "Move in with me you brilliant man," she whispered, "and together we'll conquer the world. Or at least the city."

"You spoke to my uncle?"

"I told him you're fine and not to worry. He told me about the big appointment. Field's for God's sake! Brilliant. Did I know where you were? he asked."

"You didn't know."

"Tell me. I want to know."

Jules shut his eyes and tried to call up the day's events. He put the receiver down and walked into the bathroom to take a couple of aspirin, and then lay back down on the carpet and rested the receiver against his ear. "I was in the park. The park with Göethe."

"Hmmm." Bronwyn studied philosophy and drama in college; late night Bohemians stoned and expostulating over Sartre and Kierkegaard. They were the vanguard of the Sixties, she liked to tell him. "You and Göethe, the mastermind of the German people. 'A useless life is only an early death.'"

***

Pushing the grocery cart across Halsted Street toward Bronwyn's apartment, Jules saw her walk topless past the window with a cigarette hanging from her mouth. Before, he would yell to close the shades and tell her it wasn't Amsterdam where she lived, and she would laugh and yell back about tripping on LSD while swimming naked in some cold body of water somewhere in the Midwest, sometime in the Sixties. But tonight, observing her skin from afar elicited no judgment.

After Bronwyn buzzed Jules through the door he struggled the cart on to the landing at the foot of a steep staircase. He was tired, and the thought of fighting the metal cage up three flights overwhelmed him. He stopped just long enough to determine the cart safe where it was. When the door opened Jules was sitting against the wall. Bronwyn had put on a white v-neck T-shirt that hung over a pleated green skirt. "This skirt was part of my Catholic school uniform," she said while bending down to him. "And I'll bet you haven't eaten a thing all day."

Together they walked to the front of the apartment and sunk into the couch under the picture window through which lights and traffic bathed them fittingly, as if their lives demanded urban cliché.

"What's it like right now?" she said. "How does it look?" Bronwyn believed Truth existed in every situation and Jules's Truth was his ability to transcend the mundane. Only someone of "higher consciousness" had this ability.

"I don't know," Jules said. He was thinking of his head as an hour-glass with the grains of sand dangerously close to running out. He rested his skull against the ledge of the window to stem the flow.

Bronwyn curled her legs underneath herself and leaned into him. "But what are you seeing?"

He knew what she meant. Was he seeing vibrations and colors where others saw bricks and mortar? Was he having simultaneous conversations on different plateaus?

"I don't know what happened. I never do. I need to think of what to say to my father."

Bronwyn rose from the couch and walked into the kitchen. She opened a can of tuna and began spooning chunks into a dish while discussing a Vedic poem she had just read. Jules heard her but decided to focus on the window sill's chipped paint and the strange shapes the warped panes of glass made of the colored neon sign on the Chinese restaurant across the street. When his attention returned to Bronwyn, she was walking toward him carrying a bowl and uttering strange sounds. He smiled and took the bowl of tuna chunks covered with mayonnaise. Sticking out of the bowl was a chocolate bar which Jules ate first. Bronwyn sat next to him and rested her head on his shoulder.

"'The whole world is strewn with snares, traps, gins and pitfalls for the capture of men by women,'" she said, quoting

Shaw, and then kissed him on the cheek and began rubbing his chest. "Just let it happen," she whispered. "You're unfolding, blossoming. There's nothing to fear. You don't need their world. Everything's perfect—just like it's supposed to be."

"I have a choice."

"There's always a choice. We choose everything we do."

Jules started on the tuna chunks, feeling better with each swallow. Bronwyn waited until he finished and then turned off the lamp and led him through the noise of the darkened hallway and into the bedroom.

***

In the morning, Jules lay on his side with Bronwyn spooned to his back. When he opened his eyes the windowless room was still dark except for sunlight illuminating the crack under the bedroom door. He peeled himself away and stepped naked into the brilliant sunshine and remembered it was Saturday, a day his father would be working alone behind the sliding glass doors of his showroom. He dressed and emerged from Bronwyn's apartment into the narrow stairwell where the air was dense with the smell of wet carpet. When he reached the bottom staircase his stomach tightened upon seeing the grocery cart—void of cans—turned over.

He stood the cart upright and pushed it through the door and down the sidewalk to the bus stop.

"Are you crazy? You can't bring that thing on." The bus driver shut the door.

Suddenly, the sun was hotter, whiter, and Jules's shoulders felt yoked with a heavy heat. He began walking south, toward downtown, attracting the attention of many people. The cart vibrated through his wrists. He passed a garbage can where three soda cans sat on top of the heap. He dropped the cans into the cart and looked around for more. On the street next to the curb he spotted several more cans flattened and imbedded with grime. These too he picked up. A few blocks farther a man approached and offered him a sip from a paper bag. Jules said, "No thank you,"

46

but the man continued walking next to him, talking and laughing as if they were old friends, until eventually wandering away.

Another hour passed before he reached Orleans Street. A single cabbie with his face buried in a newspaper occupied the circular drive of the Apparel Center. Through the emergency exit he dragged the cart into the nearly deserted lobby where a young Indian man sat stoically behind a counter of candy and tobacco. A giant escalator transported an endless stream of invisible buyers and sellers. Jules pulled the cart up four marble steps and then pushed it into the elevator.

He stepped off at the tenth floor and pushed the cart into the shadow of a giant corn plant from where he watched his father scrutinize one of his coat lines. Jack wore an argyle sweater-vest and baggy slacks decades out of style. The mannequins—thin, black, faceless creatures frozen in overwrought postures—carried out a macabre dance on a stage of a white marble, chrome, and track lighting.

Jules moved away from the corn plant and approached the showroom door. When the front wheels of the cart rattled across the track for the sliding glass, his father stopped what he was doing and peered over his glasses. Then he picked up a yellow packing slip and said, "You've taken up peddling, Julie?"

Jules pushed the cart to the end of the glass table where his father now sat, and collapsed into a chair. He looked around the room while Jack examined the yellow piece of paper while mumbling, sighing, shaking his head. The glare of the lights and stainless steel assaulted Jules's senses. He tried focusing on his father but the silence was terrifying.

"Your uncle called me. He told me you missed the appointment." His father had begun paging through a thick inventory list, licking two fingers before turning a page. "I thought maybe I should do something. Maybe I should talk to you. But talking never worked so good."

Jack's equivocal words tempted him. Jules thought of saying, "You're right" or "I'm sorry," but said nothing.

"You still with that girl?"

Bronwyn and his father had met once when she joined them at a Chinese restaurant where goldfish the size of tuna swam back and forth. Bronwyn only watched the meal—she was on fruit-juice fast—but engaged Jules's father with didactic inquiry about the exploitation of textile workers in far off lands and the corrupting influence of the fashion industry on young girls. Jack listened politely.

"Bronwyn," Jules said.

"Oh yes, the therapist."

Jules tried to form the words he might have said from the beginning, the only words needed to be taken back. But quickly the voice became louder and deeper. "Maybe you want to trade places with me. Maybe you would like my life instead." Something on the list caught Jack's eye and he began mumbling and sighing. Jules wanted to make his case, but his throat was too dry for speech and his mouth groped vacuously like the gold fish in the restaurant.

Jules wanted to promise to go on the road, visit small towns where salesmen learned the ropes, paid their dues, formed relationships. On the road to Benton and Vandalia, Marion and Metropolis, alone on the road with a car full of samples. Why not me? he thought and pictured himself showing the line, writing orders, slapping the backs of buyers—just like a man on the road. He felt good. He wanted to tell Bronwyn, but the inventory list closed with a thud and he suddenly saw himself lonely in a motel, depressed, rejected, tired, the television on but nothing to watch.

"And I'll tell you what," the voice boomed again, "we didn't have the choices you have today!" Jules wondered why choices for him were difficult, why his decisions couldn't be obvious. Jack leaned toward him. His voice now softened. "It's not as if I wanted nothing else in the world but to sell women's clothing. I did it to make my living..." Jules wanted to respond, but he was trapped among long, lonely, country roads, and dark, heavy skies; exile and alienation among cornfields and cafés.

"You ask too many questions," Jack said as he rose from his chair. "Just pick something to do and call it your own. That's all we ever did." Jack walked toward the back of the showroom, poured a cup of coffee, took a sip and then spilled the rest into the sink. "It may not seem like much to you, but it's mine. It's all mine," he said pointing to his chest before turning back to his papers and garments. Jack leaned over the appointment book and looked at the month laid out under his fingers. His face was a jumble of contortions filtering through his pen and manifesting on the paper as question marks, stars, and dollar signs. A sudden shift in focus drew Jules back to the trappings of the showroom—pointy black faced mannequins, enormous photos of ashen-skinned models. Am I here?

He abruptly stood, bangin his knees against the glass table top which jumped from the chrome and dropped with a loud clang sending his father's lists scattering among packing tissue and disemboweled cardboard boxes. "For Christ sake!" he heard while shuffling backward and tipping his chair over. Jules grasped the grocery cart and smashed through the mannequins en route to the hallway, an angular black model falling backward into the basket. He noted the ease with which he descended the escalator and with each flight counted backward from ten, until he reached the lobby and a line of Japanese tourists standing politely in a row, passing Jules on the way up with a nod and a smile.

He rammed the cart through the emergency exit, back into the bright summer day. Jules hurried along the sidewalks and streets, snaking his way back to Halsted, slowing down only to catch his breath before taking off again. A food vendor waved and yelled for him to buy a hot dog for his date. When he approached the park he thought he saw a couple sitting close to the statue. He walked faster. His eyes focused on the two figures getting to their feet. Are they leaving? The sidewalk grew thick with people waiting to cross to the park. "Hey you!" shouted a man in an alley, smiling, urinating on the side of a building. Jules looked at the man who gestured to come closer. He looked back to the park and thought he saw a dark-skinned woman walking toward the harbor. Was the hat yellow?

Jules walked along the sidewalk bordering the park and tried to retrace the route of the woman. He pushed the cart across the lawn toward the harbor while zig-zagging around bodies sprawled on blankets. Passing a group of shirtless teen-age boys sitting in a circle while pounding drums, a young girl with her hair stuffed into a knit cap asked Jules for money to buy dog food. She was wearing a flowing tie-dyed skirt and a bikini top. A patchwork of freckles ran across her nose. "Do you know Bea and Leroy?" Jules said.

The girl shook her head. "Why're you pushin' that thing around?"

"I need to find Bea and Leroy."

"Well, good luck," she said and skipped away.

Jules continued to maneuver the cart throughout the park while scanning the multitudes. At some point he forgot exactly what or who among the colors of the crowd he was looking for. As the afternoon wore away, fatigue gradually caught up and hit him hard. He steered his way back to the giant elm near the Göethe statue. He lay down and closed his eyes only to open them again when he heard the same girl's voice say, "Did you find them?"

Jules sat up. It was almost dusk. The rhythmic drumming permeated the park and his head. "I guess not," she said giggling.

Jules sat up and leaned his back against the elm. He watched the girl perform a quick pirouette before she lifted the mannequin from the cart, whispered secrets in its ear, and kissed its mouth. Jules's eyelids became heavy again. And as the girl pulled the mannequin tight against her thin body, he drifted off with her image dancing in a circle to the beat of the drums, holding the dummy tight around the neck.

7

When the police officer's face came into focus, another moment had ended and an interim moment had begun. That is, the ensuing period was one of transition, a moment in which not much was remembered except the physical sensation of movement, the ocular reaction to brightness, and a general feeling of corporeal surrender as his body was raised, positioned, massaged, and walked. The occasional pin-prick was the only stimulus his form answered, a provocation answered by a discharge of relief.

The better part of a week passed before cognizance returned. The efficacy of his medication combined with the familiar smells of his apartment and the intimate tactility of his bed sheets, helped bring Jules back to the present tense of life. And all through it, Jack Ellerstein sat beside him, struggling with the truth that this young man who for days had lain prostrate babbling about lost grocery carts and aluminum cans, could indeed be his relation. Not that Jack Ellerstein lacked the sensitivity to recognize the poignancy of the situation. It was just so desperately foreign, a state of affairs beyond the scope of Jack Ellerstein's experience. Snap out of it! he wanted to say, he had always wanted to say. But Jack was tired and his son was no longer a kid. He had to learn to stand on his own two feet. What else was there to say?

Gradually, Jules progressed to where he could recall events that had put him in bed while his father snored only inches away, testing the limits of his reclining chair. The incongruity of Jack sleeping somewhere besides the suburban house where Jules had grown up seemed irrational. Perhaps he was dreaming.

Then Izzy came to mind and as hard as he tried to move beyond this strange, anachronistic boy-man, he was drawn into reliving the events from the excitement of the promotion to the little bastard's sabotage. As his father snored, Jules spent only a few minutes wishing he had discussed what had transpired with McNally instead of simply disappearing and washing his hands of the whole business. He knew now the proper medication would have stayed his course and ensured a legitimate career with N&M. But thanks to medication, he didn't dwell on the past and moved to his father's invitation to "teach him the line," which brought him to his first and second missed appointments and then to closing his eyes under a tree in the park with Göethe. As for the two characters he met in the park, they must have been part of a dream, or, perhaps, they were real, but only from a distance, two people he saw while in his un-medicated state, two people from which he created a story line to serve some subconscious desire.

"Dad," Jules said, and then kicked the reclining chair with his foot.

Jack bolted upright. "Julie, are you feeling better?"

Jules noted how much older his father looked. "How come we never observed mom's yahrzeit?"

Jack searched the room with his eyes. "I don't know. We weren't religious. Are you better? You sound better."

Was he better? As if it could be that simple, as if the act of feeling better meant Jules's place in the world had been resolved and there was nothing to worry about.

"I'm much better," Jules said. "I guess screwed up again."

The suggestion of remorse in Jules's voice had a tonic effect on Jack. "Ach, don't worry about it, as long as you're feeling better," he said, smiling broadly, rising from the reclining chair, suddenly not looking quite as old. "We'll figure things out; just keep getting better."

Jack's relief was palpable; Jules could sense it ricocheting off the four walls he called home.

"You're right," Jules said, dangling a conciliatory carrot in front of his father with the hope he would follow it out of his apartment.

"OK, now take your time for chrissake" Jack said and stepped away from the chair and walked over to the window. "And don't worry, you'll figure things out, you'll find something you want to do. You could be anything you want, you know. I've always said that."

Jules nodded and watched his father fidget in the ensuing silence. "Dad, go home. You look terrible."

Jack smiled. "I'll leave you alone," he said and moved toward the door. "But let me know how you're doing, for chrissake." He put his hand on the doorknob and then stopped. "Hey, I almost forgot. I met that friend of yours. Damn it. What the hell was his name?"

Jules waited.

"Ozzy? You got a friend named Ozzy?"

"Izzy?"

"That's it! Nice kid but very peculiar."

"How the hell did you meet him? He thinks he's my friend?"

"That's what he said. He was in the lobby a few days ago and he walked right up to me and asked how you were doing. He said he worked with you at that other job. He's a schmoozer that one. Next thing I know we're talking like were old friends."

"Talked about what? The little shit stabbed me in the back!"

"I'm telling you he talked as if you two were pals, good pals. He started telling me how good you were at analyzing numbers and your potential for other things and how everyone liked you and how sad they were when you left."

Jules felt dizzy. A maliciously engineered virus had been loosed inside his system and had penetrated the inner circle of his family. His thoughts once again turned to murder. I could do it, he thought. I could really do it.

"Really do what?"

"What else did you talk about?"

"Well—it was strange because he was so full of questions and I guess I was the one he wanted to ask. And I didn't mind talking because he seemed so interested in what I had to say so he kept asking me about stuff like growing up in Chicago and the old days and how things had changed. That sort of thing. It's unusual for a young guy to ask me this stuff. So I thought it only right that I started asking him questions about himself. He had such a peculiar way about him, his voice and the way he appeared. He's just a kid but it seemed I was talking to an old man. So he's the one that caused you those problems? Strange. And even stranger was that over lunch he starts talking about Judaism—"

"You went to lunch?"

"We got a quick bite. A hot dog. He'd never had a big kosher hot dog so I treated him. But listen, he starts talking about Judaism and asks me questions as if I was some kind of rabbi or something. But I don't know that much, not really, only what I learned as a kid growing up in an orthodox house. I've told you this before how we all watched our immigrant fathers do the routines and we went through the motions just to make them happy. But this was America so things changed as you know. But I told him there are neighborhoods where they still observe the old religious ways and that he should go there and talk to the people. But he wasn't interested. He just wanted to hear about the immigrants, the way they did things. Very strange kid."

"And that was it? This idiot shows up, he gets lunch out of you and takes off?"

Jack hesitated. "Well, he came back here with me. I'm telling you he was very worried about you, Jules. And I don't think it was bullshit. He had this sad way about him. I think he was generally concerned about your health."

"He always looks that way. But how did he know I was sick?"

"I don't know. I just assumed he knew people who knew you and heard something about it. But he had to have been worried because you should've seen his expression when he saw you—"

"You brought him upstairs?"

"I thought he was a close friend. I thought this kid was gonna break down and cry if he didn't get to see you. How could he have known so much about you if he hadn't been a good friend? He knew you had a grandfather named Isadore! Why would he know that if he wasn't a good friend?"

Jack had a point. "So he came upstairs and did what?"

"He started praying. In Hebrew. And he did that for several minutes, and then he said something in English that I liked so he wrote it down for me." Jack searched his pockets until he found a scrap of paper. "He said, 'Grant me light so that I do not sleep the sleep of death, for it is You who illumines and enlightens.' Then he shook my hand and left. A couple of days later here you are, good as new."

The thought of Izzy praying over his semi-conscious body was intensely unsettling. It seemed a kind of violation for someone Jules reviled to have such access to his personal life—the place where he slept!—but who to blame?

"Promise not to bring him or anyone up here again without my permission."

"Of course. It was a dumb thing to do now that we've talked about it, but the kid got to me for some reason. He was the strangest goddamn kid I ever saw. Why does he act this way?"

Jules sighed. "It's a long story."

"OK then," Jack said and made a movement toward the door. "I'll leave you with one more thought. This anger you have. Try to get rid of it because it will eat you up alive. That's one thing I've learned."

***

A week's worth of mail awaited him. He descended the three flights to the lobby and immediately noticed a large manila envelope on the floor underneath the bank of receptacles. The envelope felt very light and was blank except for the name, "Ellerstein," written in black marker. Inside he found a photocopy of a short newspaper article in which his last name, "Ellerstein," occupied the same headline with the name "Capone."

Initially, the non sequitur quality of the moment struck Jules harder than the headline. But quickly, the infamous Scarface took hold. It didn't make sense. He tried to assemble a reasonable connection but failed. Jules knew very little about his great-grandfather beyond the tender image his father had portrayed, or the homespun black and white headshot of Morris and his wife hanging on the wall of his grandmother's apartment. Jules, however, had been perceptive enough as a child to detect there had been something shrouded about the man. He knew any time the subject of Morris Ellerstein came up his grandmother became silent, shifted in her seat, and his father would then talk about how the old man got a kick out of watching him pitch balled-up socks into the laundry basket. And then there was the book, Captive City, Jules had overheard the grown-ups talking about—a book that for years had sat upon a shelf in their den. One day young Jules decided to examine the index of the book and found several references to Morris Ellerstein, references he failed to understand since words like "boss," "patronage" and "graft" had no literal significance to the boy.

But it was his father's anger that had stuck with Jules all these years.

"Forget the book!" Jack had said angrily before grabbing the book out of Jules's hands. "Forget the book!" he said again. "You're grandmother. She's in the other room for chrissake."

Jules shrunk back. "What's wrong with wanting to know about my relatives?" he said and his father put his arm around the boy and explained Morris Ellerstein had been a powerful man many years ago, and powerful men were often disliked, and as a result, many unflattering stories circulated over the years, stories suggesting Morris Ellerstein had become wealthy through dishonest means.

"But that was a long, long time ago, in a different world, and your grandmother doesn't want to be reminded of such things. Please, forget the book. It's my fault; I should've gotten rid of it."

So Jules forgot the book. He assumed great-grandfather had been a powerful politician, one among many, long ago during a prehistoric time, and it really was not such a big deal.

But Al Capone could not be ignored.

"Jules, where art thou?" Bronwyn said over the phone. "Why did thou leavest my side?"

"I was in the hospital."

"Oh Jules, why don't you let me be your medication? You need to learn to trust if you want me to help you."

"I don't know how to think like you. Not all the time."

"My little actor. You're perfect just as you are, why not let the true you shine through?"

"My great-grandfather shared a newspaper headline with Al Capone. I found this out today."

"There's an open house tonight. Jahmal's coming through; I want you to come with me."

"Listen to this: 'Morris Ellerstein, the iron-fisted political boss of the Twentieth Ward faces the certainty of being kicked out of politics. Scarface Al Capone is to apply the boot to Boss Ellerstein, and the vice king is reputed to wield an effective toe. The changing population of the ward is responsible for the decline of the Ellerstein fortunes.'"

Silence. "That's fine, Jules. But I don't see how that's relevant to you, right now, this moment. I just told you that Jahmal is giving a talk tonight and you can be my guest, which is far more important than what you are now focusing upon."

"Can't I tell you an interesting fact without it being deemed an impediment to my enlightenment?"

"Of course you can. But we need to weigh the priorities in a given situation. Right now, I am telling you about an opportunity to hear Jahmal channeled through my teacher. Right now, I am telling you that this opportunity does not present itself to just anybody on any day. Right now, I am telling you that this single experience may very well transform your life forever. And right now, your only response is Al Capone."

Bronwyn's juxtaposing the disembodied spirit, Jahmal, with Capone sounded provocative although he knew Bronwyn was not deliberately challenging his intellect but simply speaking out of her own belief in an invisible universe Jules had yet to penetrate.

"Tell me again about Jahmal. It's a spirit channeled through somebody?"

Bronwyn sighed. "Jahmal is a dozen entities speaking as one voice through my teacher. They are here to help transform the planet, Jules. To help people like us transcend the mundane lives we live, to see the big picture, to become enlightened and walk within the light of creation with no fear. We can do this, Jules, we can achieve this state, just like Jesus did, just like the Buddha did and many others."

It was the concept Jules found irresistible, a hypothesis claiming to enable one to break free from the shackles of fear that mortality breeds, to render powerless the anxiety and alienation intrinsic to the pursuit of a comfortable life. He saw more clearly her point about Al Capone. If one truly desired to achieve enlightenment it would be necessary to pay less attention to the earthly dramas and focus more on the sublime. But Jules also knew life had moments interesting enough to divert his attention from the esoteric, moments intriguing enough to keep him content. What should be done with those moments?

8

It was one of those buildings that spoke to you like the face of an impossibly old man whose eyes were still clear and blue, a man born and raised in the same Chicago that built the park that was home to the bench on which the old man sat and watched the remaining seconds of his life tick away while wondering if it was possible he had seen as much as he remembered.

Under the archway of the building's entrance, Jules stared at the ornate symbols chiseled into the concrete. "What does all this mean?" he asked Bronwyn, referring to the carvings of a scimitar from which hung a crescent and a five-pointed star beneath the head of a sphinx.

"This building was originally a Shriner's temple," Bronwyn said and led Jules forward by his arm.

"But what does it mean. Look at this." He pointed to the phrase, Kuwat wa Ghadab, engraved into the wall.

"Who knows?" Bronwyn said. "It's Masonic stuff, it has nothing to do with Jahmal, although Jahmal liked the building and suggested we use it. They called it a very powerful structure."

Jules still struggled with the word "they" in reference to a dozen ethereal entities speaking through Bronwyn's teacher. But the building was indeed powerful if only for its intensely anachronistic ambiance, a musty, old-fashioned consciousness saturated with the Great Depression, and, of course, Chicago gangsters. The building was so solid, the walls so thick, you couldn't help but feel safe.

"This way," Bronwyn said directing Jules down a side corridor into a large room where a handful of people sat on the floor of grey carpeting. Unlike the outside of the building, the

58

room was very plain. The walls were white and bare except for several portraits of smiling, bearded men, and a few veiled women.

Bronwyn took her shoes off and placed them along the floorboard. Jules did the same and followed her to the front of the room, a few feet from a raised platform where two large pillows sat on either side of a small table.

"Wait here," Bronwyn whispered. "I'll get us something to sit on."

Jules did as he told and watched Bronwyn walk to one of the far walls where an enormous shelving unit contained all manner of seat rests. She returned with two round cushions and handed one to Jules.

"I wanted to get here early so we could sit up front."

Jules waited to see how Bronwyn used the cushion. He noticed some sat cross-legged on them while others leaned slightly forward on their knees while the cushion stood on end between their legs. Jules tried this style and found it surprisingly comfortable. Bronwyn chose the cross-legged style and closed her eyes. Jules looked around the room and noticed more people had quietly entered and were also sitting with their eyes closed. Jules did the same.

Within minutes he felt an ache in his lower back and his kneecaps hurt. He put the cushion flat on the floor and sat on top of it. A steady stream of people entering the room distracted him.

"I can't get comfortable," Jules whispered. "When does it start?"

"Sitting on the floor takes getting used to. Old people in India can squat for hours on end because they've been sitting on the floor their whole lives. And they don't develop hip and back problems like we do here."

Jules had no desire to discuss the seating habits of Indians. He studied the faces of those around him, became fascinated by the span of ages in the room, particularly the elderly men and women conversing with tattooed teenagers.

People continued filing in until there was no room on the floor and latecomers had to stand against the walls. Jules changed sitting positions several times but failed to find a comfortable arrangement. And the room was getting warm, which made it even harder for him to sit still. As he approached the point of questioning what he was doing there, the lights dimmed.

"Finally."

"Soon," Bronwyn said. "Just concentrate on keeping your spine straight."

It was a simple suggestion, one Jules embraced with renewed energy now the evening was to begin. He crossed his legs, sat upright, took slow, deep breaths, and for the next ten minutes felt somewhat content and adequately focused. But the man next to him had begun humming while rocking back and forth. Bronwyn squeezed Jules's hand. He wanted to leave but the idea of tip-toeing through the mass of people paralyzed him. He liberated his hand and was about to insist she get him out of there, when the music started.

"Listen to the music. It tells a story."

The music was an orchestral work using violins and what Jules recognized only as instruments associated with ancient Indian songs.

"This part is a depiction of joyful people living in harmony. That stringed sounding instrument is a sitar. The drumming comes from a tabla. The continuous droning in the background is from a tamboura." Then the music took on a chaotic, sinister quality. "Slowly, greed, envy, hatred and violence creep into the people's lives." A beautiful male voice sang out beseechingly in an unknown language. "This is a Vedic prayer. He's asking God to drive the darkness away, to shed light and wisdom upon us, to take away the jealousy, envy, greed and anger and fill our hearts with love and peace."

The man's voice enchanted Jules. He thought how lucky to have such a beautiful voice. Regardless of what hardships came your way, nobody could take away your voice.

He closed his eyes again. The music, the darkness, the warmth, finally succeeded in transporting Jules to a dreamy, astral world. He pictured himself back in the park looking up through the branches of the elm tree. He imagined climbing the trunk, his fingers gripping the coarse, desiccated bark, pulling himself upward until he could look out over the lake and beyond. Then he fell forward and began soaring over a bright green landscape until a sound reverberated through the park, rolled over the lake, rippled through the tree. The clangor waxed then waned, slowly pulling Jules down. He opened his eyes and saw that both cushions on the platform were occupied. On one sat a broad-shouldered woman with long dark hair streaked with grey, her face puffy and freckled, her dark eyes appearing to be permanently squinted. Next to her sat a much younger man with blonde hair parted neatly on the side, grinning through an impish face. He rotated his head slowly from side to side, scanning the room as if trying to make eye contact with each person. Both dressed in white.

"I think I did it," Jules whispered to Bronwyn. "I think I was in that deeper level of consciousness you've talked about. It was amazing."

"You were sleeping."

Her words stung. "How do you know? I felt awake, I remember thinking about things."

"I was watching you. Your head was bobbing just as we all do when we're falling asleep while sitting up. Meditation is a conscious activity, sleep is entirely different. But don't worry about it. Everyone falls asleep sometimes."

Still unconvinced, Jules turned his attention to the platform where the two sat looking over the room. The music faded out just before the woman smiled and said, "Hi everyone."

A thunderous din erupted. Jules heard Bronwyn say, "Good evening, Habiba," and was able to discern a variety of greetings, some in English, others in foreign languages. One man in the back shouted, "We love you, Habiba!" Numerous people stood up, bowed several times, while others blew kisses.

And as quickly as it began, the salutations ended and the room fell silent until the man on the platform said, "Habiba misses her children," which sent the room into an eruption of laughter lasting several more minutes until the noise died down just long enough for someone to shout, "We love you too, Adam ," which prompted another spasm of tribute.

As the room quieted down once again, Jules waited for Adam or Habiba to speak again, but the two teachers only sat with their eyes and breathed deeply.

"What's going on?"

"She's bringing Jahmal through."

He had almost forgotten his goal of witnessing the temporary occupation of a woman's body by beings divested of tangible existence.

"How will I know when it's Jahmal."

"Just pay attention."

Jules paid attention, watched how Habiba's chin lowered then lifted, then fell again, until she bent forward halfway to her knees, stayed there for a moment, and then jerked upright revealing a toothy grin which elicited a collective sigh from the crowd.

"Good evening," said the grin.

The crowd answered, "Good evening, Jahmal."

"How wonderful again to be here with you. You have questions I am sure for Jahmal?"

The room buzzed with affirmations. Jahmal's voice sounded deeper than Habiba's and seemed to have the slightest hint of a British accent.

"Who would like to start our discussion?" Jahmal said. "Yes, my precious one. Won't you stand please?"

Jules turned around and saw a pony tailed teen-age girl wearing a mini-skirt.

"You once said that the creator created so that the creator may understand itself better," the girl said. "I'm having a hard time understanding this."

"Such a gift of joy and light to experience your presence!" Jahmal said. The girl blushed. "We are all a reflection of each other, my dear. We are the reflection of all creation. We are a reflection of the creator's joy and light and breath. We are what appears behind the door when the door is opened. Think of this: a painter sitting out in the middle of the field, his oils he is desiring to paint, to put on canvas the scene before him, which is a wheat field with red flowers and other wild blossoms…"

Jules studied the other faces in the room, to make sure he was still among true-believers and nobody was laughing.

"…So as he paints, his state of being is reflected in this creation. And so another way of saying that the creator created so that he may understand, is simply what the creative process is. Do you see?"

Jules didn't really see, but oddly enough, he liked what he heard. He found Jahmal's imperfect sentence structures strangely charming, if not eloquent, which for some reason lent legitimacy to the experience. The girl thanked Jahmal and sat down. Jules did not believe the girl saw clearly, or that such an abstruse notion could be understood by a teenager.

"But it would seem that the painting has its own separateness," said a male voice from the crowd. "That the painter, like myself, has become separate from the creator."

"Yes, that is the point," Jahmal said. "In form, you are separate; you are separate from me in form only. The heart connection, my dear, when you engage in moments of stillness, and that bond and that connection, when you view great works of art and you have that elation or the sense of peace or solitude or whatever arises within you from viewing either a great sunset or a painting. That is the connection…"

Connection. Obviously relevant. Jules wondered why he hadn't thought of it. Everyone wants only to connect with something or someone. Could it be so simple?

"...As the creator created you he gave you of your own form, yet the heart connection is the energy, the thought, the intent. The painting has a different form that is separate from the painter and yet there is such a marvelous bond in the connection that there is no separation aside from the form."

"I understand that intellectually," a middle-aged woman said. "But how can I realize that this separateness is just an illusion and that I am one with the painter?"

Jules was struck by the woman's passion, how she beseeched for answers; an appeal not to an established messiah, not to God Himself, but to a voice.

"It is about receiving, my dear," Jahmal said. "However, many have been looking in the wrong places to learn how to receive..."

Receiving. Another wonderfully accessible word. How could one expect to connect without the ability to receive? "...Some learn technique, some go through formal education, some meditate, some seek enlightenment, some fret and worry about their lack of connection, some strive to make money and succeed in business or social avenues..."

Money?

"...Some spend their lives attempting to maintain strict and virtuous moral behavior fraught with integrity, honesty, responsibility, and caring for others. Unfortunately, all of these activities actually enhance the feeling of separation. How can you let the light in if you perceive the light as being something outside of yourself and not of yourself, something you must let in? You are the light. The missing link is not to search outside yourself. Not to seek enlightenment. Not to seek the light. Have the intention, and that is all it takes in the beginning. Simply have the intention to welcome and receive yourself..."

Question after question was called out, each playing off the theme established by the girl's original query. Despite having found the conversation intriguing, Jules approached his saturation point. He drifted further into a cerebrally vacant space he tended to inhabit when he could no longer concentrate. It was a vulnerable, precarious place to be, a neighborhood where the seeds of doubt were easily sown. But thanks to the pharmaceutical manipulation of his neurotransmitters, he avoided the abyss. Jules knew only he felt calm and content, a state of mind attributable to either medication or meditation—he didn't care which.

At some point there was laughter. Then some scattered clapping and then music. Jules looked at Bronwyn and then around the room. Everyone's eyes were again closed, including Adam and Habiba's. Jules closed his eyes in anticipation of the event's conclusion. But as slowly as the night began, so did it end. The music played twenty minutes before the teachers stood and tiptoed through the crowd, followed by twenty more minutes of music until, finally, the music faded out and the lights came up.

"So what did you think?" Bronwyn said.

"Lets' talk about it over tea."

"Oh, what a great idea but I'm meeting a client at the lakefront just before sunrise, so I need to sleep. But tell me what you thought."

Unsure how he felt, Jules wanted time to incorporate the evening and re-examine the emotions he experienced. "Interesting," he said.

"You didn't like it."

"I didn't say that. I need time; give me a chance."

"Don't get angry. It's an intense experience. It challenges all our preconceived notions."

"Exactly! Did you really expect that on my first visit with this 'teaching' of yours that I would be able to draw concise conclusions and be able to say once and for all that this is the right way, some kind of absolute Truth?"

Bronwyn hesitated. "You're right. It was stupid of me to assume that you would instantly be taken in. It was stupid to assume anything; we'd both be better served if I would just sit back and let things happen—or not happen. Forgive me?"

It was the first time Jules remembered Bronwyn backpedaling.

"I'm sorry if I sounded angry. Forgive me?"

Bronwyn smiled and Jules knew all was forgiven as they left the room walking hand-in-hand through the wide corridors. Bronwyn stopped several times to introduce Jules to someone in the "community," which forced him to face the same question with each handshake. Bronwyn came to his rescue and declared Jules was "still processing" which brought a conciliatory acknowledgment and allowed Jules to simply smile.

Once outside, Jules said he wasn't ready to go home and thought he might visit a nearby coffee shop. Bronwyn reminded him of her early appointment but encouraged him to sit and think about the evening.

"Can you really perform transformational therapy at five o'clock in the morning?"

"When you're devoted to helping people alter their lives, you'll do whatever it takes, and with great joy."

"I envy the true believer."

Bronwyn hugged him tightly. "I have to go," she said. Before leaving she added, "We're all resistant at first to new ways of looking at things. We don't want to let go of what's familiar, even if what's familiar fucked up our lives." She turned and walked away.

Give me some credit, Jules thought. I'm just a child afraid to go to school? What had been Bronwyn's sincerity had become Bronwyn's arrogance. Nothing was how it seemed.

***

The evening was damp. Mist haloed the street lamps. Jules cut across the busy intersection with the intention of accessing a quiet neighborhood. As he did so, he became vaguely aware of someone behind him but never considered he was being intentionally followed until the scuffing of hard-soled shoes began keeping pace with his own steps. More out of curiosity than fear, he stopped under a streetlamp at the next corner and waited. As the figure came closer Jules first noticed its diminutive stature, then how the figure's coat repeatedly flung outward as if being kicked. A few more seconds would elapse before the figure appeared close enough for Jules to realize such an ill-fitting raincoat could belong to only one person. Jules felt suddenly short of breath.

"How do you know I won't beat you to a pulp?" Jules yelled as the figure approached.

Izzy stopped several feet short of Jules but close enough for Jules to re-acquaint himself with this ridiculous caricature of a man.

"You're not a violent man," Izzy said. He stepped closer. "And I have no fear that you should become so over trivial matters."

Jules noticed numerous stains splattered across Izzy's coat. The glow from the streetlamp gave him a sickly appearance. "What the hell are you doing here? Are you following me?"

"Coincidence is the only reason that I should see you, Ellerstein."

"How the hell can you expect me to believe that?"

"I have no expectations of what you choose to believe. You were at the channeled lecture as was I—"

"You were there? The stoic Hebrew philosopher went to a channeled lecture?"

Izzy opened his raincoat and buried his hands deep into his pockets. "You disappoint me, Ellerstein. Your shallowness in matters spiritual reveals only how far you still have to travel."

The absurdity of standing on a street corner conversing with Izzy suddenly eclipsed Jules's anger. For now he was content to play the straight man.

"And for what possible reason should you care enough about me to be disappointed?"

Izzy cleared his throat. "Charity is equal in importance to all other commandments combined. I borrow these words from a very ancient text, but of course you know that. But it's more than charity, Ellerstein. For me to care is a necessary and required act. I had high hopes judging from the way you fled Nathrop & Moore—fled to better things, I assumed. I thought you would show up at the meeting cowering like a dog. Better that you ran away like a terrified child. An invisible hand was guiding you no doubt."

"So it is with a great sense of charity that you have taken an interest in my life. You're doing me a favor—"

"Forget favors! I have an obligation to help you. I expect nothing in return."

"I'm stuck with you whether I like it or not."

"In a sense. One way or another I will always be working to help you—behind the scenes, as it were."

"And when does this stalking end? You didn't have to follow me after the event."

"I spot you at the lecture and decide there is an opportunity to inquire how you're faring. I thought it better to catch up and not shout down a quiet street at a late hour, and for this I am a stalker. When the work is done, the inquiring ends."

"There are laws against this behavior, Izzy. I'll get a restraining order if I have to." Jules wasn't sure if he was serious.

"To what behavior you are referring? I attended a lecture as you did and now we're talking."

"What about going up to my father like that? And then bending his ear all day."

"Which law I have broken? Your father did not buy me lunch?"

Some anger crept back in. "You're crazy! It's that simple. And I'm crazy for talking to you. I'm on drugs, you know. It's probably the only thing keeping you alive right now—"

Izzy waved his hand dismissively. "I know all about your pills. From your father, of course. I have no judgment on this matter."

Izzy's response disarmed Jules, which angered him more. "What were you doing at the channeling? How is that remotely relevant to your Judaism?"

"As I said before, your shallowness in matters spiritual is breathtaking. Belief is not decreed, Ellerstein, but the result of investigation. The painter paints for one reason and one reason only: to reflect his state of being in his creation—and from this the painter becomes one with creation itself. The world is your canvas, Ellerstein. Maybe you should paint a little."

For a moment Jules wondered if he had missed an obvious message.

"Your talking in riddles is so damn annoying."

"From straight answers you learn nothing. This is not a classroom for the principles of cost-accounting, Ellerstein. You want me to tell you which tree to sit under from which you will receive visions of Truth. That tree you find through your own examinations. That tree may be in your own backyard. But first you have to look."

"Who told you to work in finance? From Nathrop & Moore you get visions of Truth?"

Izzy sighed. "How you make your living is irrelevant. In the scheme of creation you learn as much from asset-based lending as from prostitution. You're confused and dissatisfied, Ellerstein. For that I am grateful. From this you have a chance to learn. You fare well in my judgment. I will leave you now, although inevitably I will encounter you again."

Izzy walked away with his head bowed, his hands still in pockets, and the bottom of his raincoat dragging behind like a cape. Jules thought he would shout after him, tell him he hoped to never "encounter" him again. Instead, he said nothing and watched the figure disappear around a darkened corner.

9

Uncle Solly lived on the bottom floor of a brick two-flat he owned on Pine Grove Avenue, an apartment identical to, and only three buildings away from where he and his brother had grown up.

You would not have known it was a good investment fifty years ago, an investment being the last thing on Solly's mind when he came home from the war. Jack had thought it peculiar Solly chose to live so close, but it didn't take long for Jack to realize much seemed peculiar about Solly since his return. Even when they started to make money, Jack would ask Solly why he didn't want to move out to the suburbs and live in a house, something Jack and all their friends had dreamed about.

Solly would only shrug and comment on how easy it was to get to the showroom or he preferred taking the bus to driving a car or what would he do with all that room if he had a house? Instead, a decade later, when the neighborhood had changed drastically for the worse, he bought the entire building and rented out the second floor. It seemed like anything but a good investment. The crime rate was skyrocketing, vandalism and robbery had become common place.

"Sol, for Christ sake, get out of there," Jack would implore while reading about another murder in the neighborhood. "You like to be lullabied to sleep by gun shots?"

"I've slept through louder noises," Solly would say.

But it was Solly who ended up looking like the visionary when the neighborhood gradually became rehabbed, gentrified, a young urban professional's playground. It was Solly who found himself sitting on a gold mine in his old age. Not that Solly's good fortune altered his lifestyle or changed his mind on where his remaining years should be spent. Despite his financial resources, he still refused to leave the neighborhood.

Jules felt close to his uncle although he didn't really know him; that is, Jules had not spent very much time conversing with Solly on an intimate adult level. The main obstacle in their relationship had been logistical in nature since Jules had grown up over twenty miles away. And, of course, Jules had not yet spent much of his life as an adult.

Regardless, Solly expressed great joy upon seeing his nephew ascending the seven concrete stairs to the landing in front of the door, and after buzzing him in, he greeted Jules with a heartfelt hug.

"C'mon in, you," he said and led Jules inside. "Sit down. You want some orange juice?"

Solly's appearance shocked Jules. His face was gray and drawn. His eyes sunk inside dark circles and his shirt collar hung loosely around his neck. As Solly walked toward the kitchen, Jules saw an unnatural bulging around his hips and rear end which Jules assumed was some kind of protective undergarment.

He had not been inside Solly's home for many years and had forgotten how immaculate his uncle kept the place. What Jules had always considered Solly's old fashioned tastes he now recognized as gloriously vintage. Everything was old, but beautifully preserved. The maple draw leaf dining table, the mahogany console, the art-deco couch and chair, even the square wooden "High Fidelity" box, looked as if it had just been purchased new. Jules fingered through the vinyl record collection. The sleeves were hardly worn, the corners barely frayed. Glenn Miller and the like well dusted and in their prime.

"So, sit down already," Solly said and handed Jules a glass of orange juice.

Jules sat on the couch and put his glass down on the end table, next to an old magazine called Folies Bergere. Jules opened it and saw bare breasted women in a chorus line with feathers sticking out of their hair.

"I got that in Paris. I loved Paris, didn't want to leave. That was pornography in those days."

Jules laughed and closed the magazine.

"So talk to me, Julie."

Jules smiled and looked at the man across from him for whom he suddenly felt great affection.

"What can I say you don't already know?"

"You're getting help, right?"

"The medication keeps me from totally losing it."

"That's a good thing—not to totally lose it." They both laughed. "You know," Solly said, "people used to talk behind my back. It started a year or so after I got back. A little bit at first but as the years went by, more and more they talked. It's because I never married and didn't go out so much with women that they talked. You know what I mean, right? And you know what? I didn't give a shit. Really. I didn't give one shit what people said. So you see, it doesn't matter."

Jules thought for a moment. "What doesn't matter?"

"What you do, what you don't do. It doesn't matter. See?"

Jules wasn't sure what he saw. "But I need to do something."

"Sure, I know. We all need something. See, that's the point. But it doesn't matter, just do whatever you want."

"My brain's not wired to see things so simple. It's demanding more of something—meaning, maybe."

Solly readjusted himself in his chair. "Meaning's a tough one. You know, we have more in common than you think. You're not the only one with a brain problem."

"The army."

"We got wounded in different ways over there. Me, I didn't get shot, or blown apart, but I still got injured up here." Solly pointed to his head. "I've been lucky, though. I made it to my seventies. About twenty years ago a lot of the guys that lived through it started dropping—their hearts were giving out. Anyway, what did I ever do? I wanted to be a professor. Then the army got me and everything changed and I end up schlepping women's coats around and that's only because your father took me in. So who cares?"

"I didn't live through a war."

"You want excuses? What difference does it make why you are how you are? Either way you still have to live with yourself."

"But you made a living, carved out a life."

"So you will too."

"I haven't yet."

"It's harder now. I couldn't afford to live here if I didn't own the place."

Jules took another sip of juice. Paper crinkled in his back pocket.

"What? What is it?"

"I want to show you something." Jules took the article from his pocket and handed it over. Solly took reading glasses out of his breast pocket.

"Where the hell did you find this?"

"Somebody left it for me in my building."

"Somebody? You don't know who?"

"I don't."

"That doesn't seem strange to you?"

"It's very strange, but right now I'm more interested in the article."

Solly looked over the article again. "So what about it?"

"What about it? It's a headline with Capone, how come I never heard about this?"

Solly handed the article back to Jules. "This is something to be proud of?"

"Why not? This was the legendary Chicago, the 'vote early, vote often' Chicago, the Untouchables era. "

"Your father never talked about Morris Ellerstein?"

"Nothing like this," Jules said and related the incident when Jules asked his father about what he had read in the book so many years ago.

Solly chuckled. "I can understand his anger with your grandmother in the house."

"So tell me about him. This is what I want."

Solly hesitated. "Listen, Jules, do us a favor and forget this thing."

Jules wasn't sure what Solly meant by "us".

"Why?"

"Because were talking about gangster Jews, that's why. In this case, a Jew with our name."

"But it's our name that makes it interesting"

"Jules, people are always looking for reasons to hate Jews. We have enough problems, we don't need to be told about our crooked ancestors. I just read that now they're blaming the Jews for slavery. 'It was the Jews who owned the ships,' they're saying."

"I'm not going to write a book about him, I just want to know who the guy was."

"You're better off not knowing."

"It's too late. Capone means something, doesn't it? And my God, we're talking about people at least fifty years dead, right? Who's even alive from the family to remember anything except you and dad?"

Solly stood and walked to a framed photograph of the Ellerstein family hanging on the wall above a small book case. He stared at the photo for several minutes. "This was their golden wedding anniversary."

Jules walked over to Solly. "What year was this?"

"Is it strange that I should keep this picture on the wall but don't want to talk about him?" Solly said. "1938, to answer your question. Let's talk more about you. C'mon, let me help you figure things out."

"Not now. I need a break. Tell me about Morris Ellerstein. It's got me interested, it would be like therapy."

Solly looked thoughtfully at Jules and then walked back to his chair. Jules followed and took his place on the couch.

"It is interesting." Solly said. "If it's anything, it's interesting. But only because we're so far removed from those days. Who the hell am I to deny you what I embraced wholeheartedly? Yes, it's true. I'm a fraud. In those days, I knew all about Morris, I ate it up, I bragged to my friends even. He died in my bed, for Christ sake. It was the war that changed the way I looked at it. I didn't know what anti-Semitism really meant until the war. When I came home I wanted Jews to be only righteous people, not hoodlums. One crooked Jew creates a hundred Jew-haters. That's how I saw it. You're lucky, Jules. You've asked the right person about Morris Ellerstein. Despite the shame he brings me today, I know a lot about the guy."

"How did you learn about him?"

"From our uncles. They worshipped the guy. My grandfather arrived here penniless from Russia, and a couple of decades later he was going around town in a chauffeur-driven limousine," Solly laughed. "On an alderman's salary!

"He started as a worker for the Republican party in the 20th ward. I never knew exactly what a worker did, but in those days everything was crooked so who knows? He had a lot of strange titles during his political days. Besides alderman, he was also city sealer, city collector, and a sanitary district trustee. What he actually sealed and collected is anybody's guess.

"There was a neighborhood in the Twentieth Ward called Maxwell Street that had developed into a huge open air market where people from all nationalities came to sell their wares. You could buy stuff for a lot cheaper than the regular store fronts. Poor people didn't have a place to go back then, they depended on this type of market."

"Anyway, they would bring their fruit, or vegetables, or what have you, in pushcarts and line the street. It was said that Morris used Maxwell street as a source of graft, by making the spaces permanent shelters. Supposedly, after the produce vendors who paid the money had used them for two or three months, they were evicted and the shelter was resold for hundreds of dollars. And they did this over and over. This was public property, so a lot of people got angry.

"But it was the election day funny business that really made his reputation. Of course, it wasn't very funny. People think that the term 'terrorist' or 'terrorism' is a new invention. Not true. During Prohibition the newspapers were using those words to describe what was going on in the 'bloody 20th ward.' That's what it became known as. 'Bloody' because so many people were getting killed and beat up. It wasn't just Morris, not even close. The real gangsters, Capone and so forth, were operating down there too. Anyway, during a primary a guy who was running against Morris was gunned down, killed. Of course, they blamed Morris and he was indicted for murder. During the trial lots of witnesses testified that your great-grandfather, was the undisputed boss of the Twentieth Ward and that he placed workers on public payrolls and gave orders as to what was to be done on election days and saw to it that these orders were obeyed. From then on the newspapers called him 'Boss Ellerstein,' and the guys that worked for him were his 'henchmen.'

"One by one the witnesses told stories of being terrorized on election day. One witness was a poll watcher who said he was kidnapped at gunpoint from the polling place just as he was about to call the commissioner about voting irregularities. He was held prisoner for six hours at a safe house that turned out to be only a block away from Morris's house. The house was full of prisoners. Later that night they were threatened with death and told to leave the ward and not come back.

"The testimony went on for a few weeks, turning into quite a circus with witnesses disappearing and allegations of jury tampering. I believed Morris may have roughed up people, but I never thought of him as a real gangster who murdered. He went broke defending himself and his 'henchmen.' I admired him for sticking by the guys who fought for him, at least you can say he was loyal. Anyway, he had some good lawyers who somehow were able to link the murder to Capone who was undoubtedly trying to frame him. That was the beginning of the end for Morris. On three occasions Capone bombed his house, one time when your grandmother was home. By the early thirties, the ward had become mostly Italian. That's what the headline of the article is referring to. Capone had the votes to kick Morris out and he did. So there you have it, your great-grandfather."

Solly stood and said he had "some quick business to attend," and walked to the bedroom. Jules also stood, walked over to the Ellerstein photo, stared at his great-grandfather and tried to picture this avuncular-looking man as the iron-fisted tyrant the papers had portrayed him as. Then he looked at his father seated cross-legged on the floor in his shorts and felt a tinge of guilt. Now that Jules had acquired the forbidden knowledge, he wondered if he had committed and act of betrayal. Next to Jack Ellerstein sat Solly, smiling, his arm resting on his little brother's shoulder.

Solly emerged from his bedroom wearing a robe. "OK, good as new," Solly said.

"I'm sorry for badgering you about Morris," Jules said. "If it's not something people want to talk about, then maybe I should just shut up."

"Bullshit! We have to talk about the past, otherwise we live in denial of who we are. I realized this in the short time we've been together today. I'm glad you insisted. He's a part of you whether you like it or not. You have the right to know who or what you're made of."

Jules smiled. "I don't know if dad would agree."

Solly looked thoughtfully at Jules. "Maybe not. But you never know. People are always changing. For better or worse, they're always changing."

It was the kind of comment Jules found hard to resist since the statement's editorial slant was so uncharacteristic of how Solly usually spoke.

"How so?"

Solly put his hand on Jules's shoulder and the two walked back to where they had been sitting, although this time Solly sat next to Jules on the couch. "Everything's always changing, everyone's always changing—this I know for sure." Solly kept his gaze straight ahead while he described a sergeant he knew who had swore every day that if he survived the war he would be done with the army. "'Being in the army was like living in an insane asylum' the sergeant kept telling me. And the biggest criminals were the chicken-shit officers screwing up. So many boys got killed by American bombs and bullets, you wouldn't believe it. Sarge never got over the sheer stupidity of it all."

"He wasn't scared like the rest of us, he was just angry as hell," Solly said and then described his own astonishment when he was in the hospital recovering from prostate surgery, and while shuffling down the hall accompanied by his IV drip he noticed a man poking toward him from the other direction attached to his own bag of fluid. And thinking he would say hello to the stranger when they passed, he miraculously recognized the sergeant, who upon realizing who Solly was, embraced a fellow survivor.

"We stood there for I don't know how long," Solly said and related his amazement to learn the sergeant stayed in the army and retired as a Lieutenant Colonel.

"My point is that you never know where life is going to bring you. Just aim for something, anything. You might hit something, even by accident—if you believe in accidents."

If you believe in accidents. Who was this talking? Surely not the Solomon Ellerstein of Pine Grove Avenue, the justifiably eccentric Uncle Solly, damaged, scarred, cynical Solly.

"You don't believe in accidents?"

Solly thought about it. "No. Nothing happens by chance."

"Everything happens for a reason?"

"Yes."

"Since when?"

"It's not a new idea—that friend of yours agrees with me."

"What friend?" Jules said but by the time the words were out of his mouth he knew the answer.

"Didn't I tell you I met Izzy?"

Jules wasn't sure what horrified him more, the fact Izzy so easily infiltrated his family or the fact he was powerless to stop it. "How did this happen?"

"You're angry?"

"He's not my friend."

"Your dad gave him my number and he called me. At first, he wanted to talk about you, to see how you were doing and what I thought about what you're going through. And then he asked if he could come over and meet me." Solly shook his head. "He's an odd one alright. So he comes over and starts asking me about the war and all, and I told him a lot. I haven't talked that much about it since I don't know when. Maybe never! But he wanted to hear so I told him. I thought you two were good friends, so why not? And he starts asking me philosophical questions about living through that kind of experience and he wanted to know if I saw any of the camps. I didn't, thank God. Of course, I heard about it all, but didn't want to see what they were all talking about. That kid had a way about him that evoked emotions out of me. He asked these questions as if he had to know. There was something he was looking for. Eventually we got around to what you and I were just talking about. That things happen for a reason and not just because of chance. That kid really got to me, really got me thinking."

Jules wanted to scream that he would not allow Izzy to penetrate the psyche of his only uncle, that the idea of Izzy commiserating with his own flesh and blood on such an intimate level was unbearable. "He's not my friend," Jules said again.

"Aw Christ! I'm sorry, Julie. I just assumed since Jack gave him my number. So he's not your friend? That shmucky kid's got some nerve selling himself like that. But hey, so what. I mean he didn't get state secrets out of me. To tell you the truth, I think that kid's got real problems."

"Everything happens for a reason."

Solly hesitated. "There must be a reason. To suggest the earth pointlessly spun and orbited defies logic…" Jules listened to how he learned to cope with the past, and how history was always alive and well in the present. "There's really no disconnection. Whether we like it or not it's a part of us. But what do we do with it? That's the key. That was my luck. I had the wherewithal. Others went insane. Some temporarily, others I don't know."

Solly closed his eyes and started rubbed his forehead. "I wasn't always like this. There was one night in particular, during the Bulge, I don't remember exactly when. It was bitter cold. I was shivering in a hole in some Belgian forest, wondering how I could possibly survive long enough to get back home, and it dawned on me that nobody goes home unless they're badly wounded or dead and the only place I'm going is forward, toward Germany."

Solly took a deep breath. "It was a terrible feeling, almost more than I could take. I mean I really thought I might go crazy. And some guys did, during the shelling usually. Anyway, I know now that when you get to that point you start living on automatic pilot. Everything becomes irrelevant. What I mean is that the why's and wherefores of what I was doing in that forest go away and you just do what you have to do to survive. But there was no end in sight! That's what was killing me and right when I got to the point where I thought I might crack, I started thinking of that professor I wanted to be."

Solly put his hand on Jules's knee and turned to face him. "So help me God, I saw myself standing in front of a classroom, lecturing to all these kids who were taking notes. And then I was the student, studying, writing papers, conversing with my professors, and so forth. And for that time I forgot where I was and that I was freezing to death and there was a whole Kraut army in those woods trying to kill me."

Solly stood and walked to the window facing the street. "I think that's how a lot of us coped. I'm just guessing because I don't know what others did. I don't know shit. I lived in my mind, Jules, that's how I got through it. And I'm still there, still imagining what I could have accomplished; that's the sad part. I'm still thinking about that professor I wanted to be. I'd be in the showroom selling the line while imagining I was giving a lecture on French political philosophy."

Solly laughed loudly. "It sounds so damn funny to hear myself talk about it. I'm a schlepper, Jules, your Uncle Schlepper the rag man, who dreams about scholarship and academia. I know what you're thinking, you're wondering why I didn't go back to school when I came home. I kept telling myself that I would, that I had time, but I had been living in my head too long, I couldn't get out. It was too comfortable. I was still afraid of I don't know what. But at least I got out of the house—just down the street, but at least on my own. It was your dad that came through for me, convinced me to join him in the rag business. But I've had a lot of time to think, Jules, time to ask the kind of the questions I think you've been asking yourself lately. And I can tell you that there are no answers. Anyone who thinks they have the answers is full of bullshit. That's why trust is so important. When you can trust, then maybe you can learn something."

Solly's chin fell against his chest. He closed his eyes. Jules watched closely. He thought how different his life had been from Solly's, how the choices available to him had been so drastically inconsequential. Solly lifted his head, sighed deeply, and told Jules he needed to lie down. Then he kissed Jules on the forehead and walked to his bedroom.

Jules remained in the empty room staring at the hardwood floor. He listened to his uncle's voice as it echoed off the walls and intermingled with the words he had heard the previous day. He felt a strange awareness of himself analogous, Jules imagined, to the infinity of facing mirrors. He tried to reconcile the different statements, the assertions, until all that had been spoken became familiar and he felt, perhaps, he had heard it all before.

10

As Jules expected, his father sat at the glass table chewing on an unlit cigar while peering through bifocals into a price list. The mannequins stood in pairs throughout the room, as if a dinner party had been suspended in time.

"What's with the lovely couples?"

Jack glanced up, looked back down at his list, and said, "Julie, how's by you?"

"I was thinking of visiting with Solly."

Jack stared at Jules for a moment and shrugged. "I'm sure he'd like that," he said and walked to one of the steel garment racks where he removed a wool coat and placed it over the shoulders of one of the mannequins. "You came all the way down here to tell me that?"

"I'm hoping he'll tell me about Morris Ellerstein."

Jack began dressing another mannequin and struggled to get the arms properly into the sleeves.

"Jules, listen. We're too old for this shit. This shit was old even when I was young. Just let it go. Solly doesn't want to be reminded of hoodlum relatives, he's sensitive to this stuff. For him it's only about one thing: kike gangsters. That's it. There's no fascination, no pride with having known the man. Nothing like that. And he's fading, Jules, he's going downhill, I can see it. He won't shut up. He constantly ruminates on the past. And you know what's the latest insult he's had to endure? Incontinence. From the surgery. He spent most of his life struggling with the goddamn war only to spend his final years pissing his pants. He doesn't need this Jules. Just let him die in peace." Jack took another coat from the rack and walked to the next mannequin.

Jules observed his father's rude treatment of the garments, the way he grabbed a coat by the shoulder and yanked it off the metal hanger which then spun wildly around the chrome pole. He needed to show the dawdling mannequins who was boss.

"Who have you been hanging out with these days?" Jack shouted from across the room. "Whatever happened to Bobby? You were like brothers for chrissake."

Jack brought up a childhood name all but abandoned from Jules's consciousness. True, they had been close companions. But not unusual to boyhood friendships, a change occurred after the first year of college when the University of Chicago turned Bobby into Robert, a chain-smoking dilettante, who spent his summers in New York, sharing a Soho loft with his new "comrades" from school, wealthy New Yorkers unimpressed with provincial Chicago.

"I hear he's working for his father. Married a great gal, have a baby too, I think." Jules knew about the marriage, an Israeli woman. The baby was news. "I don't know what you got against retailing. I hear Field's has a great training program..."

Jules took a step backward, and then another while Jack worked on down jackets. Pink, orange, and mauve colored bat-winged wrappers hung stupidly on emaciated black red-lipped drones who never complained.

"Keep in touch for chrissake," Jules heard as he backed into the hallway.

<h2 style="text-align:center">11</h2>

"When my father was a kid, his best friend was Bushman, the gorilla who lived at the Lincoln Park Zoo," Jules said to Bronwyn. They were sitting on a bench in the park where Göethe lived. "He used to go to Bushman's birthday parties and Bushman would entertain the crowd by pounding his fists on his chest and jump around."

Bronwyn looked at her watch. "Why are we talking about monkeys?"

"Bushman was an ape."

Jules knew the difference. He also knew the evidence linking humans to gorillas and chimps had grown dramatically due to the increased use of molecular techniques and it was now thought all three belonged to the family Hominidae. Bronwyn had no knowledge of Jules's part-time job at one of the branch libraries since they had not spoken in several weeks. But Jules knew what he considered a serendipitous encounter with an obscure book about the Zoo's historical ownership of primates, Bronwyn would see as a destined meeting written somewhere in the cosmos.

The name Bushman had carried a mystical significance during Jules's childhood. The very mention of his name softened Jack Ellerstein's countenance, transported him to a mythical time in a fabled city, where happy children gathered around the gorilla's cage to be entertained by a simian Bozo. Inevitably the conversation would lead to life in the idyllic urban setting of Pine Grove Avenue.

"I could go to Waveland Park any time of the day and there would be hundreds of kids there," Jack would say. And from Jules's suburban house he tried to picture this world of busses and corner markets, upstairs neighbors and movies costing a dime.

"So there's no difference between humans and gorillas?" Bronwyn said.

"Gorillas are much better at climbing."

Bronwyn's shriek of laughter stunned Jules. He had no idea she was capable of such an impulsive display of mirth.

"I've taken another lover," Bronwyn said after composing herself.

The sentence sounded strange, as someone else had spoken. He had trouble with word "lover", which seemed overtly pretentious. Never had he been referred to as anybody's lover.

"No kidding?"

"Yes."

Silence, then, "So you're fucking someone else."

Bronwyn glared at him. "Do you have to be so crass?"

"You said another lover. Is he my replacement or a new addition?"

"I want to discuss that."

The idea of discussing that, of discussing his role as lover, Jules thought intensely affected, gaudy even, as if they were children playing dress-up. He hated that word, that idiotic euphemism.

"You start."

"Fine. It's all part of the growth experience..."

Jules tried to listen objectively, but she used more of those flagrant words—consciousness, oneness, human conditioning —

and after several minutes he heard nothing but sounds, long, drawn-out syllables inflected with a nasal quality that irritated him.

"And who is the other lover."

Bronwyn smiled broadly. "Adam."

At first the name registered only as another strange, nonsensical sound meant to annoy him further. But a moment later when the context for the sound revealed itself and brought with it the evening spent sitting uncomfortably in the presence of Bronwyn's teachers, it was Jules's turn to break into convulsions of laughter.

"And how did you happen to pick him?"

"We would meet in small discussion groups. We both sensed the energy between us and decided not to block it anymore."

Jules laughed again. "I see. It's about not wanting to block the energy."

"That's simplistic and you know it. We learn from these interactions. It's about attaining wisdom, learning more about ourselves. There's so much I can learn from Adam."

This was not happening. It was too ridiculous, too obvious. "You're fucking him because you want to fuck him and it has nothing to do with wisdom."

"Oh, OK. You can read my mind, you know what's going on in my head, you know me better than I know me."

"You're an educated, intelligent person. The only wisdom that little blonde gnome is giving you is through his prick. And I'm sure he has you scheduled for regular injections of knowledge."

Even Jules knew he had gone too far. So when Bronwyn stood and walked away he was not surprised by the sadness he felt or the guilt or the sense of loss or the terrifying sensation of being suddenly isolated from everything familiar.

***

What had begun as a part-time activity to give his day a little structure turned into a full-time job occupying days and then weeks before entire months disappeared from Jules's life. At first he didn't mind walking the marbled floors pushing a metal bin full of books. And there were times he even marveled how simple it was to just be. He even wondered if he could maintain this manageable lifestyle until Providence saw fit he no longer existed. This was how it had been for millions of people for hundreds of years. Why should his life be any different?

He earned enough money to pay the rent and utilities and still had enough left over to buy bread, corn flakes, bologna, cheese, bananas, orange juice, frozen lasagna, and pizza. His health insurance included a prescription drug benefit. Although the dress code was casual, he kept his suits hanging loosely on thick wooden hangers and routinely brushed them. After receiving his first full-time paycheck, he wrote a letter to his father telling him he no longer needed to send him money. Jack responded with a rambling phone message in which he wondered why a son would write a father instead of calling, and after Jules called back to explain he meant no disrespect, the two agreed to meet occasionally for dinner at their favorite Chinese restaurant.

This period of relative peace and contentment didn't last. His medication prevented another collapse, but the equanimity gradually deteriorated to a more subsistent level of existence. By his fifth month of book shelving, he no longer saw the elementary tasks required of his work as simple but necessary burdens deserving of humble respect. Instead, his job became something to endure.

Gradually, his thoughts returned to the financial life for which he had been trained, a life miraculously sensible. But as he pushed the cart down the library's corridors planning his return to respectability, he was struck with the dilemma of explaining the gap approaching eight months of unemployment and underemployment. As the minutes passed the gap quickly became a crevasse into which Jules's thoughts disappeared.

He continued his work, unaware Izzy watched him from outside the corridor. When Jules rounded the end of the aisle, he noted a pair of shoes covered by baggy gray slacks and moved on to the next subject-heading and ten-digit number. A short time later he noticed the legs of a poorly maintained Italian suit, probably too far gone to respond to conventional dry-cleaning, although a skilled professional pressing would help. The third pass finally lifted Jules's head to glimpse whoever neglected such a fine silk-blend material.

Izzy smiled. Jules had never seen Izzy smile before and this incongruous expression Jules took for a mocking gesture which, when coupled with his intense anxiety over the gap, was enough provocation to push him over the edge. "I'm here because of you!" he shouted and grabbed Izzy by the lapels and pushed him up against the wall. "You think it's funny that I work here?"

"Your work here is a blessing."

"You think you're better than me, Mr. Finance? Mr. Nathrop and fucking Moore!"

"Jules!" a voice screamed. He put Izzy back on the floor.

"My God, what are you doing to this poor man?" said Mrs. Kaloff, the reference librarian.

"It's not as it seems," Izzy said. "Ellerstein and myself are old friends. What you just now observed was horseplay, peculiar and poorly timed as it was."

"I'm sorry Mrs. Kaloff," Jules said. "It's my fault and won't happen again."

Mrs. Kaloff sternly reminded them where they were and Jules had a job to perform.

"You're lucky," Jules hissed.

"Your reaction is unjust, Ellerstein. When I saw that you worked here my heart sang out. Books can be your salvation, Ellerstein. Never before have I had such hope for you. I predict something good will result for you working here."

Jules ignored the remark. "I suppose it's just another coincidence you're here."

"That is how it would appear to small minds. If you could for a moment catch sight of the greater workings of Yahweh you would know that nothing happens by chance."

"Yeah, yeah, you poisoned my uncle with your so-called wisdom."

"Your uncle took this poison from before you were born. You should envy his knowledge."

Jules knew he was right. "You look like shit, by the way. You know what dry- cleaners are? Maybe N&M cut your clothes allowance."

"This is my suit of clothes that I wear with pride. I have nothing for which to be ashamed."

"To be perfectly honest, it's not just your clothes that look like crap. You look as gray as your suit."

"Where a small mind would see a sick man, a great mind would see progress toward perfection."

"So what do you want?"

"I have very important information for us."

"Us? There is no us in this equation, there's only you. Whatever information you have is yours, not mine."

"Allow me to quote Aristotle: 'No one loves the man whom he fears.' You have nothing to fear from the truth."

"Equating yourself with the truth is pretty arrogant, don't you think?"

"The information I have for us is the result of much study and research. How you interpret my words is your choice although what you choose, no doubt, is dependent upon your potential to understand. I think you have potential, but the will? Perhaps not."

Is there no escape from this? "Just get on with it already and go."

"The whys and wherefores of my journey have many unanswered questions. First and foremost, why Isadore Himmel? That is, of all the millions who perished why this man is the one I have chosen to honor? You would not know, Ellerstein, that the mystics clearly accept the idea that the soul can return, and not only once but several times. Yes, it's true. It's not a widely held belief but a belief nonetheless. The kabbalists have also suggested that the religious seekers of our day are the reincarnated souls of Holocaust victims who are now given a second opportunity to become what they would have been."

"What a surprise," Jules said. "You're the reincarnation of Himmel. Why don't you tell your pals at Nathrop & Moore. I'm sure they'd love to know this."

Izzy ignored the comment. "Of the six million murdered, approximately two million were babies and small children. Not only am I certain that I am the reincarnation of Himmel, I know also for certain that you are the reincarnation of his murdered son."

Jules stared into the pale blue eyes of a man whom he now thought for certain had a mental disorder. And for a moment he envied the man who could so thoroughly immerse himself into a belief system.

"If I thought I was your son in this life or any other life, I'd kill myself. How do you know he even had a son?"

"The 'know' in your question you spell with a small 'k", I assume. I use a capital letter with such words. Some things one will Know to be true, if one is receptive to Truth. I consulted with Jahmal, who confirmed what I already Knew."

 Jules laughed. "What if Jahmal had said, 'no, Izzy, you're nuts.'"

"In my world there are no 'what ifs'. We are bonded, Ellerstein, through eternity."

It occurred to Jules Izzy's bizarre behavior had become worse. This strange world he adopted had evolved into an obsession that attempted to incorporate Jules. Perhaps it was time to consult the police. "And what am I to do with this information?"

"My hope would be that you recognize our connection and desire to cultivate a relationship appropriate to a father and son that were murdered together."

Izzy's words transported Jules beyond the pale of settlement from which the surviving Yiddish-speaking immigrants had emerged and into the study of the essential nature of disease and its creepiest aspects.

"I'm going back to work now," Jules said and walked to the closest elevator, forgetting to bring the metal bin with him.

12

"I'm taking time off," Jules said. "To collect my thoughts, reassess things."

He spoke to a woman whom he thought was a few years younger than him. She was short and cute with large brown eyes and thick brown hair and spoke quickly with a voice dripping with intellectual intonation. She had asked if he knew where the reference librarian was and after he told her she commented on having seen him at the library many times and wanted to know how long he had worked there.

She giggled. "I asked how long you've worked here, not why."

Jules had seen her too, twice before, through the soundproof glass windows of one of the quiet study rooms. She stuck out in his mind because she had been standing at the end of the table, talking and gesturing emphatically to the empty chairs.

"I don't remember. How long have you been coming here?"

She giggled again. "I grew up here," she said and described her life as the only child of two university-educated "artists," an acting father and a painting mother, who didn't allow television in the house and used the library as a childcare facility. "It turned out fine because I took to the books quickly. First the pictures and then reading them. My parents taught me to read when I was four."

Jules saw a little girl sitting cross-legged on the carpet, a book opened on her lap, her brown hair falling over the pages, her small voice sounding out each word her index finger pointed at.

Her name was Candace but she insisted on being called Candy. "Because I'm so damn sweet," she said. She was an

90

actress; that is, she worked for a temp agency while pursuing the theater. This interested Jules and he asked how she came to such a path and she answered him without hesitation, describing her prep school upbringing, her Northwestern education, and her discovery of the theater scene, acting classes, and finally, a postponement of her advanced degree to see if she had any talent.

She opened her purse and took out a business card and wrote her phone number on the back. She suggested Jules call her if he wanted to talk more. Jules looked at the number and turned the card over to see a man's name who worked for company he never heard of. "It's just some guy who gave me his card," she said and smiled before walking away.

That night Jules stared at himself in the mirror, ran his fingers through his hair, felt his bicep. Candy answered on the second ring and immediately invited him to meet her for tea. He agreed to meet her at Java Jinx, a small coffee shop on a quiet side street not far from his apartment. Jules arrived early and had his pick of tables. He grabbed a copy of the Reader and chose a table near the front so Candy would see him as soon as she walked in. And after becoming unexpectedly absorbed in an article about the burgeoning rat population in the abandoned coal tunnels underneath downtown, Candy's voice startled him. "So what are you taking time off from?" She was holding a pot of tea and two cups.

"When did you get here?"

"A while ago."

"You didn't see me sitting here?"

"I like to watch first. It's just something I do."

Jules searched her face, noted the concerned expression of her eyes, the crinkle above her brow.

"You said you were taking time off," she said and filled Jules's cup. "To collect your thoughts or something."

Jules sipped his tea. It had a spicy orange flavor. "I did say that. You have a good memory."

"So tell me."

"I needed a break from the rat-race," Jules said and told a fictional story of his years as an account executive.

Candy hung on every word as he described the emptiness of the banking world, the numbing routine, the suffocating dress code. It was what he thought she wanted to hear.

"I could tell you were the tortured type."

Jules felt the sting of her amusement. "That's funny?"

Candy thought for a moment. "You looked interesting. It made you interesting to me."

"What made me interesting?"

"Your tortured-ness."

"Do I really look that miserable?"

"Not at first. Not right now. But the last couple of months it looked as if you were pushing a Buick down the aisles."

This time Jules laughed. He asked her questions and she told him about the academic flavor of her childhood, the parade of graduate-student aunts and uncles, the empty wine glasses and brimming ash trays. "I was the only ten-year-old who could tell you what a Fulbright Scholar was," she said, and then insisted Jules tell her more about himself, preferably something shocking.

"To function in society I take medication."

Candy frowned. "That's shocking? I'd be more shocked if you said you weren't."

Had Candy not been as short and cute, had she not delivered the line so deftly deadpan, Jules's laughter might have been less robust; he may have even been offended.

"Who the hell are you?" he said and was sure someone as smart as her had to know what he meant.

"What do you mean?"

"You just showed up. How could you not know what I mean?"

Candy shrugged. "I saw you. I thought you were cute. I liked the shape of your ass. I decided to meet you."

Initially speechless, he managed to say, "I think you're quite adorable, actually," and immediately regretted it.

Candy laughed. "Do me a favor." She reached into her purse and pulled out two booklets. "It's a play I'm auditioning for," she said and handed one to Jules.

"Radiation Poisoning."

"It's about this woman who pisses away her life in front of the television."

It did not seem to Jules an original theme. "Why would she do that?"

"Because she was raised to be seen and not heard in a suffocating household dominated by men. The play shows her evolution from a small child to an old woman staring at the TV. It's more complicated than that but you have to read the play."

Candy was auditioning for the lead female role and wanted Jules to read the part of the father. Candy read her first line, I'm going to the movies, that's all, nothing fancy..., a scene early in the play when her character was a teenager, and Jules followed with, You'll never be more than a one-night stand..., the first of many abusive lines the scene called for.

"You enjoyed reading the role, I could tell you were into it," she said.

Jules agreed and when she suggested he take acting classes he scoffed at the idea, saying he had too much on his mind and he needed to focus on getting some real direction in life.

"I didn't say you should dedicate your life to becoming an actor., she said and emphasized he could do something simply for the fun of it and not because it had to be the reason for his existence.

Once again Candy displayed the ability to make Jules laugh at himself, and when he caught his breath they practiced the scene a few more times and then she told him more about her other aspirations, particularly her desire to study linguistics.

"I'll need to travel, of course. I've always wanted to study foreign languages in foreign countries."

Talk of travel ambitions dampened his mood. He continued to listen, but his mind had transported them both forward in time. Candy frolicked in sunny European plazas while Jules pushed his cart of books down the dim aisles, pushed the cart all the way back to his studio apartment where he collapsed on his reclining chair and waited.

"I lied to you," Jules said. "I was an account executive for less than five months before I got fired."

"I don't remember you saying how long you worked there."

"I implied that I had been involved in this line of work for some time. As if it was truly my profession."

"Big deal."

"You enjoy hanging around phonies?"

"Like you're the first person to embellish on what they did for work? The fact you're feeling the need to reveal this egregious transgression I find very attractive."

Jules stared at Candy. "Who the hell are you?"

"We already had this conversation. Who the hell are you? And why did you get fired?" She looked at him again with that solicitous expression.

"I took off one afternoon and never came back." Jules said. He made up a story of anti-Semitic co-workers routinely using the phrase "Jewish Deal" in his presence until he could stand it no longer and fled.

"You don't look like a Jew."

His initial reaction was anger, not just at her comment, but at himself for thinking Candy was immune from making irrelevant comments.

"Thank you."

She studied Jules. Jules returned the stare until Candy said, "You didn't mean that. You're being ironic. I wasn't trying to sound provocative; I just meant that you didn't fit the stereotype of how Jewish people are usually portrayed."

He enjoyed having her on the defensive. "Thank you."

Candy wasn't interested in playing along. "You're welcome."

"I'm a little sensitive."

"I don't look Irish. I hear it all that time."

"The Irish aren't generally despised."

"Not any more."

"Where do you live?" he said and when she told him he looked at his watch again and mentioned it was getting late and she agreed. Then he asked if he could walk her home and she laughed and said it wasn't necessary. He felt foolish for thinking sex might be on the agenda for the evening. They stood and walked through the maze of tables toward the door. He knew Candy was behind him but didn't realize how close she followed until the warmth of her fingers interlaced with his. Once outside she hugged him tightly and said she would see him soon. He wanted to ask her when but she had already started walking away.

13

Jules wanted to hear Candy's voice on his answering machine when he got home. The initial disappointment upon hearing Izzy's voice gave way to dread. "Darkness is not a substance that can be separated from light, Ellerstein. You can choose to ignore the light. But whether you approve or not we are all painters creating our own canvasses. If you choose to paint a life absent of light, then the sun you shall not see. The truth you will not hear. The hand of God is a metaphor, Ellerstein. The hand that paints is only an extension of that metaphor. You are an extension of God. We are all metaphors..."

Izzy sounded more pious than usual. He cringed at the image of an unrestrained religious zealot. "...tangible things like flesh will fall to the ground, while the soul returns from whence it came—"

Cut off by the answering machine, a new male voice filled his studio. Jules tried to identify the presumptuous individual who rambled on as if he and Jules were old pals. Despite having no intention of returning Bobby's call, Jules scribbled his phone number on the back of the TV Guide. He wanted to call his father and chide him for getting in touch with Bobby, but decided against this, thinking it better to simply ignore the phone message. The phone rang fifteen minutes later.

"My father asked you to call me," Jules said.

"Don't be such a downer. I've wanted to get back in touch for a long time," Bobby said.

"You expect me to recount the last dozen years of my life so that we can be old pals again? I'm really not interested."

"I've been 'Robert' for the last dozen years or so."

"Sorry. Too late. You'll always be Bobby, I don't care what happened in New York."

"You can never stop family and friends from worrying."

"My father calls and tells you what? That Jules has gone crazy and could you help him out?"

"So what happened at Nathrop & Moore? I thought you were doing so well."

"Not interested."

"Why?"

"I'm fine."

Silence and then, "It's all about you, isn't it? You're so sure the only reason I could possibly be calling is for your benefit."

"Whose then? You need marriage counseling? You want advice on raising the kid?"

"Dahlia filed for divorce. She's fighting for sole custody."

Only for an instant did Jules think Bobby could be making this up. "I didn't know."

"How could you? Anyway, I've wanted to get back in touch for a long time. I heard that your life had become a real bummer—or if not a bummer then a time of changes or something you hadn't planned for. I thought this would be a good time for me and for you, ya know?"

In a way it was true Jules liked his life. He had become accustomed to the day-to-day activities holding little in the way of expectation. His most challenging moments occurred when pitted against the continued expansion of the "gap." The résumé itself had become an adjunct to Jules's awareness, its symbolism tempered by the isolated molecule.

"Why don't we meet tomorrow," Jules said and told Bobby about his library job and Bobby, gushing with gratitude, said he would see him there.

The next morning Candy dominated his thoughts, although her pleasant image was repeatedly interrupted with visions of Bobby Mars, specifically what his friend might look like after ten or more years encompassing a wedding, the birth of a child, and the untold events leading to the deterioration of his marriage. Bobby, an associate in a large accounting firm, said he would find Jules sometime between twelve and two o'clock. Jules hoped to see Candy in the morning, before Bobby arrived, but as the noon hour approached and Candy had not yet made an appearance, he focused on men about his age walking the aisles. He thought his friend would not look too much different—a little heavier, perhaps, with a little less hair, but still a head shorter than Jules.

"I walked right past you and you didn't even flinch," Bobby said. "You look really serious."

"Really serious," Jules repeated and then led Bobby through the stacks to one of the quiet study rooms. He looked remarkably the same.

"I'm sorry for your troubles," Jules said.

"I'm sorry for you too," Bobby said.

"And what do you know about me to be sorry for?"

Bobby shifted in his seat. "I know only what I've heard."

"I'm fine."

"You work in a library."

"Talk about yourself. That's why we're sitting here."

Bobby draped his suit jacket over the chair and started talking about going to New York shortly after finishing college. "I got caught up in this bullshit scene where I felt so cool being in New York, like Chicago was just too small-minded..."

Jules had no choice but to listen to Bobby's irritating voice and allow it to fill his world, which, strangely, it did, as a dream filled one's sleep. Jules now saw Bobby as he was a dozen or so years ago, on the south side, sitting in a coffee shop a few blocks off the Midway, looking over his notes before his last exam. Bobby's mind had already flown to New York, where Phoebe waited since she had finished her exams two days earlier. And then he was there, laying on the couch in Phoebe's Soho loft, marveling at how only a year earlier he had felt so completely lost as he struggled to write term papers and prepare for exams the University of Chicago had deemed relevant to his future. While Phoebe examined the paintings on the walls, pondered the appropriate use of white space, and phoned her mother to arrange a lunch date, Bobby basked in the glorious Truth that living with Phoebe in New York had been the most liberating of arrangements—a co-habitation that had given him a sense of recklessness and irresponsibility he found tremendously refreshing. It was no wonder he couldn't help but feel destiny was playing a role in his life.

Unfortunately, destiny had failed to take into account he was short and Semitic-looking, an inescapable fact for Phoebe who at first had seen his heritage as a daring novelty, a kind of unfamiliarity inspired by the independence of going to college a thousand miles west of where her Bryn Mawr-educated mother lived. It had been a fun year for her too, but to see him in her loft over an extended period of time, to have him in New York for more than one Autumn, opened her eyes to the subconscious motivation she saw had been operating—bringing a young man like Bobby into her life had been more a rebellion against her mother than a long-term investment.

Needless to say, her rejection dealt a massive blow, a full-forced kick to the stomach. At night, he lay in bed and felt the hemorrhaging, pictured his abdomen filling up with bloody viscous fluids draining away everything he thought he knew about himself. He was a victim of his ancestry, a culture he had given little attention but now forced him to focus inward as he tried to stanch the flow, tried to find that little place where identity was said to live—somewhere near the heart or maybe closer to the solar plexus. But after many agonizing nights he gradually saw the folly of trying to locate his identity as if it were something separate from himself, as if it would be as obvious as his liver—and what did it matter anyway where identity lived? His distinctiveness would go with him no matter where he went or what he did.

Where else to go but the Promised Land? And how lucky to live in a world where such a place existed. If he was indeed what others saw him as then he might as well investigate himself in the purest conditions, where identity and country were the same, where acceptance—he had always been told—was guaranteed as a birthright. And that's what he did, choosing the communal structure of the Kibbutz to live, where he pictured himself living the Zionist dream while planting trees, performing ethnic songs, and holding hands with tanned young women who cared not a bit for the shallowness of American life.

Upon arriving at the small agricultural community in the north, near the Sea of Galilee, while he walked on the sidewalk in front of a row of small, well kept cottages, he encountered his first Israeli kibbutznik, a husky, dark-haired man who, after observing the smiling young American, loudly announced that volunteers were not to use the sidewalk in front of their homes but were to remain on the dirt road meandering around the complex. He chose not to let this incident color his outlook. This man after all, may have fought in four wars already so he could live in one of these cottages with the sidewalk. Who was Bobby Mars to argue the sidewalk should belong to all Jews?

But not long after he settled in, the absoluteness of what it meant to live in an isolated community in the hills of northern Israel starkly contrasted the idealistic vision he had created. The trees he expected to plant had already been planted a generation or two before his arrival and most of the other volunteers were neither idealistic nor especially Zionist, but gentile kids from Europe, Australia, and Canada, on their way somewhere else but living rent free in exchange for working. And the work itself was menial, usually involving the cleaning of something or the picking of something. At times he assisted with farm animals, in particular sheep, where he stood in a packed pen ankle deep in excrement, and helped hold terrified ewes against a fence to receive insemination. This was a mysterious world for him, full of mundane physical exertions he desperately wanted to think of as honest, virtuous work. After a few weeks he was bored and sufficiently discouraged.

Then he met Dahlia, a native Israeli, the daughter of long-time members—South African expatriates who had arrived soon after the Six-Day-War—and had just returned to the kibbutz after spending three years fulfilling her military obligation. She had not personally known many Americans other than whoever happened through the kibbutz to work a month or two before leaving. He was surprised she took an interest in him and assumed it was not for his looks but more for his attitude, the way he smiled at her and said, "Shalom," in his American accent.

Dahlia took him by the hand and properly introduced him to her home, described the draining of the swamps, the battles with malaria, the danger of marauding Arabs. "You are different than the others," she told him, referring to the other volunteers whom Dahlia characterized as lazy drunkards. "And you don't complain like they do."

Fluent in three languages by the time she was ten, taller than him with golden blonde hair and green eyes, he asked how she had acquired such Nordic features, and when she responded sharply, "You can trace your roots back to Abraham?" he knew he was in love.

And it was love that brought him home to Israel, melted away the months, allowed him to experience a reality void of the material responsibilities associated with capitalism. It was a socialist type of love unconcerned with which neighborhood you lived in. It was a love embracing the early hours of communal breakfast preparation, the washing of innumerable dishes, the learning of simple carpentry, and the rigors of artificially inseminating sheep.

Not until a letter from his mother arrived on a late spring afternoon—almost a year after his arrival—that his prolonged daydream was interrupted. His trip had been a whimsical, post-college adventure, his parents had reasoned, a well deserved diversion after four years of diligent university scholarship. But it's been almost a year now, darling. Don't you think it's time to come home?

Home. The word having been written in his mother's lovely script, punched him hard in the chest. How could she possibly understand he was home? How could he explain the clarity he felt being with the woman he loved in the country considered their homeland? For his parents, the story of the homeland was not a production intended for their son's participation. It was the job of others to play the roles the drama demanded. Bobby belonged in the audience.

The thought of leaving Dahlia was more than he could bear. In a fever of despair, he told her about the letter and his willingness to forsake family and country, that he was prepared to wear the uniform of the IDF. But Dahlia remained rational.

"I can stay one year with you in America," she said and brought to him a joy he didn't know was possible. "Perhaps together we can receive their blessing."

Within a month his parents greeted them at the airport and took turns hugging Dahlia as if she were one of their own. Dahlia's charm and halting English, her ability to converse freely on any subject, the fact she was an Israeli Jew, quickly made her a member of the family. With the help of his well-connected father, he quickly found employment at a large accounting firm where his

University of Chicago education earned him a certain degree of respect and his Israeli girlfriend an equal amount of curiosity.

Many of his colleagues had been raised to look upon the homeland dream with pride but had had little contact with the Jewish state other than what they heard on the news or discussed around the dinner table. But here was Dahlia, a living, breathing, child of Zion, and not the curly, dark-haired variety, but a California beach girl speaking Hebrew accented English, the kind of Israeli American Jews wanted the world to know existed.

The future looked cloudless. His biggest challenge seemed only to be the drudgery of his job. But knowing the job was temporary, just a place hide while giving a year to his parents so they would learn the homeland was full of people like Dahlia and understand Israel needed people like himself, easily carried him through the day.

But just as falling in love in a bucolic collective settlement transformed him, so did the frenetic abundance of a large American city affect Dahlia. In retrospect, he wondered how a woman as personable and attractive as Dahlia could not have commanded such attention. It wasn't long before he noticed the heroic status Israelis were given by American Jews, as if they were a living remnant of the Children of Israel, who after carrying on the ancient legacy of fighting the righteous battle in the Promised Land, had earned the right to come to America where the least we could do was teach them to be good capitalists. Every time Dahlia spoke someone would ask where she was from, and if it was an American Jew asking the question a conversation would certainly ensue. Within an hour Dahlia had a new friend who wanted nothing more than to introduce her to more people and tutor her in the ways of the young and urban.

He had envisioned Dahlia spending her time exploring the city, bonding with his parents, taking classes at one of the many universities. When she told him she had been offered a job in a residential real estate office by one of her new acquaintances, he was surprised with her interest. "My day needs a little bit of structure," she said. "I can't be a permanent tourist forever."

He had always assumed a child of a socialist community would have been repulsed with participating in an economic process that brought material gain solely to the individual. But just the opposite was true. "How would I know what I like if I haven't done this already?" she said.

Good then, he thought, if she gets a taste of the suffocating boredom of office work, the fluorescent lighting, wearing nylons, being anchored to a desk. Arriving home after her first day she again surprised him with an upbeat description of her day including the excitement of learning the phone system, typing English on a computer, and studying a real estate contract.

"A contract? You understood it?"

"Not yet. I think soon, though."

He pretended to be pleased, but couldn't ignore the sudden wave of nausea. In time, he assured himself, she will become bored.

Weeks went by and every day it seemed she learned something new. More and more he saw his beautiful Dahlia, the woman he envisioned by his side while strolling the verdant pathways of the kibbutz, focusing on a goal irrelevant to their future.

"Let's get married," he said late one night, on the same evening Dahlia had come home from work and couldn't wait to tell him about her day spent assisting Joan, the office's top seller. "I helped show some beautiful places. And I'm learning the neighborhoods. Joan said I'm a natural."

If he could just distract her long enough so she would remember what their relationship was about; the fresh air, the stars, the homeland. Dahlia responded quickly with "Let's have a small ceremony here and then a big one later on the kibbutz." When he heard her say the word "kibbutz," his heart opened and gushed with images of their mutual happiness.

Six weeks later their small ceremony occurred at his parent's house with cake, champagne, and Dahlia's parents toasting each other on everybody's good fortune. Bobby's parents were happy too, although somewhat surprised at the diminutive affair. A few months later, he suggested they start planning the second ceremony, but Dahlia, who had been studying for her real estate licensing exam, wanted to wait. "First let me focus on this test," she said. "It's important."

Her choice of words troubled him. "Why would selling real estate be important? On the kibbutz we won't need to sell houses."

Dahlia looked up from her notes. "What if one day we decide to stay here? If I pass this test I'll be ready. I won't be only a tourist."

The nausea returned. It was the first time he had heard her describe a future not including the kibbutz. "You think one day you would rather live here than the kibbutz?"

Dahlia hesitated and then laughed. "Kibbutz life is not for everybody. We need to be prepared for you to want to come back here."

It was his turn to laugh and he did so with relief, a deep lungful of cheer vanquishing the nausea, reminding him of his luck.

***

Dahlia passed the real estate licensing exam and under the attentive eye of her "best friend" Joan, started showing properties. Although Bobby took pleasure in Dahlia's joy, he had ambiguous feelings about her sales ambition. "Selling can be very disappointing," he warned her and she accused him of trying to dampen her enthusiasm.

"If you really care, you will support me," she said, and, of course, he knew she was right. After apologizing, after emphasizing his desire that she not experience the heartbreaking aspect of sales, he realized he was struggling with the concept of selling, that closing a deal seemed too foreign a concept for a child of a kibbutz to be embracing, too contradictory of who she was—too American.

The influence of Joan also troubled him. Fifty-something Joan with her painted nails and Gucci handbags, who called Dahlia

"Sweetie" and said things like, "Do you really want to pick grapefruits the rest of your life?" She made the comment as Bobby stood in the vestibule of their first-floor walkup, about to open the door so Dahlia wouldn't have to fuss with the locks. Childless, recently married for the third time, she appeared freakishly thin with a permanent sun tan. Her long, bright yellow hair, and the artificial roundness of her nose, repulsive him.

"She looks fabulous for her age," Dahlia said every time Joan came up in conversation, a comment he thought very disturbing. And when he tried to suggest the tragic, desperate qualities about her, Dahlia would get angry and remind him Joan was her best friend.

Joan really was her best friend, the kind you brought home— to her husband's Gold Coast condo—where a professional cook served their meals under the glow of Tiffany lamps. Her husband was a real estate magnate who owned and managed properties around the world. Joan often complained of loneliness while her husband was away on business.

"And she works?" Jules said when he found out about Joan's husband.

"She's a great saleswoman," Dahlia said and he knew it was true. Getting such a kick out of schmoozing made her a natural. Women like her lived to talk, empathize, be your best friend. It was only logical Bobby should grow to despise Joan.

On the night Dahlia returned home breathless from having just closed her first deal on a three bedroom townhouse in Lincoln Park, Bobby made the mistake of again bringing up the subject of returning to the kibbutz.

"Oh not yet, not yet," Dahlia begged. "I want to see how good I can get. It's so exciting!" What could he say? That his worst fears were being realized? That he was losing the love of his life to the American dream?

"How much longer do we wait?" he said and Dahlia thought for a moment.

"Another year, maybe."

At that moment Bobby's hatred of Joan was tangible, his wife's best friend became a piece of shrapnel moving through his intestine. He agreed to another year and consoled himself by thinking a lot could happen in a year, real estate sales being the fickle line of work it was. With a little luck the markets would turn against Dahlia and the reality of capitalism's darker side would reveal itself.

The next several months brought nothing but bad news dominated by commission checks, business cards, thank-you notes, and a growing client list. Bobby did his best to appear pleased but as their bank account grew, so did the size of the shrapnel. Then, more than halfway into what he hoped would be the final "year," Bobby's spirits soared when he came home to find Dahlia lying on the couch, sobbing. A huge deal, the one involving a duplex on Astor Street, or maybe the rehabbed bungalow in Bucktown, had fallen through. He would comfort her, remind her she had spent the previous twenty-three years not worrying about rising interest rates.

He asked if something had gone wrong at work. She said no. He asked if she was sure. She was sure. He said he would wait until she wanted to talk. Dahlia sat up and blew her nose.

"I'm pregnant."

Bobby felt the shrapnel moving again, sliding down a few inches, then up again until it settled in an area just behind his navel. She had been on the pill. As an extra precaution he kept track of her cycle. He knew approximately when ovulation should begin and even tested his timing by observing what he had seen in the bathroom waste basket. And then he would start counting again, and when he guessed the egg had begun its journey he was more prone to kiss Dahlia on the forehead after joining her in bed, and then simply say "goodnight," thinking it wouldn't hurt to increase the odds just a little bit more. Not that he didn't ever want children, but he was only twenty-four, too young, he thought, not mature enough for such responsibility.

"Did you forget one day?"

"No, no, no. I did everything right."

He put his arm around her. She leaned into him and they sat quietly. He thought first of his parents, pictured what he expected to be their cautious expression of joy, and then thought of the kids he remembered on the kibbutz, the way they ran barefoot throughout the settlement, the bottoms of their feet like leather. He had admired this ability, their freedom from footwear with no fear of broken glass. He started walking barefoot himself, determined to toughen his feet so he, too, could run barefoot on the concrete or gravel or the sun-baked mud. But he failed to take into account the kibbutz child's foot had been bare since birth and the toughening of the skin was a gradual process. He learned this the hard way, walking slowly, painfully, to the amusement of others, walking as if he trod upon hot coals, walking as if he was a member of an ascetical belief. His feet raw and blistered after only a few days, he had no choice but to give in to the culture from which he had come and return to the world of shoes.

It was from this recollection a glorious insight began to take shape: what better place than a kibbutz to raise a child? The kibbutz, where children were looked after by the community, where one needn't worry about housing, education, making a living, where their child could grow up free of shoes.

"Everything's fine," he said and repeated his thoughts about raising a child on a kibbutz. "We'll have a whole community to help us. Your parents will watch their grandchild grow up. Life will have real meaning. My God, look at these feet!" He pulled off one of Dahlia's socks and pinched the bottom of her foot.

Dahlia took a breath. "I want our baby born here. I want our baby to be a native citizen of America, so it will be easier in the future—to live here."

More nausea. It suddenly hit Bobby that Dahlia didn't want to move back to the kibbutz. Not after the first year or the second year. Not ever. He wanted to lose his temper. He pictured himself shouting at her, accusing her, demanding an explanation, insisting on the truth.

"You're angry," she said and the tears began in earnest. "Please don't hate me, we'll go back, but promise me you'll wait until the baby is born. Promise me you'll wait until the baby is one-year old."

"It's always a year. One more year. Why always a year?"

"You're angry. One year is the minimum time to spend somewhere before making a judgment. You have to stay one year to begin to know something."

"It's a baby! It won't know one year from one hour."

"You don't know that." Tears fell from the corners of her eyes. "They're much more sensitive than you think to their surroundings. I want our baby to breath in America for a year, to know what it is to inhale air not filled with anxiety and fear."

It was the first time he had heard Dahlia express this type of concern. Of course, he knew anxiety from terrorism and war permeated all levels of Israeli life, but he had foolishly allowed himself to believe a background of conflict could exist benignly, without consequence. In the end, he put aside his own vision of the future and relented. He had a decent job in the United States and was soon to become a father. What right did he have to complain?

Pregnancy did little to slow Dahlia's ambition. In fact, it seemed the larger she grew the more successful she became.

"Isn't she gorgeous?" Joan would say with one hand on Dahlia's stomach and the other under her chin. "An adorable young woman carrying a child while selling real estate. Who can resist her?"

Bobby couldn't ignore how well Dahlia was doing and how beautiful she looked. He also couldn't ignore that her commission checks would soon eclipse his salary. The irony was inescapable.

How long could such a union exist? There was the child, he told himself when the crushing boredom at work became excruciating. And, of course, Dahlia herself, still a wonderful woman despite their differing priorities.

Choosing a name for the child brought on another surprisingly contentious period. From the start he had wanted a traditional Hebrew name such as Chaim or Yaron if it was a boy, and if a girl,

Shoshanna, or Shoshi for short. But Dahlia protested such obviously "foreign" names and insisted their child have a name that fit into American or Israeli life without drawing the slightest degree of attention.

"David, if he's a boy and Rachel if she's a girl."

Bobby thought them both fine names but complained of their commonness. "Don't you want something unique to the English-speaking ear? Something that will reflect both of our cultures?"

But Dahlia was adamant and he grudgingly agreed although he decided privately to discuss the names with Dahlia's parents when they arrived for the birth.

Rachel was born on schedule; Rachel, the name his in-laws expressed an immediate and exuberant fondness for, entered the world just as Dahlia wanted, as an American citizen.

Bobby focused on being a helpful father and husband, one that willingly partook in Rachel's changing, feeding, and pacifying, regardless of the hour and effect on his job performance. As the days melted into intervals relating specifically to Rachel's age—their four-week-old daughter becoming a twelve-week-old daughter and then a four-month-old daughter—he saw the current one-year deadline rapidly expiring.

He tried not to dwell on this matter of contention, tried instead to keep his focus on performing his job with distinction, something he found difficult to do as one of many associates in a large firm. He had picked accounting as his chosen profession entirely for pragmatic reasons, preferring the coursework of humanities but having no way to defend a liberal arts education to his father who was footing the bill. Meanwhile, Dahlia had returned to selling, picking up where she left off, but with Rachel swaddled against her in a Snugli, cooing and gurgling to the sounds of commerce.

As Rachel's first birthday drew closer, he made a conscious effort to ignore the subject of moving, hoping Dahlia would bring it up. But when the day arrived and the cupcakes were eaten and the new moms and dads from Dahlia's birthing class packed up their children and went home, Dahlia gave no indication she had been contemplating a change of venue. To his dismay, she seemed remarkably content and domestically blissful. It was a state of being he thought unnaturally static for a child of a kibbutz, a state of being that frightened him. Upsetting Dahlia's equilibrium could be harmful to Rachel, Bobby reasoned, since a mother's healthy state of mind was undeniably healthy for his daughter. She was playing the Rachel card, he thought, a move he hadn't anticipated before her birth. But how could Bobby have anticipated the power of unwavering paternal bonds?

What choice did he have but to wait and see? Certainly, Dahlia knew what he was thinking and certainly she hoped he would simply melt back into the culture from which he had sprung, his wife and child in tow. And that is exactly what he attempted to do, focusing first on the sheer joy of being with his daughter, playing the role of provider, watching her transformation from infant to toddler. Of course, there was Dahlia herself, glowing with both motherhood and ambition, unmistakably the breadwinner, accumulating the wealth their future needed.

Their relationship had changed but not necessarily for the worse—or so he first thought. It was true they didn't make love as often or spend weekend afternoons lying on the couch eating pizza. This change had started as soon as Dahlia passed her test and started selling on her own. But that was to be expected. Real estate sales was often a twenty-four hour job, a fact of life he thought would discourage Dahlia but ended up empowering her even more. "Money never sleeps," she started saying.

Now they both focused on their child, riveted by the smallest events such as the subtle changes in her facial expressions, the movement of her eyes, the chewing of her food, the simple fact of her complete dependence for all sustenance. But as Rachel's awareness of the world grew, so did Bobby's struggle to maintain the status quo. It was inevitable the materialism he hoped to keep away from Rachel would begin to penetrate their lives. Lilliputian-sized sneakers with Velcro straps for twenty dollars, hand-crocheted sandals for thirty dollars, socks made from organic cotton, fifteen dollars for two pair—all for a child who had just learned to walk. "We can afford it," Dahlia would say, her words slapping his face, reminding Bobby of who made the real money.

We can afford it. To Bobby, these words were a declaration of sorts, a verbal shot across the bow. What they could afford wasn't even the issue, but if he brought up the evils of a materialistic society, she countered with charges of stinginess, needlessly withholding the best from their daughter.

"Bare feet are the best for our daughter," he would say and remind Dahlia of where her feet learned to walk, and invariably the conversation would end there since they both knew in what direction the subject of bare feet would lead. Then he would have no choice but to retreat and refocus, come to grips with the fact his idealism was no match for the combination of maternal instincts and money.

Dahlia had no plans of ever leaving the United States. Again, he reminded himself how lucky he was to have everything America offered available to him as his birthright. He continued performing his duties as a father and associate accountant; he continued to bring home what he thought was an adequate paycheck. What he couldn't do was pretend to be happy. His ability to concentrate diminished. He often stopped in the middle of a project to stare out the window and watch the mania of the city. Sometimes he stared at a cloud floating aimlessly over the lake. Dahlia, busy as ever, seemed not to notice, or if she did, said nothing. Gradually, he found it more difficult to come into work but managed to do so without drawing attention to this fact. As long as he got his work done, he figured nobody would notice. But the thought of Rachel growing up to be just another cog in the capitalist machine overshadowed his thoughts. The opportunity to protect her fragile awareness, to shield her from wanton excess was passing. She deserved a childhood without shoes.

"I need to know when we're moving back to the kibbutz," he said. They had just put Rachel to bed and were sitting on the couch in front of the television.

"Soon," Dahlia said and began paging through the TV Guide.

He waited for her to elaborate but when she didn't, he asked again. This time Dahlia tossed the TV Guide on to the coffee table and looked at him. "Let's wait until she's three."

He heard himself ask "Why?" but it was a meaningless question, a final twitch from a severed nerve ending. He heard her voice, was conscious of her argument concerning language development, but her words had no meaning. Later it occurred to him there might be a pathology associated with Dahlia's procrastination, that in her mind she really thought they would one day move back to the kibbutz, although at that moment he had no doubt they weren't going anywhere.

The following months were spent managing various levels of depression, a period of time in which his relationship with Dahlia devolved into a utilitarian arrangement revolving around the facilitation of her appointments. She had lost all respect for him, he decided, which was why she had not inquired about his state of mind and his obvious collapse of spirit. Before he knew it a year had passed and then another. It was a magical time for parents who watched as their child figured out the miracle of language, developed a personality, decided on playmates. It was also a time in which he became dependent on his daughter's maturation to carry him beyond the excruciating reality of what his life had become. He continued to perform his job, albeit statically. He remained passive, uninspired to the events around him such as the promotions of colleagues or the movement of others to better opportunities elsewhere. By Rachel's third birthday he knew watching the evolution of his daughter had replaced the cosmic hourglass hanging above his head. He knew his daughter had become the gauge by which time was measured. Certainly he was aware his marriage was in trouble, but a part of him had always assumed, despite the fact their lives were moving in different directions, time had solidified a bond that over the long run would form the basis of a reconciliation or an agreement to give his version of life a try.

But soon after Rachel's fourth birthday, when she was reading complete sentences with a discernable Chicago accent, he hit a wall. The remaining remnants of hope dissolved into the final dark realization that this, indeed, would be his life.

What choice did he have but to seek professional help? When he told Dahlia he was going to see a psychiatrist, she smiled and kissed him warmly on the neck. "I think that's a good idea," she said.

The doctor came recommended from a friend of his father's who seemed to have had the doctor's résumé memorized, including all the important-sounding names the doctor had worked or studied with, names that meant nothing to Bobby, but nevertheless convinced him this man should be able to help. At their first meeting, he was struck by the doctor's age and wondered if a man well into his sixties was really the best match. He also thought it odd the doctor told him he was semi-retired and had a singing lesson scheduled immediately after their appointment. "It's not just about having talent," the doctor said. "You need a little luck, too."

Despite his concerns, he found the therapy intriguing, particularly with regard to his obsession with the kibbutz, which the doctor thought was part of a much bigger "system." The kibbutz, the doctor said, was a symbol for something unresolved, a yearning, perhaps, for a continuously peaceful mental state supported by a theoretically "abstract environment."

While he acknowledged this desire, he was conflicted over what he saw as the doctor's prejudice against it. "Why not seek to transcend the mundane?" he asked and the doctor, while recognizing the nobility in his ambition, stressed that the mundane cannot truly be transcended, that the mundane existed no matter where you lived or what you did.

"Why not focus on being happy where you are?" the doctor said.

It was sound advice although the doctor failed to take into account the ideal to which he had clung for so many years required a significant period of withdrawal, a disengagement process, a span of time to allow for the ebb and flow of bereavement.

Following the doctor's advice, he started concentrating on abandoning any hope of moving to the "abstract environment." Each time his mind wandered back to the kibbutz, or any other place beside the immediate environment where he lived, he would take a deep breath, go for a walk, remind himself how much he and his family had going for them right where they were. Withdrawal was immediate and punitive. Dahlia noticed his weight loss and asked if he should see another doctor. But he knew the problem no longer existed solely in his head, but lived in his house. How could he tell her she was the catalyst of his pain—that a man suffers greatly when having to live with the woman who just broke his heart?

"Let's talk about it," she said and when he tried to explain what he felt she assured him again when Rachel turned five they would move back to the kibbutz. Had she not then kissed him on the forehead and walked to her office, had she not then phoned one of her clients, he might have believed her this time, he might have gone back on his word to the doctor.

Change would come slowly, gradually, with no significant breakthroughs of awareness. Often, he tried to remember what he was like before he first went to the kibbutz, but could conjure up only images of pretentious behavior and juvenile affectations.

"That's all part of the system," the doctor said. "You've become so prejudiced against yourself that you now think of yourself as illegitimate."

It was true. He had thought for quite a while his life had been, somehow, invalid, a life spent asleep. How could he have done it? he asked himself. Even as a child, so full of fear, how did he get through it?

"Goals," the doctor said, guessing correctly what he was thinking. "Childhood is spent waiting for the next goal. This is what keeps us going. We think that when we reach adulthood we will have won, we will be free."

Ultimately, that's all he wanted, to be free from the stress, the worry, the fear, to not have to think about money, food, shelter, school, or how to support children. How was that possible in the society he called home?

"You're missing the point," the doctor said. "You can find joy and satisfaction in all aspects of life, even the challenges that adulthood offers..."

Bobby had stopped listening. The doctor, it now seemed, was out of touch, too old, and somewhat arrogant. "...sometimes we have to sit back and realize how good we have it..."

Now the doctor was editorializing, pushing his personal wisdom, his life experience. Therapy was finished, he decided. He wanted only to get back home and explain to Dahlia why they couldn't stay, why they had to go back if they wanted to be free.

"I can't help you if you won't let me," the doctor said as Bobby stood to leave.

"But you have helped me," he said and thanked the doctor for his time before walking out.

Dahlia was sitting at the kitchen table when he returned home. In front of her was a small pile of papers. She looked up and he could tell by her expression she was in the kind of pain he had been expecting all along, the kind of pain that arrives when a realization hits, when the thrill of closing a sale, the flush of the commission check, gives way to emotional bankruptcy.

"Don't you see?" he said. "It's all bullshit. Let's get out of here while were still young, while Rachel doesn't know better." He felt confident, animated, clairvoyant. It was all coming together and everything made sense. "You don't need all this, I can tell you don't, I can tell by the way you're looking at me."

Dahlia shifted in her seat and he interpreted this movement as a corroborative gesture which further provoked his optimism and inspired him to take Dahlia back down the road from the main highway to the kibbutz itself. He reminded her of the quaint café at the main intersection where the elderly Arab gentleman took their orders. He described the winding road they would take after hitching a ride from a fellow kibbutznik, some dear comrade who would happily transport them the two kilometers along the brown hillsides to the village they called home, the place where children ran barefoot.

He thought his description of the stars finally got to Dahlia, the truly dark sky where he got his first real glimpse of the Milky Way. "It was like being in a sparkling jar," he said and reminded her that in the city you could maybe see Venus and, if you were lucky, Jupiter, but you could forget about Saturn or the Pleiades, and the Andromeda galaxy might as well be a flagpole on the moon.

When she wiped the tears from her eyes he figured he was home free and it wouldn't be long before the three of them would be aboard an El-Al airliner on their way to their new life. He imagined when Rachel was old enough to understand, he would describe their fantastic voyage, their magic carpet ride, and how when they arrived at their new home they were greeted by old friends who welcomed them back to the land that was their home and if Rachel remembered anything, she would remember the mass of children embracing her as their sister.

The image of his precious daughter surrounded by children who would become her extended family, children who would watch each other grow, serve in the armed forces together and become adults, brought tears to his eyes. He walked behind Dahlia who was leaning on her elbows with her face buried in her hands, and wrapped his arms around her shoulders, kissed her neck, and told her how happy they would be. He waited for her response which came quietly between sobs, her accent more pronounced due to the wavering of her voice, the words, "I want a divorce," sounding surprisingly foreign.

14

Jules was aware the allotted time for his lunch break had long since expired. Bobby was leaning backward in his chair, directing his gaze somewhere on the ceiling. "So you see," Bobby said. "We're not so different, you and me."

Jules wasn't prepared to categorically agree with this statement. "We've both been through a difficult period."

"It's time for me to hear about your problems"

His use of the word "problems" annoyed Jules. "I have to get back to work."

"Well just tell me some little thing, just a detail. Are you seeing anyone?"

Jules said yes, not completely sure he was telling the truth.

"Is she Jewish?"

"Not now, Bobby." Jules stood and walked toward the door.

"How did you meet her?"

"I gotta go."

"Call me when you have time to talk," Bobby said and handed Jules a business card. "We're not as different as you think."

"We'll get together soon," Jules said and pushed the cart forward.

***

Jules didn't remember opening the door of his apartment or the thirty-minutes prior to his arrival home. So immersed he had been in a state of reflection, it wasn't until he saw the blinking light on his answering machine that his thoughts were interrupted by a rush of anticipation he was about to hear Candy's voice. When the voice was Bobby's, Jules thought their meeting had been a gigantic mistake. He had created a monster simply by acknowledging the two shared the common denominator of psychic pain.

"...why don't we get together for coffee..." Bobby suggested, wanting to talk as soon as possible, as if in Jules's "story" there contained urgent information directly affecting Bobby's life. Jules ignored the message, thinking instead of what to have for dinner and his chances of getting in touch with Candy. He dialed her number, and when the answering machine picked up he left a brief, awkward message announcing who he was and how they had met and then wondered aloud when they would meet again.

He sat in the reclining chair and thought how idiotic he must've sounded. An hour later the phone rang.

"Did you get my message?" Bobby said.

"No," Jules said.

"So let's get together. Where do you hang out?"

117

Jules wanted to say he didn't "hang out" but thought Bobby would use this admission as more proof Jules's life was in tatters. "Java Jinx," Jules said.

"That's where you hang out?"

"That's where I hang out."

"What time do you want to meet?"

The determination in Bobby's voice gave Jules the same creepy, suffocating feeling Izzy had inspired.

"My God, we just talked a few hours ago."

"We talked about me, now it's your turn. Don't I deserve the same respect?"

What Jules had failed to understand was Bobby had told his story for Jules's benefit, his story had been a gift. So Jules agreed to meet Bobby later that evening. At the very least, he thought it might look better for him not to be home should Candy return his call, which she did, just as Jules was about to leave his apartment.

"We have something in common," Candy said as soon as Jules picked up.

"Oh really?"

"I committed an egregious transgression of the truth."

"Declare to me your misbehavior."

"I've been temping in this trashy little office with this egregiously bitchy woman that I call my supervisor. At five o'clock she tells me that I need to stay and help her make copies and then organize two million packets for her boss's meeting tomorrow morning. So, I'm like a temp, right? And, like I'm gonna stay late at a minute's notice? I don't think so. 'Sorry sweetheart' I told her. 'Already got plans.'"

"And what'd she say?"

"I didn't wait around to listen. What're they gonna do, fire me?"

"You're offense being that you didn't have plans to speak of."

"Affirmative. And now you have the opportunity to make an honest woman out of me."

Of course there was the question of Bobby, whose devotion to Jules's welfare had made him a bit uneasy. Jules thought exposing Candy to the resurrected Bobby Mars came with a certain amount of risk.

"Crap. Out of nowhere this old friend got in touch with me. I promised to meet him at Java Jinx."

"You want me to become a liar? Lying is real easy once you get used to it and God only knows where it will lead."

"I really don't know the guy anymore and his wife's divorcing him. I'm not sure what kind of weird shit he's capable of saying, you know?—"

"This is your chance to save me, Jules, and you're gonna turn me away because you're afraid of what your weird friend might say—about you I assume. What're you hiding? You don't think I'm gonna find out eventually?"

"We're meeting at 7:30."

"See you there."

As he approached Java Jinx it occurred to him this place might be destined to become his official hangout. Already, on his second visit in as many nights, he felt a friendly kind of energy which gave Jules a boost of confidence when he walked in and looked around for the two familiar faces he expected to find waiting for him, two familiar faces he never thought he would find sitting together sharing a bowl of peanuts.

"There he is," Bobby said.

"You know each other?" Jules said.

"We do now," Candy said and they broke into simultaneous laughter.

Jules looked around half expecting to see Izzy. "Relax, we just met," Candy said and grabbed Jules's hand. "So sit down."

"I was just sitting here," Bobby said, "and she walks up to me and says, 'Are you meeting Jules,' and I said, 'How did you know,' and then she takes a seat and tells me how you two met at the library a few days ago, blah, blah, blah."

Again, the two broke into laughter and Jules joined in although he still was unable to be completely sure two people could get along so well so quickly.

"Oh stop it," Candy said to Jules and slapped his arm. "It happens this way sometimes. I knew you were meeting someone here, he's sitting alone, I took a chance and I was right. It's funny."

"What have you two been talking about?"

"You, what else," Bobby said.

"What has he told you?" Jules asked Candy.

"What good friends you two were."

"I owe Bobby a recap of the last decade," Jules said.

"You don't owe me anything," Bobby said, the tone of his voice decidedly cooler." The three remained silent a few moments before Bobby continued. "I got caught up in all this life and family bullshit, and way before my time, pal. I mean I'm barely past thirty and I'm about to have an ex-wife who's afraid I might kidnap our daughter and leave the country. This was never in my plan, Jules, never in a million goddamn years did I think this is where I'd be. I mean, c'mon, me? Little Bobby Mars, the smart-aleck schmuck, the nobody who got good grades and tried to be everybody's friend, the cute little Bobby with the big nose who by some miracle gets a beautiful woman to seemingly fall in love with him and start a family? In the morning I look in the mirror and I'm thinking that it's over; I had my chance. From now on I'll have the same bland bullshit life my parents had except I have the added privilege of being statistically connected to that fifty percent of divorced adults and the whole childcare scene as well."

"You don't know that," Jules said. "What you said about having the bland life and all. Dahlia saw something in you. It happened once, it could happen again. You don't know what the future holds."

"You don't want to sit through all this do you?" Jules said to Candy.

"I want her to stay," Bobby said.

They both looked at her. "OK," she said. "Bobby's my newest friend, after all."

It was a considerate thing to say, something a clever woman like Candy would think of saying when put on the spot. Jules, however, had no doubt she was serious. Jules told Bobby the story he thought he owed him, omitting the episode with Izzy and repeating the story he had told Candy.

"So there you have it, the story of my demise or my rebirth, depending on how you look at it, but certainly not very goddamn interesting, certainly not something worth writing down or bringing to the stage—except for the Capone stuff. For a while Capone was the spark getting me interested in life again, I guess I owe him one."

"Capone's cool," Bobby said. "And the drugs are cool, too. And just think where you'd be if your co-workers weren't such assholes—stuck in an office all day like me. But after a while you would have probably flipped out like you did anyway."

"Probably," Jules said, annoyed by the comment and suddenly amazed Bobby Mars could possibly have been a husband and father.

"What do you think, Candy?" Bobby said. "Glad you stuck around?"

Years later, Jules would count this moment as another of his watersheds. He would think of it as a moment transitioning him into a more definable state of mind when his search for his role in society became a search of who he was. The catalyst of this transition came from a single question uttered from Candy's gentile mouth, a question asked after Candy looked thoughtfully at Bobby and then at Jules before saying, "What's the deal with this whole Jewish thing anyway? I mean why does being a Jew have to hang above your heads like a Damocles sword or something."

Certainly Candy's choice of the word "deal" was purely unconscious and the idiomatic quality of the word canceled out any suggestion of provocation. With this knowledge Jules could appreciate the comment was spoken with complete sincerity, that it was a perfect comment for its honesty, that it was the kind of comment that could inspire fits of laughter if only because of the innocence in which the words were cloaked. And as the two men composed themselves and Bobby attempted to address Candy's question, Jules's thoughts returned to Izzy and how the strange little man had adopted the same "deal" that Candy had spoken of—the "deal," it suddenly occurred to Jules, being infinitely more complicated than he had ever imagined.

"...it has to do with culture and heritage," Jules heard Bobby say, "depending on the person, of course, whether they care or not about identity..."

Bobby struggled to help Candy understand something Bobby himself didn't fully understand. She had asked the pivotal question secular Jews had been asking themselves since the time one or more of the Chosen People chose no longer to identify with the God of David and had decided they could do just fine without having a supreme being as part of their daily lives.

"...having a culture to identify as your own..."

Jules studied Candy's face as Bobby's words filled the space between them. He often returned to the word, "identity." It was another one of those words so relevant it demanded to be spoken, as if there was no better word to explain to the world we all desired to have something to call our own.

"...Hitler being the most extreme example..."

It would always come back to Hitler, Jules thought, and how could it not? He had been the ultimate deal breaker after all, the one against whom everything would be compared. Then it occurred to Jules that Bobby's psychiatrist had been correct when he said Bobby's obsession with a homeland was part of larger "system." The system, Jules now knew, was the "deal" itself, an all encompassing consciousness, the Damocles sword Candy had sensed. Hitler, the priest, and the homeland all were intrinsically connected, all part of the "Jewish deal". It seemed so ridiculously obvious, yet peripherally so, as if to comprehend the connection one had to soften their focus and gaze just off to the side. His mind began to wander in search of the common denominator, the single unifying principle putting the "deal" front and center.

His friend was doing a respectable job, Jules thought, but like his own thoughts, Bobby's were disorganized. One moment he was marching with Nazis, the next he was on the fairways of country clubs, the kind of clubs Jews were barred from joining which became the impetus for them to build their own clubs—only nicer. Bobby was focusing on the pride factor, overcoming obstacles, persevering.

"...Do you know what I mean?" Bobby said and hesitated just long enough for Candy to interject.

"What do you think, Jules?"

He looked thoughtfully at Candy, sank into her shadowed face, her dilated pupils, studied her perky, slightly upturned nose, tried to imagine seeing the world through her eyes. He wondered if it was possible for Candy to take his words and properly translate them into the correct emotions he didn't yet know how to verbalize.

"This is a waste of time."

Bobby frowned. "Why do you say that?"

"Can you understand what it's like to be Greek or Italian?"

"It's more complicated than that."

"Exactly, it's too complicated. Nobody knows what it means. Even Jews don't know what the hell it's about."

"It's means different things to different people."

"That's my point."

"But she's asking us."

Jules scoffed at Bobby's limited interpretation and looked at Candy who had shrunk back in her seat. "Tell us," Jules said. "Did you mean us or Jews in general?" Jules regretted the question. He thought how arrogant he must've sounded in assuming she could understand the nuance of the question or even comprehend the issue had inherent distinctions. For her part, Candy remained expressionless, moved her eyes back and forth between the two men, and showed no outward sign of confusion.

"I meant you and you," she said poking her finger first into Jules's arm and then flicking a peanut across the table at Bobby. "But you're both acting like I just shoved an ice pick into an exposed bicuspid nerve. Obviously the question is much larger than the both of you."

"I don't think it's that big," Bobby said. "Not really."

"How can you possibly say that?" Jules said.

"A person chooses to identify with something for religious reasons or ethnic reasons or both—period, the end," Bobby said.

Jules shook his head, amazed at what he heard. "Like you always felt this way? Growing up you didn't give a damn, and then something happened, something made you decide needing a homeland was important. So important it's what defined your life—ruined your life, one could argue."

"I was looking for somewhere to belong. The homeland thing seemed easy, logical, a way to define myself. And then I met Dahlia and the communal lifestyle really turned me on, and everything seemed even more logical. But it was just a choice I made. It wasn't as if I fell into some weird psycho-Jew trance..."

Jules was struck by Bobby's use of "I"—But it was just a choice I made—the "I" seemed to have an extraneous quality, as if the "I" transcended the physical, provoked Bobby's easy, logical way to define himself. It was the "I" where he would find the single unifying principle. But what was the goddamn "I"?

"....maybe your drugs were making you more—"

"More stupid?" Jules said.

"More curious," Bobby said.

"More analytical," Candy said.

Jules looked at Candy and felt a touch disappointed. Her suggestion, he figured, was an implicit agreement with Bobby's statement. Jules knew it was absurd to imply the taming of his neurotransmitters had transformed his brain into an apparatus of superfluous thought patterns. He also knew neither Bobby nor Candy understood what he was looking for and the mental energy required to explain his quest was more than he was willing to expend.

"It's more than a choice," Jules said. "History proves it's much bigger than just making a choice." He hadn't planned on implicating the past.

"Watch out, Candy," Bobby said. "He's got history on his side. And Jules knows his history."

"I love history," Candy said. "Give me some history."

But Jules was used up for the evening. "I've had enough. Let's move on."

"That's it?" Bobby said. "Just like that you're giving in?"

"Yes, I'm giving in. You win, Bobby."

"No you're not," Candy said. "You just don't want to talk about it anymore."

Candy looked as cute as he had ever envisioned her only now she was smiling coyly with those black pupils sucking him in. She was smart.

"I'm not done," Bobby said.

"Sorry Bobby, I don't want to beat this horse any more tonight."

"Fuck you, Jules."

"What do you mean?" Jules said.

"I mean I'm not done, damn it all, this is important, so fuck you!"

Bobby leaned back in his chair and let his chin fall against his chest. Jules stared at him a moment and then sought direction from Candy.

"What is it you want to talk about," Candy said quietly.

Bobby raised his head. "Aren't you glad you came?" he said and laughed. "I don't mean to sound so pissed off but for fuck sake this is important. I mean this is our lives we're talking about. Right?"

The slight quiver in Bobby's lower lip alarmed Jules, and for a moment he wondered who this person was. "Take it easy, Bobby," Jules said. "We'll talk more, just not tonight."

"Why not tonight?" Bobby said. "Mr. fucking historian says my life is ruined. Why didn't you become a teacher? Instead you wanted to be a businessman! What was that all about?"

Jules waited for more but realized Bobby was expecting an answer. "Business was more practical."

"Since when were you practical? One girl friend your whole life, the same girl you met as a baby? You really thought the two of you would live happily-ever-after?"

"What the hell difference does it make?"

"I'm really concerned about you. Look at yourself, working in a library. You're wasting your life, what are you going to do?"

"What the fuck do you care? Worry about yourself. You're so fucking smart, tell me what I should be doing?"

"Work! Some kind of meaningful work!" Bobby covered his face with his hands.

Jules pushed his chair back as if to leave. Candy took his hand and shook her head. They both watched Bobby take deep breaths and loudly exhale. "She was playing me," Bobby said. "To get to the US, she played me like a grand piano."

"You don't mean that," Candy said. "She loved you."

"She liked me. I was different. An American. I made her laugh. I was easy to put up with, a small sacrifice to make to get out of there. Have I told you? Her parents have now moved here. The whole family is living in my condo. They've made it, they're in the United States with their naturalized daughter and native-born granddaughter. You're right Jules, my life is a fucking mess and who am I to give you advice? I mean look at us, you in a library and me counting beans, the lowest bean counter in the firm, going nowhere because I hate the job and everyone knows it. If not for my father I'd be shelving books in a library like you, bro."

Although he knew Candy probably felt sorry for Bobby, Jules felt only contempt. Too much drama coming after too much time had passed made it impossible for Jules to embrace Bobby's pain.

"Well, thank God for your father. So what do you want from me?"

"Are you really satisfied with just working in a library? Don't you want more from life?"

"You're starting to piss me off."

"How can I get the drugs you got? I need to get where you are. I need to get drugged up like you so I can deal better with my situation, like you're doing. But Christ don't get too comfortable, you can't just waste your life, Jules."

"Find another psychiatrist, Bobby. Just act like you're acting now and I'm sure you'll get all the medication you want."

Bobby nodded his head several times. "Yeah. I just need something to chill me out while I go through all this shit. Then, once everything is settled, I'll get off the drugs. I'm sure I'll get joint custody, don't you think? I'll get a better job and then I'll get off the drugs and I'll start over. Maybe go back to school. That's what you should do, Jules. Go back to school for Christ sake."

"Why don't we call it a night," Jules said and stood up.

"You're acting so childish, sit down and talk. What're you so afraid of? Why don't you want my help? I can help you figure things out."

"Focus on your own problems. Find another doctor, get yourself calmed down and deal with your divorce."

"But what about you. How long are you going to stay this way?"

"C'mon," Jules said and led Candy toward the door.

"Are you kidding me?" Bobby shouted at their backs. "After all these years you're just walking away?"

Just as they reached the door a pencil buzzed over Jules's head. He stopped and looked back at Bobby who held his palms up in a gesture of helplessness.

The two left the coffee shop and did not speak until they were halfway down the block. "That was really weird," Candy said. Jules could tell she was a bit shaken and he was about to agree and apologize when he felt a blow to the back of his head and heard the sound a thick glass ashtray makes when it fractures on the sidewalk.

"You're crazy!" Candy shouted down the empty sidewalk. "Are you OK?" Jules rubbed the back of his head. Candy pushed his hair away, took out a tissue from her purse, and pushed it against his head. "You're bleeding a little bit."

"Excellent," Jules said. They continued walking. This time Candy led the way, steering Jules to her apartment where she washed out the wound, applied antiseptic, and teased him about the company he kept. Jules lay on her couch with his head propped against her thigh. He apologized for exposing her to his disturbed friend, and Candy insisted despite that the "violence" the evening had been enjoyable. They talked at length of Bobby's behavior and took turns diagnosing his illness. The sincerity of the conversation gradually degenerated into sarcastic images of how Bobby would spend the remainder of his evening and soon deteriorated into uncontrollable fits of laughter.

Not surprisingly, the promise of sex was never too far in the background of Jules's thoughts and it occurred to him nothing could be more logical than for the night to end in Candy's bed. But like most intense experiences, this one lasted only as long as it took for Jules's brain to send the weakest of messages, one suggesting he was presumptuous. But Candy slid her hand under Jules's shirt and began rubbing his chest in a way that left little room for ambiguity, and by the time her fingers reached to just below his navel, Jules felt as secure about his station in life as he ever had.

15

Jules had that feeling of "otherness" again. It was an awareness as natural and intimate as the secretions of his liver or the pulsations of his heart. Where have you been? he wanted to say, but when he lifted his head and tried to make eye contact he could see nothing in front of him, just a white hole surrounded by the green of the park. He let his head fall back and then became aware of a slight pressure on his groin, not enough pressure to cause pain but enough to caution his movements. He saw Marla. She was wearing a black sleeveless dress and black pumps. She looked at him, scowled, and poked her toe into his side. Jules realized he was naked below the waist. You can fuck whomever you wish, Marla said and Jules tried to answer, wanted to tell her he knew she had been with others. But first he had to get to his feet and stretch his t-shirt to cover himself, which he did gradually but not before Marla was gone and Jules stood in the doorway of his father's showroom with his shirt back up to his waist. Jack peered over his granny glasses and shook his head. Forgive me, he said. I wasn't in World War II. Forgive me for being just a bit too young. Forgive me for being assigned to Tokyo Army Hospital in the Korean war. But I got balls just like you, Julie. And it's not a big deal. So put those goddamn things away already. Then his father stood and disappeared between rows of coat racks. Jules followed, pushed away the garments and saw Solly standing in his bedroom, about to step into an oversized white diaper. With one leg through, he stopped and looked at Jules. Just pretend I'm a sumo wrestler, he said and laughed and then placed his other leg into the diaper. Then he picked up a soiled undergarment from the floor and held it out in front of him. You live as long as you can just to end up with this. He swung the garment around his finger a few times before letting fly toward Jules who jumped out of the way only to feel another spasm of pain. I'm sorry, Bobby said, emerging from behind another rack of coats, overtaking Solly and stopping directly in front of Jules who figured Bobby was sorry about his behavior at the coffee shop. Bobby then positioned himself behind

129

Jules and closed his hand into a tight fist upon Jules's crotch. Jules wrenched himself free and awoke.

"Bad dream?"

"Are you working today?"

"Not unless the agency calls." Candy rolled back on to Jules.

"I have to go," Jules said. He hated the words for their cruelty and wished he was the type to show up late for work and not feel guilty, to feel, in fact, proud in that offbeat bohemian kind of way.

"You think you can say 'no' to me and get away with it?" Candy began applying pressure from her hips and thighs in a way that would cause Jules to be late for work, in a way so skillful that saying "no" was impossible and would remain impossible during the weeks to come when the potential consequences of arriving late for a job shelving books quickly faded in that offbeat bohemian kind of way.

***

His obsession with the widening gap faded. The gap, although growing daily, now seemed to Jules as nothing more than an obstacle to be spanned when the appropriate time arrived. The method of spanning was an insignificant detail, an irrelevant waste of thought-energy when compared to the joy he experienced on any given moment when focused on Candy.

It was ironic that when Jules wondered if he was becoming too vulnerable, he thought how nice it would be to call Bronwyn who would know how to appeal to his transcendental side to help allay irrational fears. Thus far Candy had given no indication Jules had much to worry about and if anything, she seemed to be solidifying their relationship with gestures including an invitation to meet her parents. Initially, Jules balked at such a meeting. The thought of having to explain what he did for a living and all the reasons why he existed in such circumstances seemed very unappealing.

"They don't care about that," Candy insisted. "Look at me, their own daughter. What the hell am I doing?"

"You're female. Society doesn't care what women do or don't do."

"And what do you care what society thinks?"

"I'm working on not caring. But that doesn't mean I want to talk about it."

"Then don't talk about it."

"And when your dad asks me what I do?"

"Make something up."

"You want me to lie?"

"I'll tell them not to ask you."

"Great! And then we'll spend the evening tip-toeing around the subject and they'll be wondering what the hell is wrong with me and if I'm leading their daughter straight to hell."

Not long after this discussion, Candy parked her car in the circular driveway in front of her parent's house on Pleasant Avenue, a quiet road in an old suburb where enormous oak, maple, and elm trees lined the parkways of manicured yards and formed a verdant canopy over the street. Jules stepped out of the car and surveyed the grandeur of the English Tudor structure. The house was impressive but he couldn't help notice the bushes were in dire need of clipping, the gardens were overrun with weeds, and the grass itself was uneven in length and thoroughly infiltrated with weeds.

"You didn't tell me your parents were loaded."

"We're old money." Candy pushed open the door and led Jules into the marble-floored foyer.

"Hello?" Candy shouted and the two walked into a large, stately room with gigantic windows looking over the forested backyard sloping to Lake Michigan. Jules noticed the natural light from outside was all that kept the room from being dark. "Sit," Candy said and pointed to one of several couches of differing sizes scattered throughout the room. Each couch had its own lamp. "I'll go find them."

He felt odd sitting alone in the majestic room staring down the dimly lit corridor into which Candy had disappeared. He tried to imagine how three people could occupy a house so large. After a few minutes Jules heard the opening and closing of doors followed by the rise and fall of unintelligible voices. The terrifying prospect that one of Candy's parents would appear before she returned dawned on Jules. The tortured sound of a stringed instrument being tuned periodically filled the gaps between the screech of furniture being dragged across the floor and the opening and closing of car doors.

"Jules?" a male voice echoed from the opposite end of the corridor. Jules stood, but could only see a shadowy outline of a man walking toward him. He assumed it was Candy's father.

"That's me," Jules said trying to sound cheerful. As the figure came closer, Jules processed the subtle signals of the stranger's energetic gait.

"My God, look at you," the man said emerging suddenly from the hallway into the light of the room in stocking feet, corduroy slacks, and an oversized sweater. He was much older than Jules expected, with a full head of white hair. Jules extended his hand which the man ignored, choosing instead to advance with open arms, smothering Jules in an embrace suitable for a long lost son.

"You're as handsome as Candace said you were," the man said and released Jules.

Jules, shocked Candy would have said such a thing to her father, or shocked her father would repeat it to his face upon their first meeting, could only stand still grinning stupidly. In the background he thought he heard the rhythm of footsteps and prayed they would become louder.

"I was just telling this young man how handsome he was," the man then yelled over Jules's head. Jules turned and saw a tiny smiling woman with long gray hair walking briskly toward them. She wore a white t-shirt and plaid clam digger shorts.

"Yes, I see," the woman said. "And he has a wonderful figure."

For a moment Jules wondered if he was hallucinating. "Where's Candy?" he managed to say.

"She'll be right down," the woman said. "Now let me have a look." It was her turn to embrace Jules, which she did, wrapping her arms around his waist and plastering the side of her head against his chest. "Such a powerful heartbeat!"

The thought of simply fleeing the premises entered his mind. And then, a gift. It arrived in the form of a vision eliminating any trace of solemnity from which Jules had been clinging and left only the absurdity of the scene. With the head of the woman he supposed to be Candy's mother still sealed to his chest, Jules started to laugh.

"He's alive!" the woman shouted. She stepped back to her husband and put her arm around his waist.

"Of course he's alive," Candy shouted from across the room before running to Jules's side. "I see you've met my psychotic begetters."

"Only the man begets," her father said. "And that's no way to talk about your parents. Jules would never talk that way about his parents, would you Jules?"

"Don't answer that," Candy said. "You passed the test, by the way. You didn't run away. I call it trial by humiliation. I was trying to avoid this by finding them before they found you but I blew it. Hopefully, this won't be our last date."

"Oh it wasn't that bad, was it?" her mother said.

Jules looked at Candy to see if she wanted to interject again. "No, it wasn't so bad," Jules said. "A bit strange but I'm a bit strange, too." He had no idea why he said the part about being strange, but it worked; Candy's father roared with laughter.

"You see?" her father said.

"I love the name Jules!" her mother said. "It's so Français."

"This is Paul and Diane," Candy said. "I'm their offspring."

"Come sit with us Jules," Paul said and the four took seats in front of one of the large picture windows. The late afternoon light reflected steely gray off the lake, just bright enough to illuminate their faces. Jules glanced toward the front door and could barely make out any other objects.

"You have a beautiful house," Jules said and was promptly thanked by Paul and Diane. Diane then audibly whispered to Candy that Jules had good manners and mother and daughter then proceeded to whisper back and forth. Candy first asked her to try not to act so weird and Diane said it was a sin to be ashamed of your own mother. Jules took the opportunity to study Paul who had seemingly tuned out the other's banter to focus his attention out the window. Jules became transfixed with Paul's physical appearance in the light, his thick hair shining platinum-gray, his blue eyes taking on the color of the lake. Every line in his face was suddenly apparent, telling a story.

"Oh Jules, you don't think I'm weird, do you?" Diane said.

"Not at all," Jules said, once again eliciting a roar of laughter from Paul.

"You'd have to be pretty weird yourself to not think Diane is weird," Paul said and they all laughed together.

"You grew up in this house as an only child?" Jules said to Candy.

Candy thought a moment. "As their only child, yes. But the house was full of people."

"Paul hails from the theater and I'm a painter," Diane said. "All our friends were artists of some sort, and when my father left me this house I opened it up to anyone in the arts community who needed a place to stay while visiting Chicago or was on their way somewhere. We like to say that Candace grew up in an abstract household surrounded by impressionistic dispositions."

"That's there way of saying 'dysfunctional family'," Candy said.

"Very cruel child," Paul said.

"Just kidding, Paul," Candy said.

"Yes, Jules, she calls us Paul and Diane, as if we were classmates," Paul said. "We'd prefer that she call us 'mom and dad' but she resists."

"Yes, this is normal, Jules," Candy said, "It's routine, actually, that we play out our family dramas in front of our guests. And for the record, it was Paul and Diane's idea that I call them by their first names, an idea that came about when I was a baby learning to talk and they thought that to instill a sense of equality, I should not be subjected to putting fellow humans in classifications such as 'mom and dad, aunt or uncle'. But now that I've grown up, they've reverted to some kind of sentimental fantasy world in which they've been suddenly transformed into 'mommy and daddy', whose little girl comes home to visit. What they don't understand is that it's too late. That to be a mommy or daddy, one must act like a mommy or daddy, preferably before their little girl reaches the age of twenty-five."

"Very cruel child," Diane said.

It was a family dynamic Jules had never witnessed before, although he was intrigued by what seemed to be their symbiotic relationship. Dissimilar organisms still struggling to define themselves while verbally acting out—or striking out—for their mutual benefit. As a guest you represented the audience from whom the actors solicited to hear their cases and enlist their sympathies.

"Are you a supporter of the arts, Jules?" Paul said.

"I have nothing against the arts," Jules declared.

"Good answer," Candy said.

"Brilliant," Diane said. "We'll love you no matter what, Jules."

Diane's assertion of unconditional love combined with the afternoon light that had diminished from its lustrous silvers and blues to a dingy gray, brought to Jules a new round of discomfort— a sleepy kind of malaise, as if he, too, was fading into the approaching darkness.

"I'd love to see the rest of the house," Jules said. He wanted at least to see the emanation of a single light bulb.

"Come," Candy said and reached for Jules's hand.

"Yes, give him the tour," Paul said. "Dinner's in an hour."

Jules followed Candy into the hallway where a switch illuminated a row of track lights hanging from the ceiling. The soft luminescence soaked into his eyes. The hallway came alive with colorful abstract paintings, traditional landscapes, and several large mirrors with hand-painted frames suggesting an influence of native cultures.

"Do they always keep the house so dark?" Jules said.

"Yep," Candy said. "They like all light to be concentrated only where the space is being occupied. It encourages their creative spirits to be surrounded by darkness while focusing on something that's illuminated."

They continued down the hallway. Jules was content to be led wherever Candy decided, although the doors off the hallway every ten or fifteen feet were irresistible.

"All these doors can't be closets."

"You're correct. Some are small rooms that were used as studios for guests. Each had an easel, a lamp, and a mirror. It was kind of an early sensory deprivation technique in that inside these rooms you were either painting or thinking about painting or practicing a monologue. You couldn't look out the window, open the fridge, turn on the radio. Sometimes, at the guest's request, Diane would lock the door from the outside for a given amount of time so that the person inside had no choice but to work or try to work. As a little girl I would run up and down the hallway opening and closing the doors that weren't locked, trying to guess who was inside. Some of the guests would shout and come rushing at me and I would scream and slam the door and run away only to come back a few minutes later for more. I'm sure I drove some of them crazy, or maybe saved some from insanity. Who knows?"

At the end of the hallway another switch illuminated a distant bulb somewhere up a narrow staircase. The feeble light reminded

Jules of old tenement buildings teeming with miserable immigrants.

"How the hell can you live with such pathetic lighting?"

"You get used to it." Candy led Jules into another hallway lined with more non-descript doors. One of the doors in the middle of the hall was Candy's bedroom, a queerly shaped niche resembling a capital "I". The entire east wall was a window offering the same view of the trees and lake the living room below them afforded.

"Having this room was a lifesaver. The forest and lake were my best friends."

The other walls seemed to exist for the sole purpose of supporting bookshelves of plain hardcover spines comprising volumes of literature, plays, and art history. Along with her twin-sized bed, the room contained a small dresser, a nightstand, an easel, a lamp, and a standup mirror.

"You paint?" Jules said.

"If you lived in this house you either painted or acted. Of course dancers and singers were allowed too."

Jules tried to imagine what life for her could've been like and saw Candy as a little girl sitting in front of the easel with her watercolors and a house full of people waiting to tell her how much talent she had.

"Why did you want me to come here?"

"I thought you'd want to know where I came from."

"Do I get to see the rest of the house?"

"There's really no point. It's just more rooms, pretty much the same as what you've already seen. The story is that my great-grandfather built this place to be a hotel, a place in the country for the wealthy city folks to escape to. It didn't do that well and the people who came decided to build their own homes here and eventually this fancy neighborhood sprung up around it. A fancy neighborhood that didn't want a hotel in its midst. So he lived in it with his family, all of whom eventually moved out. My grandmother hated the house, she said it was a giant mausoleum and wouldn't let Diane go near it. She was appalled when Diane agreed to live in it, as requested by her grandfather. Why it was so important to him has never really been explained to me."

"How do your parents afford the upkeep?"

"Diane's a trust fund kid. That was the agreement if she lived here. Let me show you the kitchen. It's hotel-sized and we use one sink and one stove that Diane updated. Everything else is relics. Antique appliance nuts come through once in a while and have a blast."

The house was no longer intriguing, just a huge, dimly lit box, an art-house salon of sorts, a place where a little girl grew up surrounded by eccentric adults.

"Let's stay here," Jules said and stretched out on the bed. "Do you remember looking at the stars while lying in bed?"

Candy lay down next to him. "No. But I must have."

***

The dining room was consistent with the rest of the house; a regal hall with a long wooden table in the center of the room surrounded by far too many high-back chairs than was necessary. Candy and Jules took seats at one end of the table where two lamps illuminated the place settings.

"This place is a museum," Jules said. "I bet these are the original chairs that your great-grandfather bought."

"You're absolutely right," Paul said as he walked across the room holding a large serving bowl of pasta. A bottle of red wine was tucked under each arm. "Almost all the furniture is original."

It was in the glow of candlelight Jules sat with Paul and Diane and their only child who had arrived relatively late in their lives. The four of them clasped hands while Diane thanked a nameless entity for their good fortune, and then passed to Jules the bowl of pasta. After filling his glass with wine, Paul complimented Diane on the sauce and the colors of the salad, and then reminisced about a Hawaiian vacation they took years ago, how the wild birds flew through the forest as colorful as soaring palettes. Then Diane asked Jules if he had traveled at all and Jules told them he hadn't but always wanted to, which touched off a conversation of life in other cultures, a subject Jules found fascinating since both Diane and Paul had traveled extensively. From there they spoke of politics and seminal events of the previous thirty years, civil rights, Vietnam, Watergate, and other subjects Jules was too young to either remember or appreciate. The conversation soon evolved to a point where Jules had the opportunity to talk proudly of his Uncle Solly and then about his father and the apparel business, which sparked some interest from Paul who was reminded of his role as "Biff" in Death of a Salesman. The evening progressed comfortably without questions of career goals or ambitions, only discussions and stories of the crazy world in which they lived and how important it was to find happiness within it.

Candy seemed content to mostly listen, although toward the end of the evening when a lull in the conversation occurred she jumped in and said, "Jules's great-grandfather knew Al Capone."

"How wonderful," Diane said. "Was great-granddad a gangster?"

Jules could tell Diane was not being sarcastic.

"I wouldn't say that, necessarily. Depending on one's definition of a gangster."

"Fascinating," Paul said and refilled his wine glass. "Tell us about him and don't leave out any of the gory details."

"He terrorized people on election days," Candy said, drawing a surprised look from Jules. "It was all over the papers."

"He was a politician..." Jules tried to put Morris Ellerstein into context by emphasizing the sensationalist newspaper journalism of Prohibition-era Chicago, and then related the stories Solly had told him and what he had read. "I don't know the real truth," Jules confessed. "You're right, it is fascinating, but I'm not sure how to feel."

"You feel proud!" Paul said and slapped his hand on the table. "You thank God for this man and appreciate that he is a part of you. He may very well have stayed in this house, maybe even sat in the seat that you're right now sitting in, may have cut a very important deal right at this table. Capone had the Lexington Hotel. Don't you see the interconnectivity of it all?"

Jules wasn't sure what he saw although he was pretty sure at least one of the wine bottles was empty.

"I think Paul means that he was an interesting man who lived in interesting times," Diane said. "Why not celebrate the uniqueness of your bloodlines? How many people can say they have a direct connection to a famous historical figure?"

"Thank you Diane, but it's more than that," Paul said. "Think of all the good he must've done. I'm sure he was deeply loved by his constituents and performed great services to his people..." Paul's emphasis on "his" struck Jules as cryptic, a suggestion of forbidden knowledge. "...he provided a spark for you, Jules. You could argue that he brought you here to us."

"Paul becomes very passionate when he's drinking wine," Diane said. "A philosophical artist, you might say—or he likes to think. Hopefully he won't say anything inappropriate."

"Yes, I always thought if I could go on stage after drinking a bottle of wine I could be a brilliant classical actor. I'm not drunk understand, just loose. If I continue well into the next bottle, then I will be drunk."

"Before you get drunk," Candy said, "what did you mean about his great-grandfather bringing Jules to us. That sounds like a drunken comment."

"Capone had soup kitchens, remember," Paul said. "Politicians all have their own people, especially back then. Immigrants! Where do you go but to your own people, the ones who speak your language, practice the same rituals, kept a piece of the old country waiting for your arrival. People stuck with their own, it's what got them through the hard times. Your great-grandfather rose to great prominence and for a reason: he was smart. He had to have been smart, only a smart man could've become a boss."

Paul popped the cork on the second bottle and filled his glass. "This is my last glass," he said.

"OK, so tell us about the spark," Candy said.

Paul gave Candy a savage look and then turned back to Jules. "Life must be interesting or what's the point? We all need something to strive for, something that sparks our interest. Don't you see how lucky you are to have had this Izzy character in your life?"

There was no doubt everyone at the table had heard Paul say "Izzy," although in that moment Jules's first impulse was to assume it was not his Izzy. But in the next moment he shuddered from the obvious improbability of such a coincidence.

"You said 'Izzy,' but you meant 'Morris,'" Jules said.

Paul shared his look of desperation first with Diane who had closed her eyes, and then with Candy who had her face buried in her hands.

"Of course I meant Morris!" Paul said. "He should interest you since you're one of his people, and you come from a smart group of people. It's statistically proven—"

"I think, Paul, you are officially drunk," Diane interrupted. "Yes you're a very brilliant thinker. You're Socrates in fact, but even Socrates knew when to relax."

"Am I such a sinner?" Paul said. "Can't I sing the praises of others, to help another be proud of their heritage?"

"We should probably get going," Candy said and Jules hoped Diane would facilitate their release with a sympathetic comment, which she did, offering a heartfelt, It was wonderful to finally meet you, an opening Candy took to push back her chair and stand. The goodbyes were quick. Paul had acquired a tired, crestfallen look. He smiled weakly when he shook Jules's hand.

Once outside, the two walked in silence to Candy's car. Jules let his head fall back against the top of the passenger seat.

"I know this seems really, really, weird," Candy said, "but I swear it's not what you think."

Jules said nothing.

"What are you thinking?"

"What should I think? A character named Izzy? How many could there be?"

"Before you get too angry just listen. Paul goes to one of those eclectic spiritual groups, complete with something called channeling—"

"I know what it is."

"Really? So Diane starts telling me that for some reason Paul has befriended this really bizarre guy from the channeling group. He starts having him over for dinner and they talk until all hours about spiritual things. The more Paul learns about the guy the more he's interested in him. It's like Paul became this Izzy guy's student. So I go over for dinner one night and there he is, dressed in this huge suit and talking like an old man. This guy is weird. I mean all night I have to listen to Paul and Izzy talk about every esoteric thing there is. Now here's the weirdest part. He starts talking about you! I didn't know it was you at the time, he just starts talking about his 'friend' who he used to work with at some finance job but who now works at the library. I'm not sure what discussion it came out of, but he starts using you as an example. He kept calling you a 'hero,' and that you did heroic things and that he owed you and that because of your 'heroism' he was able to do something, or I don't know what. So finally I asked him what was so heroic about you and he tells us the whole story about the priest saying Jewish deal, and how it changed him but that it took an act of treachery on his part to get you to be inspired enough to take off and work in a library. And for some reason that's heroic. Yeah, I know it sounds too bizarre to be true, but I swear it's the truth. So I'm really curious because I do go to the library to study and work on my monologues. So I'm thinking I must know who this person is. And then I saw you and you fit Izzy's description and I knew it had to be you. The rest is history."

"Why didn't you just mention Izzy from the start?" Jules said.

"I figured you would mention him to me eventually and that we'd have a good laugh. But when you told me your experience at the job but didn't mention him I got really worried and realized Izzy was either lying about your 'friendship' or just completely wacko. But I wanted you to meet my parents, and then Paul opened up his mouth and here we are."

Jules's life had become a series of coincidences. "But what was all that 'spark' stuff," Jules said.

Candy put the car in gear and pulled out of the driveway. "All I told him was that when you talked about your great-grandfather you lit up. That's all. I didn't say anything about a 'spark' getting you to go somewhere or do something."

"It's OK," Jules said. "It's fine if you told them more. It's only natural they'd want to know who their daughter is hanging out with."

Candy stopped her car in front of Jules's apartment building. She took his hand and then slid next to him.

"What about the 'luck' thing. What your dad said about being lucky to have had this great-grandfather."

"Who knows?"

Jules grunted his concurrence although he wondered if it was correct to assume he would have taken the library job had he not already uncovered the facts about Morris Ellerstein. Not that a connection was obvious or even conceivable except to the most hypothetical minds, but nothing in Jules's world was obvious.

"Maybe I am lucky," Jules said and thought in the broadest, most peripheral sense, his interest in Morris Ellerstein could be responsible for having Candy's hand now on his thigh. But the more he focused on finding this connection the less obvious things became.

16

His apartment seemed unfamiliar, absurdly smaller than any living space should be. The previous three nights he had spent at

Candy's apartment, a spacious two-bedroom with a balcony the size of Jules's studio. He wondered how long he could live cooped up inside these same four walls. Some people lived their whole lives surrounded by the same four walls. As long as he worked in a library his options were limited.

He noticed the frantic flashing of the number "4" on his answering machine. He pressed the "play" button and heard only a scuffling sound intermixed with background murmurings and an occasional breath. The next message was the same, as was the third, and then came the voice of Bobby Mars.

"Jules, how are you? Can you find a little place in your heart to forgive my abominable behavior the other night? My mind was fried, Jules. Try to understand what I'm going through. Can you? You say you can but I'm not sure. It's an anger thing that I'm now trying to deal with. I found a doctor Freidman but he wants to see me twice a week. Twice-a-fucking-week! I told him the yakety-yak approach doesn't work for me. I just need some chemistry adjusting, like what you got. Then he goes into this crap about what are my passions, and why I'm not still playing the piano like I did as a child. Can you believe that shit? And then he has the fucking audacity to give me a piece of paper with a list of symptoms associated with OCD. Ten fucking minutes into the session and he's got me all figured out! Hi I'm Bobby Mars, obsessive-compulsive sufferer, it's so fucking easy, see? All neat and tied up in a little fucking box! So I told the good doctor that if he had been played by some Israeli bitch, and had his daughter taken away, he'd be acting like he had a rubber band strapped around his nuts too! I just want some drugs, like Jules got, I said, but that's not his way. He has to see me twice a week at a hundred an hour. So finally I told him what a stupid kike-cunt he was and left. From now on it's only goyim doctors for me. Hey that girlfriend of yours is something else. Beats the shit out of Marla, that's for sure. Anyway, call me for chrissake."

The following morning, Jules attributed his sour mood to having spent the previous days completely in Candy's attention. He was just experiencing a letdown common among couples still immersed in the excitement of early relationship passion. By the third day of his funk, Jules realized his letdown had more to do with the reality of his life when he wasn't with Candy than anything else. Nothing had really changed. They still saw each other several times a week, his job was as non-threatening and predictable as it always had been, and all his material needs were being met.

Candy, too, noticed he seemed a bit more tortured than usual. "I thought that turned you on," Jules deadpanned which elicited only a measured response of laughter because it really wasn't funny.

"Maybe your meds need a tweak," Candy said and it occurred to Jules she might be right, although making an appointment with his doctor at his girlfriend's suggestion bothered him.

A native of India, Dr. Ramakant reminded Jules he had to do some of the work too, that the medication alone was not enough to keep his life on the right track. "You must practice looking for the positive pathway in which to travel," the doctor said. "The medication will help you get there. But if negativity is what you are seeking, then that is the path you will find.

He left the office liking the idea he still had some control over his brain activity, but thought an increase in the strength of his prescription would have been easier. Was it really up to him? he wondered and concentrated on thinking of positive things, reminded himself he was educated, intelligent, personable. It was time to look for a job, he thought and once again pictured himself wearing a jacket and tie, carrying a briefcase, having a pile of money in the bank.

The vision felt fresh and had a restorative quality that quickly improved his mood. Then Jules sensed the gap's approach. That's just negative thinking, he thought and visualized being interviewed in a downtown office by an older man who admired Jules's honesty about the gap. I took some time to reevaluate what was important, Jules said and then explained how much he had learned from his time off, which the interviewer saw as a sign of confidence and maturity.

The afternoon sailed by with a brashness reserved for those who had a direction in life. Fuck the gap, he confidently told himself.

When he arrived home his first thought was to call Candy and tell her how good he felt. The number "1" was flashing on his answering machine. "Listen to this," Bobby began, "so I found a doctor Gladstone, definitely a goy, an old-world goy, you know, silver-haired, chiseled chin, and older, much older. 'What the hell was he doing working at his age?' I'm thinking. But so what. Anyway, I sit down in his office and he's got pictures of Ford, Reagan and Bush everywhere. One with Reagan shaking his hand a million years ago, another with Bush and the doctor and some kind of priest, the kind with the purple clothes. Anyway, I have to ask him about this, why he's such a Republican and he keeps trying to steer the conversation back to me. That makes sense I know, but hey, he's got the goddamn pictures on the wall for everyone to see and I need to know about the guy before I can trust him. So I asked him if Iran-Contra bothered him, and he shrugged. And I asked him about all the marines that got blown up in Lebanon and snubbing the constitution to give money to drug-running death squads and the big tax cuts for the wealthy and the Tiananmen Square massacre and why we're kissing China's ass and so on etcetera, etcetera. And all he can do is shrug or mumble some bullshit about how money trickles down and the importance of oil and free trade and who the fuck knows what else. So I know who I'm dealing with now and I straight out ask him if I can get the kind of drugs to help me like they helped you, Jules. And he wants to know why I'm depressed and I told him that my wife just got a restraining order, as if I'm a terrorist. I can't even go near my little girl I told him, and he wants to know more and more, yakety-yak yak yak until I got angry because he kept ignoring my question, and I just got up and told him to go fuck himself and left. Jules, you gotta help me out. If you've got any humanity left in you, give me your doctor's number, will ya?"

Jules considered calling the police. Instead, he called Candy with the intention of showing off his good mood.

"The gap has been reduced to a crack in the sidewalk," Jules said when Candy answered the phone. "I stepped over the crack without missing a beat, with no interruption to my swagger; I am a fully capable and worthy unit of the system."

"Yes?" Candy said laughing and then listened to the story of Jules's triumphant battle with himself.

When he finished, her response was not as immediate or as enthusiastic as he had hoped. "I didn't know there was this gap in your life."

"Are you busy tonight?"

"Actually, I'm going to a GRE class." The three letters smacked Jules across his face. "I'm getting my stuff together which is why I might sound a little preoccupied."

"Really?"

"Don't sound so surprised. I told you I was going back to school."

"I think it's great. What was it you're going to study?"

"Linguistics."

Jules sensed impatience in her voice.

"Let's talk tomorrow. I'm glad you had a good day."

Mobility was a big issue, Jules thought. Movement was good, he reminded himself, but movement for Candy seemed both figurative and literal. The Graduate Record Exam was a springboard to anywhere in the country—she was rich, after all, she could go where she wanted. Movement was good, he said again, and saw himself stepping over the crack, briefcase in hand.

He fell into his reclining chair and allowed the day's fatigue to settle in. Then he imagined numerous miniscule silent explosions in his brain, each eruption spitting out a viscous fluid coating the countless number of pointed gray nodules that had started taking on a reddish hue, as if they had been rubbed too hard with a coarse material. And with each burst and excretion, the fluid soothed the nodules, healed their chafed casings, and returned the color to a healthy gray. Gradually, the world of his brain faded into background noises from the other side of his four walls, and then back to himself and Marla as children, the two looking at each other across a dining room table full of adults.

The phone rang. "Julie, let's have dinner, I haven't seen you in over a month. You're free tonight?"

Jules said he was free and didn't buy his father's attempt at sounding surprised.

17

Jack was sitting at their usual table when Jules walked into the restaurant. "Well? How's by you?"

"All right."

"Still dating that new girl?"

Jules said he was still dating Candy and then Jack asked when he would get to meet her.

"Do me a favor. Call Bill Mars and see if he knows that Bobby is shopping for a psychiatrist."

Jack thought for a moment. "It's nothing to be ashamed of. Raising a family is pretty stressful, especially now with the cost of everything."

"Then ask him if he knows his son is cracking up."

"Whaddya mean 'cracking up'?" The waitress approached and they both ordered their usual meal.

Jules told his father an abbreviated story of meeting Bobby at Java Jinx and then about the rambling phone messages. "Did you know he's getting divorced and in a custody battle?"

Jack looked blankly at Jules. "What are you talking about?"

"I'm talking about Bobby Mars, my childhood friend who you told to call me."

Jack searched his son's face. "I see Bill on the train two, three times a week and he never said a word about that. He says only how great everyone's doing. Bobby told you this?"

"Bobby told me this."

Silence. "I don't get it. And what do you mean I told him to call you? I haven't spoken to him since you two were kids."

"That's not what he told me," Jules said, eliciting another blank stare from his father.

"I don't know. Maybe he is cracking up."

"Call Bill Mars. I don't want anymore of his psycho messages on my answering machine."

Jack thought about it. "Why don't you just call him back? It sounds like he's asking for your help, and that's what friends are for, right?"

"Dad, listen to me. I'm not his friend and I'm not Izzy's friend and I don't want to be their friend, I want them out of my life."

Jack looked at his son as if he didn't recognize him. "Whaddya carrying on like this?"

"Because you're not taking me seriously."

"Alright, I'll talk to Bill. But there's something I need to tell you. Solly's in the hospital. He's got an infection. Everything down inside is irritated or something. The doctors don't seem to know for sure what's going on but Solly's got a hell-of-a-fever and his gut is killing him." Jack blinked back a tear. "I'm afraid we'll be saying kaddish for him soon."

Jules hadn't realized how much time had passed since Solly had been in his thoughts. He also hadn't noticed how downcast his father looked. Already he felt guilty for asking Jack to get involved with his business with Bobby. Jules didn't know what to say but in his father's gaze he saw his uncle, the two brothers playing out the drama of their lives as if under contract to a theater production, as if a document had been signed before they were born stipulating the two would travel through life together.

"I'm sorry. Is it OK if I go see him?"

"Sure," Jack said, his face perking up.

"Forget about that crap with Bobby and talking to Bill. I'll
deal with it."

Jack shrugged. "I'll see him on the train. We'll see what
happens."

***

Jules wasn't prepared for his Solly's cadaverous pallor. For a
moment Jules thought death had already visited, but after stepping
closer, a single blink of Solly's opened eyes told him otherwise.
The blink pulled Jules closer to Solly's bedside where he saw his
uncle's mouth ajar, his front teeth tapping lightly together.

"Uncle Solly," Jules whispered. "It's Julie."

Solly's eyes narrowed and darted about. "I'm here," Jules
said. "I'll be with you every day."

Solly blinked several times in succession. Jules examined the
side of Solly's face, the ashen flakiness of his skin, his almost
translucent whiskers. He thought back to their last meeting. Solly
was sick but he was full of life; he wanted to remember Solly
being full of life.

"Julie?" said a voice, weak and gravelly but a sound with
identifiable resonance. "You're still there, Julie?" the voice said
again, this time louder than a whisper, loud enough to make Jules
think it came from the body on the bed, which seemed impossible.

"I'm here," Jules said and leaned closer.

"I think I understand better now," Solly said. "Things are very
simple, not confusing. Pain makes things simpler. Everything is
raw; my organs are crumbling. I can feel the antibiotics fighting
but the battle is too costly, too draining on my resources. Supply
lines spread too thin. I thought I could coast into an easy death
without too much fighting, just slip on through. I thought I could
walk right into the cheering crowds, the flowers, the wine. That's
my best memory. It was lovely. I was lucky, I thought. That was
my mistake. That's when the enemy is most desperate, when your
confidence is highest, when you think all the hard work is behind
you, then they attack and you're surprised, your morale collapses,
you panic and run for your life to the rear without thinking of the

150

others, just your own skin. Killing's as hard as getting killed, nobody talks about that, but they're bleeding me white as the snow..."

Gradually, his eyelids closed and his voice trailed off until the resonance faded into a throaty mumble and then nothing at all. His mouth remained open. Jules could hear Solly's breath pushing through his teeth. He wanted to believe he rested comfortably. He watched hoping to see Solly rebound into consciousness but after an hour passed with no visible sign, he stood up only to be surprised by the figure of his father slouched in a chair outside the entrance to the room.

"Dad?"

Jack lifted his head. "I should have warned you about how he looked."

"Why didn't you come in?"

Jack rubbed his eyes, peered into the room. "I don't know. You looked caught up sitting there. I thought maybe you wanted to be alone."

It didn't sound like something his father would say. "Were you here when he started talking?"

Jack shook his head. "Doesn't surprise me, though. Yesterday he just started talking out of nowhere and scared the hell out of me. He was just going on about nothing I could really understand. I should've told you more about what to expect."

Jules appreciated his father's sincerity and told him it wouldn't have mattered, nothing could've prepared him to see Solly in such a state. "I've never seen a dying person before," Jules said.

"Of course not, why should you? Listen, I know you don't care for the kid, but I spoke to Izzy again."

"That asshole called you?"

"Relax. I called him."

"For what?"

"I wanted to talk to him! OK, so you think he's nuts, and maybe he is, but I liked talking to him and he seemed knowledgeable about philosophies and rituals, and I decided to talk to him about Solly. I wanted to hear what he had to say."

It was an act of betrayal that Jules's own father would embrace his enemy. "What did he tell you?"

"We talked about dying. He reminded me that death in our view was like going from one room to another room, only to a nicer room. 'The world was just the lobby on the way to a great palace.' That kind of thing. I like that stuff. And hearing it from this kid helped. It's something about his voice. I felt like a sweet old rabbi was holding my hand."

Jack told Jules to go home, that he would take the next "shift." As appalled as Jules was, he kept his feelings on the matter to himself and embraced his father before leaving.

The contrast to those living outside the hospital without the thought of bed pans or bags of fluid dripping into their veins was now so glaringly obvious, Jules wondered how he could have lived this long without seeing it. His uncle was reaching the inevitable conclusion of his life in the manner most would one day become acquainted with. It seemed impossible, absurd this was the truth, and the vast majority of people will live their lives to end up as institutionalized mounds of flesh. But what was the alternative?

As he walked home, each person he saw became another body destined to end up like Solly. His thoughts turned to the millions of Holocaust victims, whose deaths made more sense if only because they died at the hands of people who wanted them dead, people who had devised ways in which to facilitate their deaths. The idiocy of such logic was not lost on Jules.

Regardless, the two developed a routine over the following weeks in which Jack would arrive at the hospital sometime past six o'clock, exchange compassionate conversation with his son, offer a few more pearls of wisdom from Izzy, and then relieve Jules on the death watch.

At first, Solly's verbal outbursts would occur at least once during each visit. By the second week Jules noticed the duration of each event didn't last as long as the previous day's, until sometime during the third week Solly spent the entire two hours silent.

"It won't be long," Jack said when Jules reported the change.

During this time, Jules's contact with Candy was limited to conversations a few evenings a week where Jules would spend fifteen or twenty minutes trying to describe the turmoil inside of him, a conflict he came to call "the futility of death."

Candy listened and pointed out the foolishness of his comments.

"There's nothing futile about dying," she said. "Death has a useful purpose. Think of what a hell-hole our world would be if no one died."

"But nobody wants to die and we do it anyway. Death doesn't solve anything."

Conversations like these took their toll on Candy which Jules realized when she finally told him it was living he saw as futile because if one lived, one was required to die. "That's called depression, Jules."

But he didn't feel bad, he argued, only conflicted.

"That's the medication working for you," Dr. Ramakant said. "Without it you would undoubtedly be experiencing the kind of severe episode that first brought you to me. Your panic-depression-psychosis is being inhibited by the drugs."

"But what about my confusion, my questioning, my dissatisfaction?"

"The medication was not designed to take away your humanity."

"I'm obsessed with this death-thing and the infinite possibilities that I connect with it. I think I'm going crazy."

"You're preoccupied with your dying uncle. You're seeing death for the first time."

"I don't like how I feel."

Dr. Ramakant stared at Jules. "If the absence of strong emotional reactions is what you desire, I suggest you have the frontal lobes of your brain severed. Part of being human, Jules, is learning to deal with the conundrum of what it means to be alive."

Dr. Ramakant made no excuses for his belief that the proper neuro-chemical relationship held the key to sustainable mental health. Jules never took personally the doctor's bluntness or apparent lack of empathy.

Arriving at the hospital that evening, Jules was surprised to find his father already there.

"A nurse called me. She said his blood pressure had dropped dangerously low and that I might want to come down."

He looked at his uncle and searched for something recognizable, but saw nothing remotely familiar, only mottled gray skin draped over delicate bones. Most disturbing was his uncle's mouth, no longer ajar but wide open.

"I've been preoccupied with Solly's dying," Jules said.

Jack said nothing, then, "That's understandable. Watching someone die will do that."

"How do you watch someone die like this and not think of yourself one day in the same situation?"

Jack frowned. "Don't think about that. Don't dwell on the future that way, just worry about what you have to deal with right now and try to be happy and leave the future out of it."

"You watched mom die and now you're sitting here watching your brother die whose only a couple of years older than you—"

"He's not in pain, Julie, he's just waiting around. They have all kinds of drugs to make it painless. Sure, I think about it, but it might not be this way, it might be a quick death, like turning out the lights and I'm gone, but I don't worry about it and you shouldn't either. For chrissake relax already."

They sat for several minutes staring at Solly until Jack broke the silence. "Really Jules, please. Don't think about this morbid shit, you're a young guy with your whole life ahead of you, there's no reason for it."

"I still haven't figured out who the hell left me that article about Morris Ellerstein."

Jack's face lightened. "He died in Solly's bed, you know. That's how it was done in those days. He got sick and moved in with us. He wanted to live with my mother and father; he loved my mother the best. He was a big shot for all those years but died in a fifteen-year-old kid's bed. As good a place as any to die, I guess. You didn't need a hospital to die. You didn't need a hospital to live. Your grandmother was born on a kitchen table."

Silence again until Jack said, "There's no reason for you to sit here. Go home and eat. I'll call you if something changes."

An envelope taped to the mail receptacle greeted Jules as he entered his building. Inside was a handwritten letter from Bobby. The familiar sick feeling returned as he climbed the three flights wondering if this letter represented a new level of derangement.

"Dear Jules, because you refuse to return my phone calls I have no choice but to write this letter with the hope that seeing your old friend's handwriting on a piece of paper might stir up a little compassion, or maybe even some gratitude that you undoubtedly owe me. Not that I think you are solely responsible for my happiness, but goddamn it don't you think I deserve a little respect? I'm not asking you to save my life. No, that would be too easy. It's easy to ask for help, just look at all those bastards on the street corners shaking cups in your face and asking for change. You think I'm a beggar, don't you? But does a beggar tell you their intimate secrets, reveal their souls to their old friends? You're being so childish, Jules, the way you refuse to face your fears. I can only help you if you let me. You're hiding behind your drugs. You think you can just walk away from your responsibilities because you pop a few pills? The shoemaker's children also have shoes, Jules. Remember our Hebrew school carpool? Remember Bradley Rabin who never said a word, just sat there staring into space? He's a fucking rabbi! That's right, he turned out to really give a damn about his religion. He found himself, Jules, he discovered his true identity. So can you, you know. I can help you get there, if you let me. You can help me too, I'm sure..."

Jules let the letter fall to the floor; he had no appetite for the rest. He closed his eyes and thought of the different issues demanding his attention: Solly, Bobby, Candy, his job. His job. Ever since Candy started studying for the GRE the issue of Jules's job had slowly resurfaced. It was much easier to embrace an uninspiring life alone, without an equal to compare oneself. Eventually she will leave, he thought, and it wasn't a pleasant thought, not only because he would miss her but because her movement would be more evidence of his inertia.

He reached for the phone and dialed her number fully expecting her answering machine to pick up, but heard Candy's voice after a single ring.

"Hi," Jules said and Candy responded enthusiastically, the exact way Jules hoped she would respond.

"It won't be long," Jules said and briefly described his uncle's condition before asking how her studying was coming along. Candy responded halfheartedly, which Jules appreciated, although he was aware her reaction may have been affected. Then she turned the subject back to Jules, wanting to know how he was doing, and Jules told her he was fine and wondered aloud when he would see her again and Candy told him her evenings would be taken up with studying for the rest of the week although they could probably get together over the weekend. Jules couldn't be sure, but he thought Candy had hesitated before answering.

"You're upset," Candy said.

Jules denied feeling any such emotion and Candy reminded him how important the GRE was to her dream of a linguistic career. There was a sharpness in her voice, an edge on her tone that sliced into Jules.

"You sound angry," Jules said and Candy disagreed, although she did acknowledge some frustration.

"You can't expect me to stand still while the world spins around us," Candy said. "And it's not like we have to have this conversation now. It's a good year or two before I get accepted somewhere and leave—if I leave. I could go to Northwestern or Chicago, depending on my scores."

Jules liked what he heard, but he knew they had taken a turn. It was now clear their relationship would never be the same, and with this understanding came calmness.

"You should go to the best school possible, no matter where it is," Jules said, offering this concession with his new, confident voice eliciting a heartfelt "thank you" from Candy whose own relief Jules thought to be evident, indicating she, too, knew their relationship had changed. They cheerfully parted ways for the evening with Jules apologizing for being too needy and Candy telling him how important he was to her. And while Jules enjoyed hearing Candy's avowal, he knew her words couldn't be trusted, that in effect, he was now alone.

He decided to spend a relaxing night in front of the television and was pleased to find a holocaust documentary to occupy his attention. Despite the shocking images—naked corpses bulldozed into giant heaps, smoldering ovens filled with charred bones—Jules watched with semi-detachment, his morbid fascination commanding only a simple majority of his neuro-transmitting activity. Solly resembled those dead bodies, he thought.

The phone rang at three a.m.

"He's gone," Jack said and Jules, mouthed the words, "I'm sorry," over and over, unsure whether he could be heard or not.

As Jules approached Solly's room he saw his father outside the entrance leaning against the wall.

"Dad."

Jack looked up and said, "I called you, didn't I?"

Jules could see the confusion in Jack's face. "That's why I'm here."

"I thought I did but I can't remember. I was sleeping in the chair and woke up when the nurse told me he was gone. And all of the sudden I'm standing out here and you're walking down the hall."

Jules peered into the hospital room and saw a little man dressed in black sitting in a chair next to Solly's bed, praying quietly.

"He wanted to sit with him," Jack said, and Jules knew it was Izzy. "It's part of the tradition."

Jules nodded, content to include Izzy in this moment if his father so desired. But how was it possible that Solly had lived this long only to leave as if in a dream?

The funeral was a brief graveside affair, sparsely attended since Jack followed his brother's request that only relevant friends attend and to keep those with guilty consciences away. Jules recognized a few faces from Solly's apparel days, sun-tanned, craggy-faced old men who flew in from Florida to pay their respects to one of their own. One of them recognized Jules and approached him with a determined look. "He was a mensch, your uncle," the man said and cupped Jules's ear. "You should be lucky to know men like him your whole life."

Jules agreed. Then the man turned and walked a few feet away and as if on cue, stopped and turned back to face Jules. "He was a mensch!" he said loudly and then dabbed his eyes with a handkerchief.

17

The phone rang again. Jules heard it from deep within his dream where he stood watching a table full of men wearing white shirts and black vests with scoop necklines. At his side was his grandmother, looking the way Jules had always remembered, her face slightly pouched, a bit saggy, yet still charming and graceful.

"There's the phone again," she said.

The sound annoyed Jules, interfered with his concentration on the men around the table. The next ring was the loudest. Jules lifted his head and reached for the receiver.

"Hello Jules," a female voice said. "I hope you haven't forgotten what I sound like."

"Candy?"

"Candy! What a cute name. I hope she's special to you."

The voice had a throaty, sensuous quality intimately connecting with Jules, a voice reeking of recognition but struggling for a name. "Bronwyn?"

"Oh, thank you, thank you, thank you—for remembering me!"

"How are you?"

"Well," Bronwyn said and Jules heard her take a deep breath. "I've been really, really good. And you?"

How was he? It was an asinine question at seven o'clock on a Sunday morning. But what could Bronwyn have known of Candy? How could Bronwyn have known she had been as cute as her name, she had been cute enough to have penetrated Jules to the marrow. Certainly Bronwyn could not have known of Bobby's now weekly letters, and that Bobby's sole mission in life had become the deliverance of his friend from the horrors of a piddling, pedestrian life. Bronwyn had been "really, really, good," after all, much too busy screwing her teacher to care Solly had withered away and his father had sunken into a bitter funk despite inheriting his brother's assets, the paper value of which made Jack a millionaire. Then, of course, there was Jules and his inability to re-ignite his career search, which wasn't completely true since he had produced a rough draft of a resume he kept in a manila folder on top of his dresser.

"I'm OK."

"You don't sound OK," Bronwyn said in that affected tone of someone who had all the answers and thought it their duty to stand in front of you, look you square in the eye and insist on helping you because, after all, they were doing really, really, good. "It's been so long," she continued, "I think enough time has passed that we can re-establish some kind of connection."

Silence. "Why?"

"You're upset, and that's good. Emotion is important; it's what makes us human. It's emotion that made me decide to call you and see how you are. Imagine a world without emotion."

Jules had no concept of worlds other than the one he lived in, although he couldn't deny his ongoing curiosity of Bronwyn's world. Of course, Jules knew she would try to equate his un-medicated state with freedom, and say his true emotion could only be expressed without the artificial manipulation of neurotransmitters.

He agreed to meet for lunch if only because it had been two months since he left the third of three messages on Candy's answering machine, the last message being a simple request they at least talk about what they both knew was happening.

He stood in front of a popular restaurant, as Bronwyn requested, so she could approach him slowly from down the sidewalk and have him come gradually into focus as she started her re-connection process. So he waited for the familiar figure of a woman to appear, which she did only minutes after his arrival, her lovely smile clearly visible as it bobbed in and out of view from behind the multitudes enjoying a beautiful Sunday afternoon. When the smile was upon Jules and held him tightly around the neck, it seemed impossible so much time could have passed since their last embrace. Instantly, any residual anger was vanquished by the power of familiarity.

Sitting on the restaurant's patio, they held hands over the table while Bronwyn apologized for hurting him and Jules apologized for the hurtful comments he had made.

"Tell me about Candy," Bronwyn said and Jules launched into his story of meeting Candy at the library, Bobby's reappearance, and Solly's death.

He felt good. He felt so good even her quirky behavior didn't bother him, such as when she informed the waiter she wasn't feeling well and would like a lunch consisting of one-half of a baked potato. It was a request the waiter pointed out was not a menu option.

"Have you ever asked anyone if it was OK?" Bronwyn said and the waiter mumbled he would check with the manager and walked away. During their relationship Jules would have been embarrassed, felt empathy for the waiter and informed Bronwyn you don't come to a restaurant to order one-half of a baked potato and that he would have been happy to buy her a sack of potatoes. Instead, he was drawn to the intricate muscle maneuvers of her nose, upper lip, and chin, and then the slight movements of her forehead, eyelids, and brows. All these aspects came together to create this person called Bronwyn, this beautiful woman who in the end would get her one half of a baked potato.

As expected, Bronwyn was full of compassion, encouragement, and compliments for what Jules experienced the previous seven or eight months, and when he told her it was time to hear what her life had been like, he said it fully aware she may include carnal references, fully aware what she had experienced might have no resemblance to anything Jules knew outside of magazine articles and salacious innuendo.

He was surprised to hear Bronwyn had left the teaching of Adam and Habiba for another spiritual "community," one incorporating everything she had learned but focused more on the "physicality" of enlightenment. "There's a real emphasis on physical fitness," she said. "Running, swimming, climbing, weight lifting, any physical activity that gets your heart pumping and your muscles sore is encouraged. Check this out." Bronwyn offered her bicep for Jules to feel.

Jules associated an athletic wholesomeness with Bronwyn's description which was reinforced when it occurred to him she hadn't had a cigarette since they'd been together. And when he asked if she had quit smoking she emphatically nodded her head and chastised herself for having participated in such a degrading habit.

She no longer lived in the Halsted street apartment. "Members of the community share homes," she said but didn't elaborate except to say she cohabitated with three other women and the community's teacher. Jules imagined her new teacher as the peak of health, one who lived the life she taught, someone who was up with the sun and made sure her girls ate properly and exercised regularly.

Well into their second hour together, Jules's thoughts gradually turned to sex, which seemed to be a logical part of such a reunion. After lunch he thought they would walk the neighborhoods, have a cup of tea somewhere, and end up back at his place. His sudden focus on sex with no regard for a re-definition of their relationship was not typical of Jules. He had never been the type to be on the prowl, looking for sex like a drunken college boy, but this afternoon was different. The universe had returned him to Bronwyn, a woman whom Jules thought he could handle since he knew she was someone he could never totally trust and she would never completely belong to anyone.

About the time Bronwyn finished picking the potato clean and had started cutting the skin into small squares, the waiter approached and handed Jules an envelope.

"Some guy just asked me to give this to you," the waiter said. The letter was addressed to Jules and included a first-class stamp but had not been post marked.

"Bobby?" Bronwyn said excitedly. "The old friend you were just talking about?"

Jules folded the letter in half and in half again before sliding it into his back pocket.

"You're not going to read it?"

"Later."

"Read it now. Please, please, please, please!"

"Why?"

"Because it's interesting. Human beings are really interesting, especially when they're out of whack like this guy."

Jules sighed and extricated the letter from his pocket. "Dear Jules," the letter began on a memo pad page from the pizzeria across the street. "While walking to mail you this letter, I happened to see you eating lunch on the patio of that burger joint, sitting with some woman who I know isn't Candy. I'll just assume that Candy probably realized what a prick you are and ditched you. Good for her. Watching you eat that burger was pretty disgusting also. This letter really starts on the next page."

Jules folded the page back and noticed Bronwyn struggling to contain her laughter. "Dear Jules, You'll be happy to know that I have found a doctor! At least I think you'll be happy to know. Actually, probably not, since once I am properly medicated we will be equals which probably doesn't sit well with you since you always liked being better than me. A better athlete, better looking. Take away your drugs and it's a different story. You're knocked down a few pegs. I've traveled, I've seen other cultures, I've seen the miraculous effect of my seed germinating in a beautiful woman. I have a daughter, Jules. Face it, you'll never be the man I am, no matter what drugs you're on. You think there's only one doctor that can do the job for people like us, you think you're the great veteran of the ballgame, but you're wrong because now I have one and from now on we'll be equals. I lost in court, by the way. I can see Rachel only every other weekend and only supervised. They think I'm not stable. That shows you what filth she's put in their heads. Once I get appropriately medicated they'll see how wrong they were which brings me to something else. Do you know any good lawyers you might recommend? I'll need another one in a few months to try to get a better deal out this custody thing..."

Jules crumpled the pages into a ball and tossed it on Bronwyn's plate.

"It's really not funny," Jules said.

"You're letting it ruin your day. That's your choice."

"You see what my life's become?"

"You're a grown man, anything can happen."

It occurred to Jules he'd never thought of himself as a grown man, or at least not very often. "Let's walk," he said and Bronwyn reached for his hand and led him to a leafy sidewalk bordered by ornate wrought iron and mature oaks towering in front of large Victorian three-flats with arched doorways and three-window bays.

Jules imagined they were all newly renovated with bamboo hardwood floors and Tizio lamps.

"I love this neighborhood," Bronwyn said. Jules knew what she meant because everybody "loved" these neighborhoods for their quaintness and charm. These neighborhoods brought out the cynic in Jules because behind the beauty he saw greed and privilege, arrogance and oppression, human traits he had seldom thought of while pursuing his MBA. How easy it would have been had Jules merely stayed the course with Nathrop & Moore. Despite his hatred of who he tried to be, the simplicity of it all came flooding back as he walked with his beautiful older woman. How easy it would've been to play the game, to perform the job as best he could and then produce a down payment on the verdant street just off the busy avenue with the shops, the parks, the elevated train, and plenty of others just like yourself, establishing their claim on the city.

"Where'd you go?"

Jules looked into her face. He hadn't noticed the freckles before, a couple dozen reddish dots scattered across the bridge of her nose. How could he have missed it? "I was thinking about how nice it would be to live on this street."

"Start manifesting. Picture your name on that mailbox."

He wondered what names were on the mailboxes and guessed others prowling the neighborhoods scrutinized those names, were quick to assign assumptions with some names while having no reaction to others. Jules knew his name elicited inferences and if his name was on that mailbox some would view his residence as logical in a dark, rapacious way, as if there weren't enough names like his attaining such good fortune. At the same time, Jules hated those same names for the same reason and couldn't help but wish they were found in less desirable communities—which he knew they were—but what would it matter? He also knew names like his carried a special status. No matter where he lived assumptions would follow. Living with assumptions was part of the deal.

"Let's go this way," Jules said and gently tugged Bronwyn's arm to direct her north along similar side streets with more

Victorian three-flats but also brownstones, row houses, some one-story red brick homes that cooked you alive in the summer, and a few bland utilitarian low-rise apartment buildings with an air conditioner sticking out each window.

"Where are you taking me?"

"Let's go to the park near your old place," Jules said. He knew how close the park was to his apartment which stoked the incendiary feeling he had earlier, only this time it was enhanced by his anger at the unfairness of gentrification, the futility of trying to change the system, and, finally, his disgust that anger and sex could have a symbiotic relationship.

"You seemed so content at lunch and then I made you read the letter and everything changed," Bronwyn said. It wasn't the letter, he told her. But how could he try to explain what he felt to a woman who had an esoteric answer for everything and anything? Just considering the amount of mental energy required to explain what was going on in his head exhausted him, exacerbated the very point he didn't know how to explain. He'd been born a time bomb, defused by modern chemistry, but now vulnerable to the world, defenseless against the standards of the system, the arbitrary practices, and the inherent inequities.

"Tell me more about your teacher."

"My teacher is a brilliant dispeller of darkness," she said, "a true leader in every sense..." Jules listened, struggled to conjure up a realistic image to blot out the blonde, braided überfrau. "My teacher is a scholar who has studied all the masters..." She spoke as if in a trance, as if reading from a script. Her voice lost its personality, reminded Jules of the channeled voice of the pale lady. "My teacher throws the I Ching, interprets the changes..." She droned on as they walked, still hand-in-hand, until Jules stopped and took her by the shoulders.

"What's your teacher's name?"

Bronwyn looked puzzled. "What difference does it make? And why are you looking at me that way?"

Because it was only logical to expect someone to have a name, he wanted to say, normal people didn't ramble on endlessly about someone without referring to a name, everybody had a name, every thing had a goddamn name. But Bronwyn wasn't a normal person and Jules knew the rules didn't apply to her. Names weren't important, were meaningless, in fact, and if anything, were a sign of human weakness. In Bronwyn's world only one name could exist for everything since everything was all there was. But what was that name?

"I'm sorry. Go ahead."

She continued where she left off, not missing a beat, "...my teacher moves through the water without resistance, like a dolphin slicing through the ocean of life..." Jules liked dolphins—who didn't?—with their perpetual smiles, their ecstatic leaps through the air, acting as free and unfettered as any mammal could. "...each life is like a wave, Jules, rolling, swelling, cresting, and then sinking back into the ocean of oneness to live again as another wave..."

It had become cliché to him, the word "oneness." The word made Jules sigh, feel a tinge of annoyance. The word, he realized, now represented Bronwyn, represented all the banal ideals unable to address the tangible realities of life. For what reason do I desire her company? he thought, and expected to find the answer in a long complicated thought pattern, but found it quickly on the natural red highlights of Bronwyn's hair, the fullness of her breasts, the shape of her lips, the curve of her buttocks. It was simple yet it was complicated. There were countless chemical processes at work, processes not involving the synthetics he was every day introducing into his bloodstream. He wanted to lose himself in the precious hours they would spend in bed, to look forward to an evening in which nothing mattered because they were so focused, so intent on pleasing each other they didn't talk, didn't discuss complex issues like oneness.

As they neared the park and Göethe came into sight, Jules tried to imagine an unattractive Bronwyn, tried to separate her personality from the body she carried. The image wasn't pleasant, and worse, he found her personality intolerably pretentious; within his repulsion he included himself for going along with it all, for compromising his intellect for a biological process—for being a man.

She was a drug, the most dangerous kind, a drug believing in itself, a drug with a mind of its own, a drug Jules knew he needed to stop abusing. And it was there, walking past the statue of Göethe he swore he would stop. This evening would be his final dose of Bronwyn. Just one more time, he promised, one more evening with the woman of oneness, and then he would walk away for the last time with no fear of going back, feeling much more confident he could change his life.

"...at some point you need to surrender to a teacher, Jules. I can be your teacher if you allow me..." They sat in the shade looking over the harbor, talking as if there was nothing more important in the world than describing her teacher.

"Is this why you called me? To get me to join your community."

Bronwyn thought for a moment. "I never considered our relationship over or completed. Having you meet my household would be the most I could expect of you right now. It would make me very happy."

His first inclination was to offer himself to her community that very night, but the implications of such behavior reinforced his disgust for himself. Am I that desperate? he thought, fully aware the idea of Bronwyn being a casual sex partner was appealing despite only moments before having sworn this night would be their last together.

"Well, I'm free tonight. I would really love to be with you tonight, wherever you want."

Who the hell am I? he thought, powerless over the proceedings taking place in the core region of his brain, defenseless against the neuro-chemicals that vertebrates used for sex-related social behaviors. Surrender, Bronwyn had said, to a teacher, to the one who would dispel darkness. Jules had no choice but to surrender to forces inside of him, dark forces, he imagined, for they had to be dark forces since they kept company with anger and violence.

It was not like Bronwyn's heart could be broken, he reasoned, since her heart belonged to everyone, existed in oneness. She was his drug of distraction temporarily erasing his problems. With Candy it was a purely tactile act in the physical realm, an event occurring as a natural extension of the day. Candy was of the world. Bronwyn was the anti-Candy, an independent actor who chose her performances and then scripted the scenes.

"Enough time has passed," Bronwyn said, "where I am confident you can keep your emotions from interfering with what's really happening. Come to my house and see what it's all about."

She was singing the siren's song and Jules could not have been happier.

18

They were holding hands again on the elevated train as it made its way into neighborhoods Jules only knew from newscasts or a relative reminiscing about this neighborhood or that being so different from when they were children. Bronwyn led him off the train into a foreign landscape, an "historic neighborhood," a sign read, full of modest but well-maintained homes each with a perfect square of grass and several sculptured juniper bushes in front.

"This way." Bronwyn took Jules down a street where a huge church in the gothic revival style took up half the block. He was drawn to the masonry construction, the vertical proportions, and the tall pointed windows filled with stain glass and elaborate tracery. The soaring bell towers and enormous gargoyle heads gave him the creeps. Somehow beautiful yet horrible, he thought, and was reminded of the ignorance and cruelty of medieval Europe.

"You're supposed to worship God in a building like this?"

Bronwyn giggled and tugged on his arm. "C'mon," she said and pulled him past the church to the next block. "You're safe now," she said and stopped in front of a one-story bungalow.

"Isn't it beautiful?" Bronwyn said and Jules agreed although he wasn't sure why. The enormous stone planters and exterior wood moldings and trim were interesting and the decorative features were fancy, but the brick façade and low-slung roof weighed Jules down and brought to him a stifling sense of monotony.

They entered through the kitchen, a large square room overlooking the backyard. Not a single scuff or scratch was evident on the black and white floor tiles. It was the cleanest kitchen he had ever seen.

"We spend most of our time over here." Bronwyn led him into the living room which occupied the entire front of the house. The oak floor was also spotless, as was the dark wood trim bordering white walls that reflected the light of a single lamp sitting on a small table in front of the windows. Under the table was a small stereo. There was no other furniture although cushions lined the floorboards.

"There was a dining area that separated this room from the kitchen. But the community knocked out the walls and combined the rooms since the kitchen was big enough to be a dining room also."

"Where's your bedroom?"

Bronwyn pushed on a door off the living room that he had thought was a closet. The door opened halfway but no further. Then she pulled him on to the wall-to-wall bed in the windowless room and kicked the door closed. "This is where I sleep," she whispered while maneuvering over him, kissing his neck, pinning him down with her pelvis.

It was very dark. The crack under the door gave off the only light. Groping in the pitch-black, wriggling against the pressure of Bronwyn's body, Jules tried to surrender to her touch and allow the woman of oneness to dispel his darkness, at least for a while.

But oneness would come at a price.

The darkness got to him first as they blindly explored each other. It had never been this way in his relatively limited experience. It had never been so anonymous in such a small dark space with no windows, no obvious outlet to fresh air or anything connected to the natural world. It was too warm for such a dark room.

Bronwyn traveled on her lips and tongue down Jules body. He imagined that was all she was, a mouth and nothing more, or maybe someone else's mouth. The big red-lipped mouth of the Chinese woman who sat across from them on the train or the teenager holding the baby. What difference did it make in such darkness? A warm mouth was sustenance, he thought, nourishment for his soul—if he believed in such things. And as the lips moved across his abdomen, a word came to him, a terrifying word, but a word describing perfectly where he was—the word womb being the only place such darkness and warmth should be felt.

Jules had no use for wombs. He wanted to breathe oxygen from the cool air and not from strange liquids transported through tubular portals. He wanted nothing to do with wombs, they were smothering places for those not ready for the world, a place to hide while you were given everything you needed, a place to be coddled until you acquired the audacity to appear and demand more. Fetal images began to float past, images of translucent alien beings having nothing in common with Jules, creatures sucking greedily and giving nothing back. When the mouth found its target the intense pleasure overtook the womb inspiring the most horrifying thought of all: Bronwyn was a manifestation of some twisted mommy fetish, an unfulfilled desire acting out in an artificial womb of Jules's subconscious. Is it Bronwyn? Is it?

"Turn on the light!"

"What's wrong?"

"I need the light Goddamn it!"

Bronwyn felt along the wall until she found the switch for a bulb hanging on the ceiling. Jules struggled with the brightness to identify her face. He looked into her eyes, touched her nose, her chin, her lips, sought tangible proof Bronwyn was the legitimate reality.

"It's you, right? I mean you feel like yourself, don't you?"

"What's going on?" Bronwyn gently pushed Jules on to his back and lay beside him.

That's how easy it was for Bronwyn, a simple decision to wait, a quick acceptance that Jules was experiencing something. With the light on he was able to recognize the strange emotions as an absurd paper tiger of neuro-transmitting chaos.

"I can't tell you exactly what happened," Jules said and decided to just repeat what he had seen, knowing each image, each symbol he described would be a spore landing on the fertile soil of Bronwyn's belief system.

Lying next to Bronwyn while she ministered, interpreted, evaluated the materializations of his brain, he felt the relief of facing one's worst fear only to survive the encounter intact. He couldn't imagine anything psychically worse than what he had experienced when the lights were out. He didn't remember dreaming, only hearing the sound of footsteps and then hushed voices. When Bronwyn lifted her head he was awake but confused. She now sat toward the end of the bed on her knees with her legs tucked under her. "They'll be making dinner soon," she said and reached for a hairbrush from a shelf hanging beneath a small mirror.

"I should leave."

"Of course not. You're my guest for dinner and to stay the night if you want."

Jules agreed to stay but felt nervous knowing there were now people on the other side of the door that a few hours earlier had been the opening to his imaginary womb of horrors.

"You have nothing to worry about. You're perfectly safe."

He wondered what Bronwyn really meant by "safe," and was amazed he didn't already know the possibilities the word offered. Of course he was safe in Bronwyn's world, because everything happened for a reason; to all actions would come a righteous and judicious outcome. There was safety in oneness.

"I meant I felt awkward, not afraid."

"But why would you feel that way if something wasn't causing you fear?"

Jules pictured himself stepping into the large room as the intruder, the foreigner to be surveyed by those already schooled in the ways of Truth. "I mean what's the worst thing that could happen? I'm going to step out this door and drop dead?"

"It's all about the fear of death. Everything we do, all our motivation revolves around this fear. Get ready to face death."

She opened the door to reveal the large, immaculate room he had seen hours earlier, only this time with six women seated on cushions along one of the walls, apparently meditating.

He was struck by the youth and beauty of the women. All appeared to be no older than twenty-five with slim, athletic builds and long satiny hair either falling over their shoulders or tied back in a ponytail. None of the woman seemed to notice Jules and Bronwyn entering the room. They sat against the opposite wall and closed their eyes. It was never his intention to spend any part of this Sunday meditating. In fact, Jules had not spent any part of any day meditating since the night he had attended the channeling session.

"How long are we going to do this?"

"Not long."

A woman opened her eyes. She glanced Jules's way as she stood and walked to the kitchen. She looked no more than twenty, her body a perfect sculpture of athletic American womanhood.

No longer content to wait for whatever the evening would offer, Jules stood and walked to the kitchen where the woman spooned some kind of granola-like mixture into bowls. He stared at her backside a while, admiring her light blonde hair and how it hung neatly between her shoulder blades. She wore khaki shorts and a black tank-top. On the back of her shoulder was a small tattoo of a butterfly.

"Can I use the bathroom?" Jules said and waited for the woman to turn around. He had anticipated some kind of recognition but received only an extended arm with a pointed finger. The blue and yellow butterfly still faced him, offering no hint of acceptance.

He walked to one of two doors in the direction she had pointed and turned the knob only to be met by a steep staircase from which soft music and incense emanated. "The other door," the woman said in a mousey voice full of anger. He entered the tiny room that contained a toilet and sink. The woman's chilly response was mildly upsetting, but at the same time she piqued his curiosity. Her aloofness acted as a provocative gesture and said to Jules she was nobody's spiritual "fuck buddy," and the pursuit of oneness was serious business.

A few minutes later Jules exited the bathroom and did his best to walk though the kitchen as if the tattooed woman was of no consequence to him. The others were still seated with their eyes closed. Bronwyn, however, was stretching her arms above her head and smiled as Jules approached her.

"What's the basement for?"

"That's where our teacher lives. Someone you'll see later. There's going to be a party tonight."

Jules tried to imagine what kind of party he could expect on a Sunday night and wondered what they all did for work.

One by one the others opened their eyes and stretched their limbs. Each acknowledged Bronwyn their own way with a quick wave of the hand or a soft "hello" or direct eye contact and a smile. Jules noticed nothing in the way of recognition. They acted as if strange men often appeared in their home.

"This is my friend, Jules," Bronwyn said and Jules thought he heard one of them say, "Hello," and then another asked Bronwyn if she was going to get up early tomorrow and swim laps with them. After Bronwyn said "Yes," another started describing a dream she had the previous evening about swimming in the ocean and how when the enormous waves were about to crash over her she shot up to the top of the crest and glided down smoothly, as if flying. The others nodded and sighed and told similar stories of astral gymnastics involving running or cycling or swimming.

Jules took it all in as if listening through an open window from outside the house. Who are these people? he thought as the women talked on and on about how important their workout routines were in understanding who they were. The intensity in their voices reminded Jules of the way people spoke at the channeling event although he felt more intimidated by these women; the severe austerity in the way they spoke left no room for the gentle compassion or empathy elicited from Jahmal's discourse.

The woman with the butterfly tattoo entered the room holding a tray of bowls which seemed to be the signal for the others to move to the center of the room and form a circle. Jules followed along and waited as the butterfly woman placed a bowl in front of each person. He watched closely to see if some other ritual was required before eating—a prayer, perhaps, or some kind of affirmation supporting a common athletic goal. When Bronwyn began to eat Jules did the same. He first tasted a sample from the end of his spoon that revealed no distinct flavors Jules could readily identify beyond an initial hint of cinnamon. The texture of the gruel was more watery than Jules would've liked but he ate it anyway. For several minutes the only noise was the clinking of spoons until Bronwyn announced she had made swimming a mile her new goal which elicited an eruption of encouragement, each woman taking turns describing how they will help her, how they will work with her the entire time until her goal was achieved.

Jules stared at Bronwyn and tried to digest this new path she had chosen, tried to find a parallel between talking to disembodied beings for spiritual guidance and swimming a mile. He reminded himself that trying to understand Bronwyn was silly and he didn't have to understand her because he just wanted to have sex. Any knowledge he acquired along the way should be considered a bonus.

Bronwyn laughed. They all laughed, rocking back and forth in their cross-legged seats, and just as the laughter died down, just as they each spooned another helping of the bland porridge, a blast from an electrical buzzer sent a spasm through Jules heart. Immediately, one of the women, a tall brunette whom Jules thought to be the youngest of the group, stood, and without a word, walked through the kitchen and disappeared.

"What's going on?"

"It's her night to take care of Jeb."

Jeb? Where Jules had failed in his assumption he knew Bronwyn well enough not to be surprised, was now ridiculously obvious. Her "teacher" was a man, of course, a beautiful Adonis, most likely blonde, blue-eyed, an über-guru right off a Teutonic propaganda poster, a young woman's sexual fantasy providing not only physical eroticism but an intellectual and spiritual thoughtfulness.

The allure must've been overwhelming, he thought, especially for the younger ones who probably had estranged relationships with their fathers and looked to Jeb as not only their spiritual guide but their spiritual daddy, someone mature beyond his years, an older soul who brought to this incarnation Knowledge acquired only by the relatively few who could claim such a legacy. Add Jeb's athletic prowess and physical beauty and you have an irresistible teacher whose female students will view getting fucked senseless as essential to their spiritual growth.

This was just how things were, Jules decided. For women seeking oneness, sex could be simply employed as a learning tool, an instrument used to shape, form, and finish the experience of emotion. Men, being less inclined to recognize the symbolic potential of a sexual experience, may claim to know romantic love, perhaps, but most likely know only what they feel physically, at best lingering momentarily on an emotional aspect, if lingering at all.

Those finished eating now milled about the room or washed dishes. Only Bronwyn and Jules remained on the floor.

"You didn't tell me your teacher was a man."

"The gender of the teacher is irrelevant as is his name. Outsiders get caught up in the physical realities and start making judgments. Learn from our actions and words, Jules, and don't get caught up in the flesh and blood aspects which change over time—the truth never changes."

Jules had almost forgotten how good she was, had almost forgotten how in Bronwyn's world anything having to do with the body was of no real consequence to the big picture. Oneness justified all action, all emotions, all sensations, all desires. There was no right and wrong, there was only choices.

"When it's someone's night to take care of Jeb, what exactly is required?"

"That depends on what his needs are at the time. We bring him his meals, his protein shakes. We bathe him, massage his muscles after a run, sing to him, make love, or just talk. It all depends."

Jules had reached the evening's crossroad. Should he reveal the disgust he felt, admit to what he thought were nauseating images flashing across his brain, he knew he could quickly find himself standing on the El platform waiting for a train.

"It's all part of the teaching. Wisdom can be imparted in different ways. It's not all just listening to talks and then taking advice. Sometimes wisdom comes from being in service to your teacher, cleaning his room, cooking his meals, making him comfortable in every way possible, and, yes, engaging in sexual union."

Jules managed to process her information with the appropriate tact.

"What night is yours?"

"Thursday nights."

For the first time since reuniting with Bronwyn, he questioned whether it was all worth it—the masquerading of his feelings and his phony interest in Bronwyn's world in exchange for the potential of having a casual sex partner, whom he now knew he would share with untold numbers.

Why he felt suddenly dirty, crude, primitive, was not immediately clear since blaming sex and the lengths men would go to experience it, seemed too easy. He could, after all, count on one hand the number of women whom he had engaged in sexual intercourse with, a pitifully small number when compared to an average American male who had just begun his fourth decade of life. And what of Bronwyn? Jules had always assumed her lifetime had included enough partners to populate a room the size they were now sitting in, but he also assumed beyond her introductory experiences, beyond her early attempts at envisioning the one great love that all little girls had been raised to expect, sex had long ago moved into the experiential realm, had become one of life's irresistible learning tools.

Their worlds were incompatible. Deep down he probably had known this to be true for some time, but not until this moment sitting on the shiny hardwood floor of a bungalow in a foreign north-side neighborhood, Jules was able to see clearly enough the processes at work. It was better to walk away, he decided, to not give in to the humiliating blackmail of his sex drive, and leave Bronwyn's world once and for all.

More people began to arrive. More attractive, fit, men and women, smiling, happy, many carrying bottles of liquor. "What's with all the booze?"

Bronwyn shrugged. "These parties are about having fun. A few drinks to lower your inhibitions won't hurt anybody."

It was hard for Jules to believe members of this community needed help lowering their inhibitions. The hypocrisies would stand out and the inconsistencies would gnaw at him. But it was just one evening and he was determined to have fun.

As more people entered the house, Jules and Bronwyn joined them in the kitchen where many had congregated and had started pouring drinks. Music was also playing loudly from the stereo. Bronwyn introduced Jules to several people, whom unlike the women who lived in the house, made friendly small talk, as one might expect at any party. Marty was a carpenter who ran marathons. Lisa was a college professor who also competed in cross-country bicycle races and so on. Many expressed curiosity toward Jules, specifically wanting to know his connection to Bronwyn, what he did for a living, and what he thought so far of their community. When Jules told them he worked in a library the reactions were surprisingly enthusiastic with each person commenting on how wonderful it would be to have a quiet, simple job surrounded by interesting works in every subject imaginable. Jules appreciated their "support" and suggested jobs like his were plentiful, a suggestion that elicited a nod and a smile.

As the night wore on and people continued arriving, Jules thought the house was beginning to resemble a college party. With the liquor flowing freely, many had started "dancing" wildly— jumping spastically into the air, spinning and jerking their bodies in every direction as if possessed. Jules had lost sight of Bronwyn but guessed she was among the throng. He also realized he was probably the only sober person in the house which was an intentional condition given the strict warnings attached to his medication.

Typically, he wouldn't care about drinking although on this night with all the craziness around him, he thought a few drinks would enhance his experience, allow him to understand better what it was these people were after—ultimately, lower his inhibitions. He thought hard about what the warning labels had said but could only remember something about the liver. The liver was important, he knew, but he reasoned thus far in life his liver had suffered little from the indignities of alcohol and a few drinks at the only drunken party he planned on attending would pose little risk. He reached over to the part of the counter where several rows of shot glasses filled with a pink liquid sat on a cloth towel. Quickly, as if he had been doing it all his life, he gulped down one of the drinks and braced himself for a burning aftershock in his throat. When all he experienced was the sweet taste of watermelon, he gulped down a couple of more—they were awfully small, he reasoned—and waited for the effects while watching as the frenzied "dancing" continued without any sign of letting up.

It wasn't long before the kitchen became very warm. It didn't bother him too much although Jules was suddenly curious as to what he looked like. He took a step toward the bathroom and thought the tile floor slanted a few degrees to his left and then corrected itself. Upon reaching the bathroom he conceded he was a little bit drunk but was not concerned because his mind was still clear and he had complete control over his thoughts. He looked in the mirror, studied his face, and then pushed his hair around for a moment before heading back to the counter where a petite woman with strawberry blonde hair and wearing a ruffled mini-skirt now stood.

"Hi," she yelled over the music and Jules smiled at her, watched her quickly down two shots. "I love these parties," she said. "I wait all week for them."

Jules downed another shot. "This is my first party," he said and then she asked how he had heard about these parties and Jules told her the abbreviated story of his relationship with Bronwyn whom the woman said she had met, whom the woman said she envied for being allowed to just jump into "it" so quickly. When Jules asked what she meant, she said only a select few were allowed to live in Jeb's house and she hoped to one day be one of them.

"Can you imagine the intensity of living here?" she said and then downed another shot before introducing herself as "Dina."

"Jules," he said and admitted he couldn't imagine what it would be like.

"Let's dance, Jules," Dina said and pulled him into the living room where she instantly began jumping, twisting, and twirling so effortlessly it seemed she floated on the air.

Jules blended into the crowd and found jumping, spinning, and gyrating to the beat of the music was remarkably simple. Dina smiled, giggled, crashed into his hips. And while her white cotton panties flashed shamelessly from under her flailing skirt, Jules realized how much fun he was having. So acute was his realization, that for a while he felt out of himself, amazed at how far he had come since his life with Marla, someone whom he had never danced with.

How lucky he had averted from the Marla course and put himself in the perfect situation to trigger the change in his chemistry which allowed him to become sweaty, unbridled, a lover of life. Not that he needed this stimulation, but he was here, after all, surrounded by so many lovely, perfect bodies encased in tight-fitting stretchy material, sexy young women all here to have fun. He could have fun too. He could experience what the others experienced and wake up in the morning and resume the part of his life required to function in society.

So he spun and jumped and shook, stopping only once in two and a half hours to drink a couple of more shots and get another glimpse of himself in the mirror before returning to the dance floor to whirl himself into a sweaty exhaustion until the music stopped and Jules looked at Dina who was still giggling as she fell into his arms. "I really want to get to know you," she said. Her words served as the crowning achievement of Jules's evening and he imagined the words spinning around his head as he held on to her, felt her delicate body pressing against him. He thought if he squeezed her any tighter she would disintegrate.

The slow, harmonious sounds of Native American flute music filled the room as the crowd relaxed and began milling about. Jules surveyed the scene and saw Bronwyn across the room leaning backward into someone's arms. She seemed to be looking directly at him, smiling broadly, almost laughing.

"So what happens now? Is the party over?"

Dina lifted her head away from Jules's chest. "Now we wait for Jeb to make an appearance," she said. "He likes to walk around and look at everyone. We're like his family coming to visit. He's really, really, loved. I can't wait to be able to live here. That's gonna be so cool."

Dina returned her head to Jules's chest and initiated a slow dance, which is what many others were doing. As he followed Dina's lead with her rhythmic swaying, he glanced at his watch and was shocked to see it was after midnight. He thought about what time he would have to get up for work and then became aware of a slight nausea creeping upward from his stomach. He knew as late as it was, it would probably take an hour to get home. He tried to calculate how much sleep he could get if he left in the next ten minutes. An hour earlier he had envisioned inviting Dina back to his apartment where he thought he would start the first of many forays into his newly adopted world of unrestrained sexual promiscuity. It was a world where he would keep one foot while continuing his search for the niche in society where he belonged.

But the queasy throbbing in his head had re-focused his thoughts back to the immediate comforts of what he could expect when he arrived home—his own bed, his own bathroom, four walls of privacy, a place to be sick. Yet his curiosity to observe Jeb among those adoring him, kept Jules in place. He fought the nausea with deep breaths, fought the fear that running off and vomiting would bring ridicule, as if his intestinal rebellion was evidence of a greater weakness, a spiritual deficiency—that he was simply ordinary. The real issue, he knew, was why he should care what they thought. What did he give a damn if he retched out his guts all over their shiny wood floor? And with his anger came a momentary settling of his stomach, the result, he thought, of eliminating his fear from the emotional mixture, although the relief was short-lived and followed by another nauseous wave.

"Hey there, are you OK?" Dina said.

Just as Jules was about to admit he was not OK, the crowd began to part, splitting open as if commanded to make way for the arrival of Jeb. He wondered if the woman who had disappeared into the basement would appear with Jeb, as an escort say, or if she had already re-joined the crowd. He searched the faces in the room and saw how intently they stared into the kitchen anticipating something magical, something life-changing. Jules became entranced with several of the female faces, young, enchanting, healthy, beautiful faces, the kind of faces young men dreamt about then obsessed over.

Who was this man? Jules demanded through a haze of nausea, and within the film a figure appeared from the kitchen, small and naked, a large hooked nose, a head of black frizzled hair merging with a billowing beard of the same color and texture. He walked in quick bursts a few steps at a time, his hands resting on his bony hips, his shriveled penis a bobbing mushroom in a twisted pubic nest. Each time he came to a stop the man stared at a one of the young bodies while his head jerked about every which way as if plotting coordinates on a map. His incisors were conspicuously evident like some kind of bearded rodent. Jules re-checked the faces in the room and when he saw no sign of repulsion, when he realized their expressions were, if anything, more adoring, he knew their teacher had arrived, a fact containing enough shock value to temporarily displace his nausea. How was it possible? he thought, and kept repeating these same four words while watching the movements of the hairy troll as he three-stepped his way through the crowd.

Jules tried to keep an open mind, tried to rationalize the laws of attraction as simply part of the greater mystery of life, part of the same mystery that encompassed the beating of the heart and the infinity of space. Who was Jules to judge God's intention?

For the moment, he no longer worried about the distressing pictures his brain processed. Instead, he saw an opportunity to create his own reality by simply refusing to believe what he saw, refusing to give the disturbing images any power at all. Dina, for example, had left his side and was following closely along Jeb's path. But Jules didn't believe it and imagined she still clung to his body with her eyes closed, her hand exploring the small of his back. There was a surreal quality with this pursuit that took Jules on his own little trip. Even when the nausea returned, its effect helped to detract from the image of a tall brunette's hands sliding along Jeb's sunken chest. But Jules was just a dabbler in this realm of creativity, a skill belonging to those with much more experience in psychic drilling. Gradually, the nausea became an equalizer and then a multiplier, and finally a catalyst for a host of negative biological processes associated with Bronwyn's familiar backside. Her beautiful chestnut hair stuck to that sweaty, pathetic chest, interwove with that coarse, hideous beard, and then went down, until her hands groped the troll's buttocks, the same hands that only hours earlier had explored Jules's body with the same sensuality. The evil, fetid odor of the troll filled his nostrils just as Bronwyn's mouth approached the most loathsome part of the troll, just as she was about to bury her beautiful face into that bristly crotch from hell—he could take it no more. He barely made it to a small strip of grass outside the door when an acrid flow of undigested food spilled out of him and his abdominal cavities heaved relentlessly, purging the day from his cells, dissolving all the horrible images into a liquefied pulp. Let them laugh, he thought between spasms, let them dance and drink and screw, he thought as water poured from his eyes, dripped off his nose. Just get me back to my studio apartment, my four walls; back to my world.

19

He had vague images of himself sitting on the El platform, then sitting on an empty train with the side of his head leaning against a window, and then walking into his apartment and collapsing on to his bed. They were memories that came when he found himself pushing his metal cart of books down an aisle. On the morning after the party, the library felt safe, as if in the company of old friends. It was true his head pounded and even the most amorphous scent of anything edible instigated a surge of nausea, but for Jules this condition only served to intensify his feeling everything he had experienced from the day of his birth until that very moment had been somehow contrived by an unseen authority, ostensibly for his benefit.

The feeling sustained Jules while he went about his task of shelving books and enabled him to maintain a certain degree of numbness, as if the feel of the books themselves—their sober, staid, predictable presence—reinforced his security. The books reminded him of the original plan: to work an unchallenging job as the world spun around him, all the while leading a respectable life, until he eventually died and moved on to whatever was next. It was not a realistic way to think, not a healthy way to think—what intelligent, educated person could maintain such an underachieving point of view?—but it served a purpose by combining with his medication to bring him through those periods where the choices available to him appeared to have passed him by. And when the spell wore off, when a friendly smile or familiar song brought him back to the land of possibilities, Jules could only shake his head and marvel at how egocentric it was to think the whole world existed just so he could experience it. Maybe life really was just a dream, or maybe a thought, perhaps, in some collective consciousness called God.

Gradually the nausea decreased, the throbbing abated, and the environment around him moved back to the forefront of his vision. The Book of Bronwyn had been closed, he decided, once and for all, and with this closure he included her world, or her interpretation of her world. He should focus on getting his life back to mainstream respectability; he was still young after all, still intelligent, still educated, still a good investment. There was the problem with the "gap," he knew, which had grown considerably. But if he just persevered something good will happen, someone will see his potential and give him the chance he deserved.

That evening he called his father to set up a dinner date. Jack sounded pleasantly surprised to hear from him and they made plans to meet later in the week. Initially he felt good after he hung up the phone, but as the evening wore on and he replayed their stilted conversation in his head—the same conversation they had been having on the phone for eight or ten years—he couldn't help but have the feeling his father wanted to get off the phone.

But what did he expect? Could it really be possible Jack Ellerstein was now the father who knew his son, understood it wasn't simply a question of snapping out of it, that the chemicals in Jules's brain came from somewhere and, perhaps, the responsibility should be shared?

Nevertheless, Jules was glad they were getting together and at work the next day he occupied his mind with ideas and strategies he would present to Jack regarding his approach to pursuing a career. Jules would get out there, show his face, shake hands, ask questions, request informational interview. It's about hitting the streets and selling yourself, Jack will say, and Jules will agree and the two will become excited because they both see the value of the old-fashioned face-to-face, show-me-what-you've-got attitude.

And he had some experience. Sitting in Java Jinx he knew he had some real life experience. Wasn't it Jules who had discovered who Tri-Cal had been borrowing money based on phony assets? Wasn't it Jules who had sent in the auditors when he suspected his client's cash-flow problem was the result of their largest customer closing its doors? It was inevitable the question of Izzy would present itself and bring with it all the events Jules associated with his life becoming permanently altered. Izzy was the catalyst, the adulterator; Izzy was ground zero.

But what should he do with him? He could sit and think about the past eighteen months or so, remember once-upon-a-time his life had been defined exactly how it was supposed to be defined, yet he had no logical explanation as to why his brain cut and ran the way it did, sabotaging everything familiar. And what did it matter? The damage was done, he was a different person despite not knowing who this different person was. Life was less complicated before he had met Izzy. He had been on his way after all! And how easy to blame Izzy, as if Izzy had put a spell on Jules, had unleashed the changes in Jules's brain, turning him into a pharmaceutically-dependent slacker.

It was bound to happen, one way or another, sooner or later. Jules didn't really believe Izzy held the key to his destiny. The revolt of his brain chemistry could've happened while standing in front of a room full of vice presidents, or on an airplane en route to give the most important presentation of his life, or while holding his and Marla's child. Marla, he thought, and shuddered at the commotion his transmutation would've caused had Marla been his wife, the mother of his child, when the rebellion broke out. The thought of child support payments, legal bills, and all the emotional and traumatic histrionics associated with such matters— the weeping, the in-law anguish, the accusations, the financial considerations, the regrets of time lost, the continual speculation and endless ruminations of what went wrong, the friends taking sides, the friends disappearing, and everything else Jules thought to be abhorrent.

That such unpleasantness had not occurred to him before seemed astonishing, almost as astonishing as how clear things suddenly looked. How could he have missed such obvious luck for so long? And what was he to do with such obvious luck now that he recognized it? The very idea of expressing gratitude toward Izzy was repugnant and only reinforced his anger and bitterness. He became filled with indignation and disbelief he should be indebted to that clown, as if his life had been reduced to being a player in some moralistic fable. Things happen, he thought knowing full well in Bronwyn's world Jules was supposed to have met Izzy. But Jules had renounced that world although he couldn't deny he was still attracted to it.

"You're trying too hard," said a voice from over Jules's shoulder, a voice so unexpected that despite hearing, You're trying too hard, a second time he still didn't turn around which prompted the voice to repeat itself once more, this time directly into Jules's ear.

"Oh Jesus Christ," Jules said and looked at Bobby who wore a black armband with a white swastika.

"Heil Hitler mein jüdischen Mensch," Bobby said and took a seat opposite Jules. "I'm telling you exactly what you need to hear and all you can say is 'Jesus Christ'?"

"Are you out of your mind?"

"You look absolutely tortured like one of those Spanish Inquisition Jews on the rack."

"How the hell could you wear that?"

"Don't you see what a slave you are? 'Arbeit macht frei!'"

"Please, just go away." Jules didn't feel like fighting. The idea of owing Izzy a debt of gratitude had sapped the last of his strength.

"Don't you see the freedom in this? We're allowed to get away with this shit. Look, if I call your wife a slut, I'm in trouble. But if you call your wife a slut, who cares?"

"Don't you see how sick this is?"

"I've been watching you sitting here, torturing yourself over who the hell you are. Just take the path of least resistance otherwise it's that Newton's law thing about equal and opposite stuff. I was acting out, you know? It was a reaction to the events around me. But I'm doing better thanks to you."

"I made you a Nazi."

"The drugs, bro. I finally hooked up with a doctor who understood a little bit where I was coming from. He's not a big talker but he listens which is cool because he could see what was going on with me. I'm not perfect, but I'm more even, I'm seeing much more clearly."

"Wearing a swastika is an indication of your clear thinking?"

"It's freedom. Why are you missing the point?"

"Does this mean you'll stop with the goddamn letters?"

"You could've called me back, eh? I mean it wouldn't have killed you. Like I said I was acting out, you know, looking for the right doctor, the right meds, and then it took a while to kick in. I had to express myself and who better to hear it than someone who'd been there? You can't take that shit personally because I'm not who I used to be. Like you I've gone through a change, and like you I'm getting better. So you see, we're the same now."

"What do you want?"

"I'm checking in! I've been hanging out here a couple of hours every day just waiting to check in with you again. We can't give up on each other, not now while were getting better; let me help you, bro. And I'm sure you can help me too."

"I'm fine."

Bobby laughed. "Bullshit. You're trying too hard. You want to know who you are and what you should be doing and all that. I know you Jules, I can see it in your eyes. You're suffering, and you know why? Because you're trying to be something you're not instead of just going with the flow of who you already are."

Once again Jules wore a straight jacket while morons told him how sick he was. "And now you're a goddamn expert."

"I got a ways to go, but right out of the chute this stuff took away my blinders and let me see the basics."

"Really? And now you're qualified to tell me who I am. So who the hell are you?"

"I'm one of the six million! Why do you think I'm wearing this arm band?"

"Of course, it's so obvious."

"It's who I am. And it's who you are."

"And how is it that you're suddenly defined this way?"

"It's not my definition," Bobby said. "It's the world's definition. It's how history has defined us. And you know what the craziest goddamn thing is? The definition has no meaning." Bobby laughed and nodded his head. "I've been thinking about this forever and the drugs finally brought it home. The whole world thinks they know us, they think they know what a Jew is and even though the whole world is full of shit it doesn't matter because we're gonna be whatever they want us to be."

Jules tried to assess whether he was listening to a coherent individual or a ranting fool. "So what's the point? How is this relevant to me?"

"The point is that it's relevant to you because you insist on fighting the world. You probably think I'm talking bullshit. And that's the crazy thing, it is bullshit, it doesn't make sense, so why fight it? If you weren't fighting it, it wouldn't be relevant. Just go along with the world, just accept how things are. Accept you're a victim of history and forget about it already."

"You've lost me."

"Jesus Christ Jules, just be a goddamn Jew already! Stop thinking so hard and play the game—enjoy life. Look, the world says we're money-loving, war mongering, bleeding hearts, whiners, Christ-killers, Zionist spies; we control the money supply and we control the media which we use to promote our Zionist propaganda, and this is all designed for an eventual takeover of the world. We're spawns of Satan, Jules, preparing to rid the world of Jesus, and that the northern Europeans are the true descendents of the twelve tribes..."

Jules did his best to listen but found the more Bobby spoke of Jewish blame—the Black Death, both world wars—the less confidence he had that Bobby's prescription had been the appropriate choice.

"And I'm part of these conspiracies," Jules said.

"We have no choice. Because that's who you are and who I am. It's not my choice or yours it's what everyone will say you are. History makes the decision about us Jules, we have no say, we having nothing to do with it."

"There are plenty of money-loving, war-mongering, whining, bleeding heart gentiles."

"But they're not Jews. There's always a difference, there's always something that justifies our behavior and that's what being a Jew is. There's no escaping it bro. It's a definition with no meaning."

"So what do you want me to do? How should I utilize for my own good the meaningless definition that makes up my existence?"

"Free yourself," Bobby said. "You can't be happy working for bullshit money. It's not in your makeup. Your great-grandfather, for Christ sake. You think he sat around questioning who he was? You think he gave a shit how he got his money? You think he thought about whether he was happy or not?"

"You're telling me there aren't poor Jews?"

"You're not one of them. If you were we wouldn't be sitting here talking, you wouldn't be so screwed up."

Despite the conflict and frustration, Jules had always thought of his condition as a healthier state than the typical man going through the motions of life without challenging his own motivations. There was something noble with questioning, with seeking a deeper meaning. Bobby argued the Jew questioning deeper meanings was a waste of time.

"Only gentiles are allowed to question."

"So let them question," Bobby said. "The word 'gentile' isn't synonymous with blood-sucking, Christ-killing, thieving, and backstabbing."

"Your entire thesis seems to be based on what others think," Jules said. "All you care about is how we are viewed by the rest of society. In your world what others think of you is more important than what you think of yourself."

"Everyone cares more of what others think and those who deny it are full of bullshit. There's no shame in making money, which you seem to think. Anyone who looks down on you for making a lot of cash is jealous. Period. The end. You want to be a librarian and make bullshit? You're doing it because you see some bullshit nobility in poverty, but who's the nobility for? It's not for you, it's for others to see, others to admire, others to talk about. And where does it get you? Nowhere, because you're a Jew and that's it. You can be a rich Jew or a poor Jew, but either way you're still a Jew and I have about a thousand years of proof backing me up."

A thousand years was too much time to cover in what was left of the evening. In a way, Jules was glad he had run into Bobby, if only to know his old friend had chosen some way to define himself.

"We'll talk again soon," Bobby said and Jules nodded but knew he would prefer never to see him again.

20

Jules's encounter with Bobby was still on his mind the following evening as he walked to the Chinese restaurant where he expected to see his father already seated at their usual table. It wasn't enough that immediately preceding Bobby's appearance Jules had been battling with the irony of owing Izzy a debt of gratitude for bringing out his illness before he had become entrenched in the complications of marriage and fatherhood. Now Jules was faced with trying to recapture the enthusiasm of the night he had called his father to set up the date, an enthusiasm he couldn't immediately account for as he walked through the door and saw his father peering at a menu.

"How are you feeling?" Jack said as Jules approached the table.

"Fine," Jules said although Jack's question stung for its shallowness. Those on medication weren't allowed to feel the normal ebb and flow of emotions without it being a question of disease. "How are you feeling?"

Jack shrugged. "Good. Except playing landlord is a pain in the ass."

"Just sell the building and live the good life already."

Jack asked if he was still dating Candy. When Jules said "No," and didn't elaborate Jack seemed surprised. "What happened?"

"Nothing happened."

"OK," Jack said and returned to the menu. A minute later he said, "On the phone you sounded good. I thought maybe it was because of the girl."

"I just thought it was time to get together."

"Me too," Jack said and started waving his arm to get the waitress's attention.

"You know," said Jules. "In the long run I think all this mental crap I've been through might have been a blessing. I think I'm coming out of it stronger than I was, smarter in a way, smarter for the experience, I mean."

Jack smiled. "Listen, I've screwed up many times over the years, but I learned from my mistakes and that's what's important. When I first started selling I would try to load everybody up with as much merchandise as possible not thinking that if they didn't move the goods how pissed off they'd get. These retailers can't have winter coats sitting around all spring and summer, that's money tied up, and then they'd have to mark it down and next time I came through they'd only buy half as much thinking they could just re-order the most popular styles. What a pain in the ass that was, trying to get a couple of coats shipped across the country in those days. And if they arrived at the end of the season, they didn't want them anymore. Sure, I know what you mean. We all do shmucky things. The key for me was to sell just enough, not over load them but make sure they kept their racks full. But it took time, I had to learn the business."

"I'm talking about learning about myself," Jules said. "Learning about who I am, what it is I want from life."

Jack looked thoughtfully at his son. "You never talked this way before you got sick. I didn't know you didn't know what you wanted. You always seemed to know what you wanted."

"That's what I mean, the getting sick. It was probably a good thing since I started to look differently at the world. I've started learning more about who I am."

"I thought you're feeling better. When you walked in the restaurant you said you were feeling fine."

It was about feeling fine; that's all it had ever been about. As long as Jules felt fine Jack didn't have to worry, didn't have to wonder what would become of his son.

"I'm feeling fine," Jules said, trying to keep the tone of his voice even. "But what I'm talking about has nothing to do with feeling fine. A person can feel fine and not be satisfied with their life."

"What would make you satisfied?"

"I don't know. Did you think about satisfaction when you went into the apparel business?"

Jack sighed. "I wanted to make a living. I liked selling. That was all I thought about. That was all the satisfaction I needed. Money brought satisfaction. A house, a car, providing for your family brought satisfaction. Having a baby brought satisfaction. This is life, this is what's offered and if you look around the world you'll notice it's a hell of a lot more than most have. And it's a hell of a lot more than our ancestors had. They came here with nothing but the rags they wore and the skills they had. Give them a bed to collapse on at the end of the day and that was satisfaction. They worked and worked and succeeded. They saved their money and opened their own businesses and many got rich and many more were at least middle class which was rich compared to the shit holes they came from. I guarantee you they were pretty damn satisfied. And when law firms and the accounting firms wouldn't take us, they started their own firms, and when they weren't allowed into the country clubs, they built their own. And you know what? Theirs were better and fancier. That's satisfaction, making something of yourself, getting money in the bank, no matter who says what. You just do it because that's the life that's available if you want it. If you don't want it, then I don't know what to tell you..."

With each word the uniqueness of Jules predicament became more apparent. It occurred to him how special he was to have his own world where he suspected others resided, but a world in which he didn't personally know anyone. And how contradictory was his world! How absolutely antithetical his world seemed compared to all the other worlds and while his father droned on, energized, no doubt, with the knowledge his son was "fine," Jules fantasized one day he would occupy his world with a woman who was as screwed up as he was, a woman who sat with her mother or father or both and thought how she didn't belong in her parent's world or her friends' world or any other world she was aware of.

With the arrival of their food Jack stopped talking. But Jules knew his father was not one to simply back off a subject once it had stirred his passion. He knew at any moment his father would plunge back in, and while Jack's head hung over his plate, his jaws working hard on a mouthful of Mongolian beef, he formulated what to say next.

"You just can't go changing your life because of some fantasy that popped into your head." He looked up from his plate. "We're not the kind of people that just go around acting out dreams, like if you want to go live in the Bahamas and be a beach bum. Those are the losers who can't make it here..."

Losers? The word had a harsh finality to it. Jules imagined drunken sots stumbling across a park, in particular a black woman and a fat white man who remained suspended in his thoughts. He watched as they stumbled through the grass pushing a grocery cart from which a pathetically small number of soda cans bounced inside.

"You're wrong," Jules said. "And what the hell do you know about people changing their lives? I've seen people do it, happy people, people with a purpose and not losers either. Screwed up like me maybe, but not losers."

"Whaddya mean 'screwed up?' You're not screwed up, you're doing good, I can see it and you said so yourself. And I never said you were a loser."

"Of course I'm screwed up, but so what? It's a good thing I'm screwed up otherwise tell you about some people I met in a house in Roger's Park just a few days ago. Normal people, dad, and you know what their lives are about? Exercising and screwing. That's it. They do one and then the other. Everyone screw everyone. But most of all they screw their teacher, a hairy little hooked nose bearded rabbi-looking guy. The ugliest little kike you ever saw. Joseph Göebbels couldn't have asked for a better poster boy. You couldn't have dreamed up a more repulsive little Jew to terrify any self-respecting gentile. And there he is, screwing their willing daughters every goddamn night of the week and probably every day too. And I'm not talking dogs either. These are babes, dad, the kind of girls we men fantasize about, the ones we jack-off to in our dreams."

"Jules—what are you talking about?"

"And as screwed up as these people are, as revolting as this little hairy beast was, I envy them. At some point they said, 'Fuck it, there's more to life than just making money.' And a lot of them do make money but so what? It's not the only reason they get up in the morning it's not the only reason they're alive."

"Jules, take it easy already. What's this all about?"

Jules stared at his father, the man who wanted to know what it was all about. But what was there to say? He could continue informing Jack of how the others lived, how there were plenty of others out there, educated people who talked to a collective of disembodied beings who spoke as one voice through a person they called their "teacher." Or he could talk about his father's inability to understand because his generation was too steeped in eras requiring capitalization; Great Depression, Second World War, Cold War. They were handicapped, he thought, numbed to understanding how their children couldn't just be satisfied to live safely in a safe world.

But his father looked so bewildered, so helpless, so pitiful with his lips smeared with soy sauce.

"It's not about anything, dad. I'm fine, everything's fine. I just had a bad day."

Jack nodded. "Listen, we all have them. I've had many a bad day," he said and returned to his Mongolian beef.

21

Jules didn't remember the steep stairway extending to the sidewalk outside the building. For a while he watched the non-stop progression of sharply dressed men and women walk through the revolving door. He was curious if any of the austere faces looked familiar, but it was the kind of gray, wet day that turned everybody the same color.

On the twelfth floor he stood in front of the counter surrounding the receptionist, a young woman whom he did not recognize.

"I'd like to see Isadore Himmel. Izzy is what he's called, I think."

She thought for a moment and then picked up a phone list. "I don't see the name listed. Did you have an appointment?"

"Look under Williamson. James Williamson."

She did as told but found no listing for Williamson. "Are you sure you're in the right place?" she said.

"Yes I'm sure," Jules said with an edge in his voice he didn't intend. "I used to work here."

She leaned back in her chair and crossed her arms. "I'm new. Forgive me for not knowing who you are."

"I didn't mean it that way. Are you sure that's a current phone list?"

She picked up the list and pointed to the lower right hand corner of the page where a recent date was printed.

"How about Pelc? Does Brian Pelc still work here?"

"What's your name please?" she asked and when Jules told her she picked up the telephone receiver.

"He'll be right out," she said. Jules thanked her but received no reply.

Pelc appeared at the end of the hallway joining the reception area. "Come on back, Jules."

"No, no, no," Jules said and motioned for Pelc to come to him. "I just need to ask you a quick question."

"How are you? We were all wondering what the hell happened to you." Pelc spoke louder than Jules would've liked.

"Does Izzy still work here?"

Pelc looked blankly at Jules for a moment. "Oh, the little guy with the baggy suit. No, he left not long after you did."

Jules thought he was joking. "Where did he go?"

"No idea. He just up and left. So what have you been doing?"

Looking into his former co-worker's eyes, Jules remembered it was Pelc who broke the news on that crucial day many months ago—that Izzy had left for the airport—thus sealing Jules's fate. "By any chance do you know where he lives?"

"No. But he's listed because I had to call him from home once."

It turned out Izzy lived on the tenth floor of an older medium-rise apartment building a few blocks from a neighborhood some would consider "changing" while others might call "eclectic." The lobby was small and depressing with scratchy tile and a couple of padded benches covered in vinyl where elderly women sat staring at Jules while clutching their purses. Jules thought Izzy must've fallen on hard times since he could think of no other reason why a young, single, male would choose to live in this building.

He pushed the button next to "I. Himmel" and waited. To his surprise the lobby door immediately buzzed open. Jules walked into the elevator vestibule where the flickering fluorescent light played tricks with his eyes against the yellow wallpaper. Stepping out of the elevator he was assaulted by the antiseptic odor of industrial strength cleansers. The ammonia smell combined with the glare off the white linoleum floor made Jules wonder why anyone would live here if they didn't have to.

On the door post to Izzy's apartment hung a mezuzah, a sign of the resident's faith. A Jew must live here, Jules thought and pushed a black button under the peep hole producing a tinny "ding-dong." Jules waited nervously for the door to open and when it did the little man showed himself to Jules once again, this time leaning heavily on a cane.

"Ellerstein," Izzy said and smiled weakly before turning around and walking back into his apartment. It was the first time Jules had seen Izzy undraped of the corporate costume. It was also the first time Jules had seen him unshaven, which for the baby-faced Izzy could've meant a solid week without shaving—the reality of which, combined with Izzy's current outfit of tan polyester slacks and a v-neck t-shirt, presented to Jules a shocking picture.

"Is this your way of inviting me in?"

Izzy turned part way toward Jules and waved him forward. "If the door's open you're invited."

Jules walked into Izzy's home, a sparsely furnished one-bedroom apartment with low-pile blue carpeting. "Sit," Izzy said and pointed to a sofa decorated with all types of wildflower designs stitched into the fabric. Izzy sat in an overstuffed chair opposite the sofa and waited.

"You're not going to ask me what I'm doing here?"

Izzy shrugged. "You're not going tell me?"

Jules once again marveled at Izzy's peculiar manner of speaking, how he could make the most trivial of statements sound condescending.

"What happened to your leg?"

"Ach! They think some kind of gout or rheumatoid something or other."

"Why did you leave Nathrop & Moore?"

Izzy narrowed his eyes and frowned. "For this you out-of-the-blue come over?"

"I'm curious. They told me at the office you weren't there any more. Isn't it logical to think I would be curious?"

"I think it more logical you don't care."

Was it worth it? Jules thought, meaning the aggravation, the madness of communicating with this freak. "I need a reference, Izzy. I went to the office to ask you for a reference."

Izzy nodded. "I see a small amount of logic. When I returned from my nephew's first communion and was told that you had disappeared, McNally called me into his office to ask me if I knew what had happened. I told him you could not find the presentation you were to give and that I was responsible for it missing. He asked me what I meant and told him what had been happening to you, how you had become so single-minded on your career that you neglected even to honor your deceased mother. Only the walking dead could ignore the death anniversary of one's mother, I told McNally, the very womb from which your life had sprung. McNally nodded in the fashion that he always did although I was very sure that he understood little of what I was saying. 'How is this your business, Ellerstein's mother,' he asked and I again tried to explain only this time I told him about the time I was a little boy and my parents took us skiing for the first time.

"I was the youngest and much smaller than the rest so my mother spent the day guiding me up and down the bunny hill while my older siblings and father spent their day on the much steeper turtle hill. When it was time for lunch my mother took me to the resort's restaurant where she sat me on a stool at the counter where, among other things, the French fries were prepared. After ordering me a hamburger sandwich, I noticed that the basket holding the already-cooked fries was suspended over what looked to be a few ordinary light bulbs. It didn't seem possible that the important task of keeping the fries warm could fall on such a common household appliance. I asked my mother if this was indeed the case and I never forgot the look of excitement on her face at being able to affirm my wonderment.

"It was the look of love, I told McNally, the love only a mother could know from giving joy to a small child who asked a simple question. I thought foolishly that this small story would be enough to provide a little inspiration for McNally, but this was not the case since McNally then asked why you did not just tell him what had happened and go from there. Of this I had no opinion for McNally although our conversation brought to me a changing of perspective for myself. I began to question if I really wanted to spend my days working for people like McNally whose insight into the world rivaled that of a dried fig. Looking back, I owe you a debt of gratitude Ellerstein, for not returning to your job. Your not coming back became a statement of defiance that ultimately provided me with the realization that we can all walk away if we choose."

Jules let a few moments pass to make sure Izzy had finished. "So you just walked away? A sparkling career waiting for you and you just walk away? What're you gonna do? How do you support yourself?"

"I had saved an amount to invest conservatively and still get enough of a check every month."

"Enough of a check to live here? This is like a broken down retirement home."

"What is it that I need? I got a roof over my head, a warm bed, a table to study. Yes, I study, that's what I do. I study the ancient books, Ellerstein, the Talmud, the Kabbalah, the five books of Moses. From this I receive my sustenance. And what is it you want me to reference?"

"I'm going to start looking for a job and I need a professional reference, someone who worked with me and will vouch for me in the finance world."

Izzy remained expressionless and sat staring into the carpet as if pondering a complicated question.

"I want a reference.'

"It's my blessing you want," Izzy finally said. "I will give you this since you were once my son."

"Are you kidding me? I want a reference; it's the least you owe me."

"You want me to tell you it's OK to go back to that world when I know otherwise. I won't give you my blessing for your own good; I won't be a part of your self-destructive behavior. No father would."

"You're crazy! "Absolutely goddamn crazy. You're out of your mind, an idiot acting like an old Jew. Taking the name of a dead Jew, for fuck sake. What the hell's wrong with you? Now you're a retired old Jew living in a shit house apartment and for what? What're you, twenty-four? Twenty-five years old? You're dead, Izzy. You're the walking dead living in a dead life and for what? So you can read those goddamned books and talk the way you do and tell people how to live their lives because you study, you know all the answers you know the truth. You're an arrogant bastard. What did your parents do to you? How screwed up were they to raise a son like you? Maybe you were just too smart too soon. You did too well in school and your brain fried out. I'm just asking for a goddamn reference, just to have someone say I can do the job because they saw me do the job. Can't you just do that for me? Is this asking so goddamned much?"

Jules leaned back and then let his head fall forward. He knew Izzy was still sitting in the same position, still staring into the blue industrial carpet at some point a few feet in front of him, midway from his chair to the tiny kitchenette with its floor of black and brown linoleum squares, its stove with four coiled burners, its metal cabinets with the shelves lined with a patterned sticky paper.

"Some people are so afraid to die that they never begin to live," Izzy said quietly. "One may live as a conqueror, a king, or a magistrate; but he must die a man."

Jules said nothing. He had come to the end of something. He had no reason to stay, no reason to dialogue with Izzy, no reason to expect anything at all.

"It runs in your family, your fear of death," Izzy said. "If asked where it started I would say with the politician. A Russian immigrant born under Alexander II's reforms which, as usual, backfired leading to more anti-Semitism. And then Alexander III, a Jew-hating bastard if there ever was one, the Czar that the immigrant remembered best when he arrived in Chicago. Who could blame him for being afraid? And what was Chicago in 1883? Compared to Czarist Russia Chicago was a walk in the woods. He was a smart man—fear does that to some, makes them smarter. So afraid and smart he was, that he built his empire, surrounded himself with other fear-mongers, others willing to kill and terrorize, becoming the very thing that he fled..."

Jules stood in between at three worlds at once, hop-scotching a triangular pattern. One foot landed in the sphere of success—Jules the provider, the keeper of the assets, the wearer of the clothes in a place with sparkling lakefronts, stylishly-dressed women and mature landscaping. The other foot was in the pale of the meek— Jules the servant, the thinker, the self-possessed among gritty streets and corner lots full of weeds. Then both feet were in the realm of the dead—Jules the defender of the tribe, the keeper of the flame, the historian among the ruins, a victim of the Jewish deal. Izzy's words moved freely within each area, passing easily through the borders of connective tissue holding everything together, making sure each world was relevant to the other. From this Jules emerged with a victorious insight.

"You sent me the article!"

"Who else? How better to learn about someone than to study their family? And why should I want to learn about you?— you're wanting to ask. I can only tell you it had more to do with the timing of your coming to Nathrop & Moore than anything else. My changeover was in process; I was becoming something other than what I was raised to be, and watching you, Ellerstein, sitting in your new office on your first day, a Jew among gentiles, I couldn't help but be struck by your air of complacency and conceit. Relax, Ellerstein, to your ears that sounds presumptive, I know. But Kabbalah teaches you to look beneath the surface and when I looked at you I couldn't deny I was disappointed. But I gave you a chance to show me that you were more than just a job. When you disappointed me I was reminded that my first impression had been the correct one. But why should I care?—I'm sure you are wanting to ask me this. Why shouldn't I care? Why shouldn't I lash out the way I did? Not that what I did was the honorable thing to do, for it wasn't. In the cab, on the way to the airport, I thought over and over that I will apologize upon my return.

"But you were gone when I returned. I sensed that for you to give up so easily, a much greater insight must have occurred. There was no other explanation. Had you returned and exposed me for the sin I committed against you, I would have been the one without a job. And as the weeks passed with no mention of your whereabouts, I slowly came to see that you had freed yourself from the shackles of these Pharaohs and perhaps you were wandering in the desert in search of your promised land. Don't ask me how I come to know such things because I only know what I feel and it's all affirmed in the books, Ellerstein, I'm just a vessel for the knowledge already written down.

"So I, too, broke free of the irons and fled the sting of the taskmaster's rod, stopped slaving away making bricks from mud and straw. I followed your example, Ellerstein, but I didn't really know you. I didn't know who you were or where you had come from and I wanted to know. One should always know who it is he is following, for fear of following a false prophet. So I did a little research. In today's world getting information on people is more than a little easy. And through my search I came across Morris Ellerstein and learned of his power. My hunch was that he was in your bloodline, although I didn't know for sure until this very day, just a few minutes ago. The newspapers had many accounts of this man, none very flattering but that's another story. I chose to send you a copy of the most provocative headline, the headline that had your name along side the gangster Capone.

"It was my way of reaching out that I should send this to you. It was anonymous because it was easier that way, which I am not proud of but that's another issue. I thought if you didn't know already about your relative that you should know and that, perhaps, it might help in directing your wanderings. Morris Ellerstein's building of his hoodlum empire was constructed from a lifetime of knowing only fear and death. His life was a castle of fright. I thought maybe it might help you realize that your fear of acknowledging your mother's death was a display of your own fear of death. And that your desire to acquire money and material goods was also a demonstration of one's fear of death. How lucky you are, Ellerstein, to have such an example in your bloodlines. Most go through life ignorant of one's past beyond shopworn stories of immigrant quirks. If anything, I hope you can see how lucky you are."

Jules watched Izzy lean back in his chair and close his eyes. "And it all started with the Jewish deal," Jules said.

Izzy opened his eyes. "It did. Two words spoken by a person whose job it was to act as an agent between man and God. It's a shame you don't see the significance. Your shallowness is unending."

"But you're wrong. I've been thinking long and hard about those two words for many months."

"And what have you discovered?"

"That it encompasses everything," Jules said. "There was a period where I was trying to find a single unifying theory that would explain being a Jew and I think the theory and the Jewish deal are one and the same."

Izzy nodded but said nothing.

"For some reason you'll always be looked at differently if you're a Jew. I don't understand it but that's just he way it is and it's all part of the deal. Even thinking about it and not being able to explain it is all part of the deal. The priest saying Jewish deal is part of the deal. It's a condition, a state of being. You'll never really be a Jew, Izzy, because you weren't born into the condition, you just adopted it. That's just part of the deal, too. And I can never stop being a Jew no matter what I say or do or believe— history has proven that over and over. That's also just part of the deal."

Izzy seemed pleased. "It's a dialectic," Izzy said. "A cannibalistic dialectic. A condition that's only obvious long enough for enough exceptions to devour the original theory— although the original theory is still relevant. You're a microcosm of the dialectic, Ellerstein. The Jewish stereotype is the thesis. You are the antithesis. And the synthesis is the Jewish deal itself. It means nothing and it means everything. Deep down we're all Jews, this I've long ago decided."

"You're nuts."

"I'm a reflection of the world," Izzy said. "Had there not been a Holocaust there would not be an Israel. Nowadays we need gasoline powered engines to push the leaves from our lawns. In Florida, citrus trees are destroyed if a fungus creates spots on the skin of the fruit. The fruit is affected not the least. But people don't like spots. So the trees they cut. One man's sushi is another's lasagna. You wander about asking yourself where it is you belong. Maybe better to ask yourself: who is asking the question? Perhaps you should get out of town, Ellerstein. Start over, reinvent yourself somewhere else. Put your single unifying theory to the test. Really, what's keeping you here anyway?..."

The little man was indeed out of his mind, Jules knew—Jules had always known. But for some reason, for some crazy, unexplainable reason, Izzy was starting to make sense if only because Jules couldn't help but listen, couldn't help but remember his words long after he would leave his company. Izzy's suggestion he should reinvent himself sounded particularly intriguing. It was, no doubt, just part of the deal.

Like his character Jules Ellerstein, Marc Krulewitch, the author of *Maxwell Street Blues, Windy City Blues, Gold Coast Blues, Doubt in the 2nd Degree,* and *Something to Call Your Own,* is descended from an infamous Chicagoan. He grew up in Highland Park, Illinois, and now lives with his wife in Colorado.

Thank you for reading my book. If you enjoyed it, won't you please take a moment to leave me a review at your favorite retailer?